Praise for Jillian Hunter's Tales of Romance and Laughter

"Jillian Hunter has just become one of my favorite authors!"
—Teresa Medeiros, author of *The Bride and the Beast*

INDISCRETION

"We could all use a little more Jillian Hunter in our lives. . . . *Indiscretion* is a sexy, funny, fast-paced read that is sure to please."

—*The Oakland Press*

"The thrill of this book is . . . the banter between Patrick and Anne as they try to best each other and find instead, the best in each other."

—*Heartland Critiques*

"A wonderful Victorian romance. . . . Anyone who reads this enjoyable tale will immediately hunt down previous novels by delightful Jillian Hunter."

—Harriet Klausner, Barnesandnoble.com

DELIGHT

"*Delight* is, well, a delight. Funny, touching, sexy, and tender, this is Jillian Hunter at her fairy-tale best. Somehow she has found a way to create stories that speak to the nineties woman, but sound like a fairy tale of old."

—*Romantic Times*

"*Delight* is just that. . . . [A] funny tale. . . . The ever sly Hunter has a field day."

—*Detroit Free Press*

"This hysterically enchanting story was pure fun to read. . . . Ms. Hunter tells a 'delightful' tale of love, romance, and adventure. A must-read!"

—*Old Book Barn Gazette*

"Hilarious from beginning to end."

—*Rendezvous*

"The captivating Ms. Hunter once again enchants romance readers with a delightful tale."

—*Affaire de Coeur*

"This story is ripe with humorous misadventures."

—CompuServe Romance Reviews

"A humorously warm historical romance. . . . The story line is fast paced, filled with action, and loaded with jocular ripostes. The warmth of the characters is a Jillian Hunter trademark. . . . Very highly recommended."

—*Under the Covers Book Reviews*

DARING

"Jillian Hunter's distinctive voice has never been brighter or clearer than in *Daring*. With a winning combination of characters, plot, and quirkiness, she simply works magic on your heart, bringing joy, a smile, and perhaps a tear to make it a special day. . . . You'll be charmed, captivated, and utterly enchanted with Maggie and Connor, the entire plot, setting, and, most of all, the special pieces that make a Jillian Hunter romance a rare treat."

—*Romantic Times*

FAIRY TALE

"[A] delightful tale full of wonderfully warm characters who make you smile and laugh out loud. It's a must read."

—Janet Carroll, Romance Writers of America's 1996 Bookseller of the Year

"*Fairy Tale* is a hoot, but it's also touching and a wee bit magical."

—*The Atlanta Journal-Constitution*

"*Fairy Tale* is sheer magic! [It] bewitched me from the very first page. It's one of the freshest, funniest, most delightful romances I've had the pleasure to read. A tender, endearing love story blessed with unforgettable characters."

—Teresa Medeiros, author of *The Bride and the Beast*

"Exquisite. . . . You'll be surrounded by enchantment from first page to last. . . . *Fairy Tale* is a story that beguiles, enthralls, and captivates the reader by its sheer beauty and warmth. This is a 'feel good,' heartsoaring read that will remain with you for a long time. Read it and savor the pleasure."

—*Romantic Times*

"Jillian Hunter [weaves] a spell whose threads are mystery, deep emotion, and the relationship between . . . very vivid, very human, very amusing and touching characters."

—Kathryn Lynn Davis, bestselling author of *Somewhere Lies the Moon*

"Hilarious. . . . The characters come to life in this unusual story."

—*Rendezvous*

"Jillian Hunter is a master of her craft."

—Katherine Sutcliffe, bestselling author of *Hope and Glory*

Books by Jillian Hunter

Fairy Tale
Daring
Delight
Indiscretion
Abandon

Published by POCKET BOOKS

JILLIAN HUNTER

Abandon

SONNET BOOKS

New York   London   Toronto   Sydney   Singapore

This book is a work of fiction. Names, characters, places and incidents are products of the author's imagination or are used fictitiously. Any resemblance to actual events or locales or persons living or dead is entirely coincidental.

An *Original* Publication of POCKET BOOKS

A Sonnet Book published by
POCKET BOOKS, a division of Simon & Schuster, Inc.
1230 Avenue of the Americas, New York, NY 10020

ISBN: 0-7434-1790-9

First Sonnet Books printing May 2001

10 9 8 7 6 5 4 3 2 1

SONNET BOOKS and colophon are trademarks of Simon & Schuster, Inc.

Cover art by Tom Hallman

Printed in the U.S.A.

In memory of my father,
Harry Joseph Gardner,
July 8, 1924–October 1, 2000.
You are a hero to
your country and family, Dad.
I will love you forever.

I could not send this book into the world without expressing my appreciation to two extraordinary women who have helped me during a difficult year:

Andrea Cirillo, my agent, tough and tender, warm and wise, with my deepest gratitude and respect.

—and—

Kate Collins, my editor, who is smart, supportive, and insightful. It is my privilege to work with you.

Thank you both.

1

The Scilly Islands
Cornwall, England

The castle servants had warned him that he would pay for ignoring the girl. On the very night he took possession of the ancient keep, the domestic prophets of doom surrounded him in the hallway. They assured him that the girl possessed some vague magical powers which she would use against him for turning her away.

"And what sort of magical powers might those be?" he had asked out of amused curiosity.

"She brings rainbows to the sky after a storm," the castle housekeeper said proudly.

The coachman nodded. "She causes flowers to bloom where nary a weed could grow before."

"Oh, my goodness," Anthony said, hiding a grin. "These are terrifying powers, indeed. Is it safe to leave my room?"

"And she's under the protection of the sorceress Morgan le Fay, King Arthur's own sister," a chambermaid piped in ominously.

"Not the same King Arthur who lived in Saxon

times?" Anthony walked the small group of servants into the bronze umbrella stand, his voice rising. "Who probably never lived at all and, if he did live, would have banished the lot of you to the dungeon for aggravation?"

"The one and only Arthur," the housekeeper said, adding under her breath as she hid behind the coachman, "and old Annie Jenkins has had a vision that you and Miss Halliwell are destined to marry."

"Marry?" Anthony muttered to himself as he waved the absurd little group away. "Now, *that* is a terrifying thought."

Still, inspiring his own brand of terror in the much-beloved Miss Halliwell was probably what he needed to do to get rid of the girl once and for all. Ignoring her for a week obviously had not worked. In fact, the thunderous echo that resounded through the walls this very moment could have been caused by the brutal Atlantic breakers that pounded at the foundations of the castle. Or they could have been her again.

The persistent young woman had demanded, and been denied, an audience with him for more than a week.

Anthony Hartstone, third Earl of Pentargon, sat unmoving in his balloon-back chair, his brandy untouched. The coal fire highlighted the cynical humor on his angular face as passionate voices rose from the bailey. Ah, yes. One o'clock. His feminine tormentor had arrived right on time.

Foolish girl. Brave girl indeed to beard the lion in his den. It sounded from the fracas as if she had finally brought reinforcements to plead her case. Which, of course, was a waste of time. Anthony could not have helped her even had he so desired.

His lips curled at the corners as a man shouted, "Over my dead body! You are not to disturb his lordship!"

Vincent, his valet, butler, and former butcher, was apparently losing his temper, which never boded well for the object of his annoyance. Under different circumstances, Anthony might have enjoyed watching the spectacle between the Cornish Titan and the infamous Miss Halliwell. Vincent would not raise a finger to the lady; one shake of his meaty fist would probably send her scurrying.

A belch of thunder broke overhead, portending another storm. The waves below the cliffs threw white flecks of spume high against the mullioned windows. The room darkened.

Anthony put aside the letters of condolence he'd received at the same moment the door behind him flew open.

"My lord." Vincent's bulky frame shook with indignation. "The tethers of my patience are stretched to the breaking point."

"Admittedly thin threads to begin with."

Vincent's cheeks reddened under his bushy whiskers. "The woman refused to take no for an answer."

"Until you escorted her back to the beach. In the most polite way possible, of course."

"She poked me, my lord."

Anthony sat forward, his face delighted. "She what?"

"With a parasol. In the—the hindquarters." Clearly distraught, Vincent pressed his intimidating bulk against the door panels. "Prepare to defend yourself," he managed to shout seconds before a petite bundle of gray-blue muslin burst into the room. "We are *besieged.*"

Besieged.

Anthony shot to his feet, frowning in displeasure at the intrusion. The bold invaders, three in all, stormed into the library, defiling his male sanctuary and mood of private mourning for his recently departed brother.

Actually, it was their female leader, face concealed by the intriguing shadows of a bonnet, who stormed the room. Her two male escorts more wisely crept behind her, darting apologetic glances his way. They, at least, possessed the sense to be afraid of him.

The young woman was either too spoiled or too thick-headed to recognize her social limitations.

"Forgive us, my lord," the eldest of the intruders said, a portly man in his sixties with a trim white beard.

The other man was in his early thirties. Tall, dark-haired, and blinking nervously behind gold-rimmed spectacles, he stammered a sheepish apology. "We shouldn't have come. We shall return at a better time—"

"Do be quiet, Elliott." The young woman tapped her parasol on the floor for emphasis. "He's intimidating you, and he hasn't said a single word. For all we know, his lordship is the kindest man in the world. For all we know, we shall be warmly received."

"Leave."

Anthony pointed to the door, no hint of the hoped-for warmth or kindness on his lean face. "I do not have time for this nonsense." He peered into the shadowed cavern of her bonnet. "Good-bye, Miss Hollywell."

"That is Halliwell, Lord Pendragon. Morwenna Halliwell."

He smiled coldly. "Pentargon."

"Oh." She gave him an insincere smile. "Sorry."

"Sir Dunstan Halliwell." The older man extended his hand in a gesture so patently humble that Anthony could hardly refuse. "An honor to meet you, my lord. A rare honor."

"Elliott Winleigh." The slender man with ink-stained fingers turned from examining the watercolors on the wall. "At your service, my lord," he said, bowing.

Anthony nodded. "At any other time, I should be glad to receive you, but my day—my entire week—is filled with business."

"But that's why we've come," Miss Halliwell said in exasperation. "On a business matter."

Then, with an ingenious flick of her hand, she pushed the bonnet down onto her nape, revealing herself with artlessness that was more disarming than a frontal attack.

His frown deepened as he stared at her. His thoughts seemed to collide one upon another like an avalanche of boulders at the bottom of a hill, faster than he could hold them at bay.

She was beautiful, he could not deny that.

Green eyes that gazed at him with irresistible innocence and struck a chord in his distant memory. Chestnut-gold hair too heavy for the twisted knot at her nape. Features so clean and fragile she might have been carved from ice—if he breathed on her, would she melt, he wondered? Most alarming was the fact that she looked so familiar.

"Have we met?" he said in confusion.

She looked at him as if he were a bit of an idiot. "I just introduced myself a few moments ago. I have begged an audience with you every morning for a week and been refused by Jack the Giant Killer at your door."

"Morwenna." Her uncle gave a discreet cough. "His lordship is a busy man. Get to the point, my dear."

"There is no point." Anthony turned back to his escritoire, his voice dismissive. "There is no point in any of us wasting our time. I know what you want. It is impossible."

Morwenna stared at him; heat rose to his neck at the intensity of emotion in her eyes. "Perhaps you knew my father, Sir Roland Halliwell," she said. "He was a great scholar and antiquarian whose books a learned person such as yourself may even have in your library. *Passage to the Land of the Little People.*"

"*Excalibur in England,*" Elliott added helpfully.

Morwenna swept her parasol across his desk in a burst of enthusiasm. "In fact, your own dear brother said he was reading one of Papa's books a fortnight before his tragic death."

Anthony swore softly, watching the bottle of ink she had knocked over saturate his letters. "*Damnation.*"

"We are sorry about your brother, my lord," she whispered, staring in chagrin at the slow-moving stain on his desk as Elliott rushed forward with his handkerchief to sop up the mess.

Anthony turned and tugged at the bellpull for his housekeeper. "I cannot help you, Miss Halliwell. I understand why you are here. However, the contracts for the sale of the island have already been drawn up by an army of lawyers."

"Is your behavior not rather impulsive?" she said. "You have hardly left this castle since your arrival. Your brother adored Abandon."

His blue-gray eyes darkened in warning. "And perhaps if he had not secluded himself on this god-forsaken pile of granite, investigating ridiculous phenomena such as mermaids, he would still be alive today."

"He seemed happy here," she said in surprise. "Although I did not know him well, the islanders liked him very much, and I believe he would not have wanted even one stone to be removed from its place."

He gripped the back of his chair, assessing her face with a ruthless scrutiny that would have reduced most men to powder. "My brother is gone. The sooner I am shed of this island, the better."

"How can you be so callous? There are entire families at stake."

"I do not need to explain my actions to you," he said in astonishment.

"I think you do," she said quietly.

The clatter of china from the doorway broke the dangerous silence that had fallen. Outside, even the storm seemed suspended as if nature held its breath, awaiting the outcome of a battle this bold girl could not win.

"You wished for tea for our guests, my lord?" Tillie Treffry, the castle's pretty Cornish housekeeper, entered the room with an approving smile, elbowing Anthony's brandy decanter aside on the table to lower her tray. "Scones fresh from the oven and clotted cream."

She cast a covert glance at Miss Halliwell, which Anthony interpreted to mean a conspiracy was afoot. "I did not ring for refreshments, Mrs. Treffry," he said. "I would like you to clean my desk. Our guests are not staying."

"Not staying? But how can they row back to the other side of the island in the rain, my lord?"

"The same way they rowed here, I imagine." He looked directly at Sir Dunstan. "Please understand I am obligated to supervise certain improvements on the island. They were promised as a condition of the sale."

Sir Dunstan moved to the door, frowning at his niece. "Come, Morwenna. We should perhaps have stated our case to his lordship in a letter."

Morwenna refused to move. "If you sell Abandon to a stranger, Lord Pentargon, you are condemning the islanders to a fate as awful as the Highland Clearances."

Her eyes reminded him of oil upon the surface of the dark green Cornish sea, changing with emotion. "The Marquess of Camelbourne is hardly a monster. No one will be smoked out of a cottage or sent to Canada."

"Lord Heart of Stone," she said. "That is what you are called. I discounted the warnings. I did not believe it fair to judge you until we had met."

He laughed shortly. "One can hardly fend off progress with the parasol."

"Perhaps not," she said, her eyes narrowing, "but one can certainly make a few good dents."

"I can attest to the truth of that," Vincent muttered from the hall where he evidently stood eavesdropping.

Anthony had a sudden insane urge to scoop Miss Halliwell into his arms, drop her on the sofa, and—well, he refused to let his imagination go any farther. He was a gentleman, after all, even if this slip of a girl did arouse the barbaric undercurrents of behavior that lurked beneath the surface of every red-blooded male.

He gave her a stare designed to crush her spirit. "I have made a bargain, Miss Halliwell."

"With the devil, I do not doubt," she retorted.

"That is enough, Morwenna." Her uncle took firm hold of her arm, dragging her toward the door.

"I won't leave until he listens to me," she said, continuing to stare at Anthony as if she could not believe what an evil entity she had encountered.

"Then I shall leave," he said simply.

Silence fell as he moved past them. He wondered if she noticed that his gait was slightly uneven, and he wondered why he should care. Then he caught the faintest hint of lilies on her skin. The fragrance was so elusive he barely identified it as he glanced back at her.

Their eyes met. He thought for an instant she might bash him on the skull with her umbrella, the bent tip of which had no doubt left one of her aforementioned dents in Vincent's tough flesh.

But it was the shy-looking Elliott who stopped him, with the most outrageous remark Anthony had ever heard.

"I—I should like to sketch you, my lord."

Anthony stilled. "Excuse me?"

Elliott flushed. He still held one of Anthony's ink-stained letters in his hand while the housekeeper covertly cleaned up the mess on the desk. "I should like to sketch you in costume for the book I am illustrating, to be published at the beginning of next year. It is about Arthurian legends and their connection to Cornwall. Miss Halliwell's papa had almost completed it before his untimely death, and I w-would be honored to use you as a model."

"A sketch. Of me. I am flattered, Mr. Winleigh," he

said wryly. *Stunned* was more accurate. Having overcome a handicap in his childhood, Anthony did not think of himself as a handsome man, although women seemed to find him reasonably attractive. "But I hardly have the time, nor do I see myself in such a heroic role."

"I think you would make the perfect Sir Gawain for the book, my lord," Elliott said. "You have the physique of a knight, and a face . . . a face that not only brings to mind a warrior but which reveals a remarkable depth of character."

"Oh, Elliott," the girl said in an angry whisper. "You carry artistic obsession too far. How *could* you? Besides," she added a little spitefully, "he would make a better Mordred than Gawain, and Gawain was fair."

Anthony almost laughed. He knew just enough of Arthurian lore to remember that Mordred was the archvillain in the legend, the treasonous nephew who had delivered a deathblow to the king.

"You are too kind, Mr. Winleigh," he murmured, closing the door on the trio of apprehensive faces. "Far too kind."

The girl had made a muffled sound behind him, a combined huff of dismay, indignation, and disbelief. He had laughed then, chuckled all the way up the tower stairs to the battlements where he and Vincent stood in the rain for several minutes as the unsuccessful party took its leave.

"Why should I care what she thinks, Vincent?"

"You should not, my lord. Not a jot."

"I have only done what needed to be done, and the matter was decided a month ago."

"Indeed it was, my lord."

"Look at us, Vincent, standing here in the rain. Blast that silly creature for raking me over the coals of my own conscience when my motives are pure. I am not selling this damn island for profit."

"Of course you are not, my lord."

Anthony frowned. His younger brother, Ethan, had died several months ago, leaving Abandon, a tiny isle off the Cornish coast, to Anthony. Ethan had fallen off a cliff one morning and drowned, presumably during his absurd search for mermaids. In Anthony's opinion, a man like Ethan, disabled by an army injury, should never have come to this wretched place to begin with, and the sooner it was sold, the better.

In fact, Anthony was amazed when he received the offer, ecstatic when he discovered the buyer was an old acquaintance, the politically powerful Marquess of Camelbourne, a master statesman and personal friend to Prince Albert. For two years Anthony had been trying to find a political ally to ensure that his child labor reform measures would be passed.

A deal was struck. Abandon would be sold to Camelbourne in exchange for political support, and countless innocent children would be protected from inhumane conditions.

"Has the girl never been taught that one must make sacrifices for the greater good?" Anthony asked himself aloud. "Does she not understand that one does not always have a choice?"

This time Vincent did not respond. He was too busy watching the sturdy rowboat that had just taken to the sea. A small cluster of servants also stood watching on the castle causeway. The girl in the bonnet bobbed up and down in the boat. Her profile seemed pure even at this distance.

Vincent lifted his spyglass. "The staff accused us of sending them to their deaths, my lord."

"The storm appears to be passing," Anthony said, secretly relieved that he could see a mass of thunderheads moving away from the castle. "They might have stayed in the drawing room until the rain stopped, I suppose."

"I suppose we could have suggested it, my lord."

Anthony looked at him. "Except that Jack the Giant Killer and Mordred the King Slayer could hardly be expected to play the perfect hosts."

"Still, we would not want them to be drowned, my lord."

"No," Anthony murmured, "we would not."

The rain had died to a drizzling mist; the sea below still churned, the green waves so glassy one could see the ocean bottom. Anthony gazed across the sea at the girl in the boat and felt a sudden stab of concern for her. Nuisance she might be, but he did not wish her harm.

Then, suddenly, she looked up at him. She looked at him, and the wind carried the scent of lilies, lilies and a rush of images from the past so poignant and overpowering that he felt himself carried away by their spell.

Children's voices clamored in his mind, excited and impatient with anticipation.

"Bring me a sword, Ethan! We're playing King Arthur in the forest, and last one there has to be his dwarf."

He heard his brother Ethan's voice. "Well, wait for Anthony, you idiots. He can't go as fast as us."

"Do we have to bring him, Ethan? He's always falling down."

"We *have* to bring him. He's my brother." Then, in an annoyed undertone, Ethan said, "Get up, Anthony. Make an effort to climb over the wall. I'll push you from below."

"Just go, would you?" Anthony pressed his face into the dirt. "I don't want to play, anyway. There never was a King Arthur, you know. It's a fairy tale for fools."

Ethan stared at him. "I am going to help you over the stile, but you have to climb the wall yourself."

"Go to the devil."

"Ethan! Ethan!" The other boys were calling him from the edge of the forest. "Your governess is coming—hide in the trees, or she'll take you in."

He waited until the other boys had vanished before he scaled the wall; flushed with victory, he dropped to the other side only to run three hobbled steps before he stumbled over a shovel.

He heard the boys laughing from the leafy depths of the forest, and he gritted his teeth. The new governess, a determined woman, was scaling the wall in her voluminous skirts to catch her charges.

His chest ached with the effort it took to hold back tears. He was nine years old, the eldest son, a weakling who suffered from a muscular myopathy which made playing sports such a painful challenge that his father had forbidden him to participate. Most people thought that the earl had imposed this restriction because he did not wish his heir to suffer injury. The truth, as Anthony knew it, was that his father was ashamed of his son's clumsiness and contrived to keep him invisible as much as possible.

The governess had found him. He lay facedown in the grass, pretending to ignore her. Humiliation washed over him as he felt her hand on his shoulder. "You are not hurt, my lord."

Strange, only now in retrospect did he hear the words phrased as a statement, not a question.

He would die of embarrassment if she tried to help him up with the others watching. He scrambled to his feet, giving her an angry look.

Her gaze scanned the trees. "You're not going to play with your friends?"

"They're not my friends, and I don't want to play King Arthur. It's a silly game. There was no such person."

She picked up a fallen branch from the grass. "Your sword, brave knight."

Her hair was hidden beneath a huge bonnet, and her eyes—had they been green, or was he recalling that other girl's remarkable features to fill the gaps in memory?

"No governess stays with us for long," he said confidently, ignoring the proffered branch. "My mother is addicted to laudanum, and my father frightens them off with his temper."

"Your papa is going away to conduct some business affairs in China." Her voice was low, hypnotic almost. "He will be gone a long time, my lord, and during his absence you will grow so strong he will not know you when he returns."

She had not put down the branch. Anthony wanted to hit her, or run away, but couldn't seem to move. "I'll never be strong. You—you're stupid."

"You will practice swordplay and become the bravest knight in King Arthur's court. It will be your solemn duty to defend the weak and protect the innocent. Always do what is right, young lord."

"Nobody wants to play with me. Except Ethan."

"You will practice with the fencing master who has been sent for this very morning."

She was mocking him, or she was mad. He took a stumbling step back. "Shall I knight you, young lord?" she asked. "Kneel, then."

"Me—kneel before you? You're a servant." Yet when he took another halting step back, his hip locked, and he went down on one knee, blinking in disbelief. The branch touched his shoulder, and he felt a bolt of power go through him, or perhaps only his hope, that with a touch of a magic wand he would arise, whole and unafflicted with his disability, like the other boys who mocked him.

He lurched to his feet, filled with bitter disappointment to realize nothing had changed. He was still uncoordinated, half lame, so consumed with despair that he barely heard her speak again.

"That was stupid," he whispered.

Only now did Anthony remember that the governess had left the scent of lilies in her wake. At the time, he had not cared. He'd wanted to shout at her that she was wrong; he would never be strong or ride into battle.

She left their Devon house three weeks later, and there was no time to wonder at her mysterious disappearance. The fencing master arrived the day she left, and the following week the earl inexplicably employed a new groom, a half-gypsy former jockey from Wales who gave the boys riding lessons.

Over time, while Anthony's mother languished on laudanum, he developed physical strength, but the change was so gradual that he barely noticed it. Then, one day, he got into a fight with a boy who had blackened Ethan's eye, and his life changed.

"You almost killed him," Ethan exclaimed as the other boys gathered around the fallen bully in awestruck silence. Anthony cradled his aching wrist. He still walked with a hint of a limp, nothing would change that, but his shoulders and chest had broadened, his face had matured. He stood a foot taller than the rest of them, and nobody could outride him except Leon, the half-gypsy groom, who congratulated him after the fight.

Anthony had not heard from the governess once in all those years. Not when his parents had died and he had inherited the earldom. Not when Ethan had gone off to fight in India and, ironically, had returned to England a partial cripple from a bullet lodged in his spine.

No, Anthony had not even thought of the bold-hearted woman again until the girl today reminded him, with her connection to King Arthur, the elusive perfume of lilies, and her unseemly spirit, which said: "I will not accept the world the way it is."

The spell was broken. Anthony released his breath. "What did my brother find in this dreary place to make him happy?"

Vincent, clearly only half listening, squinted into the spyglass. "Some people find peace in simplicity. Good heavens, the young woman has taken up the oar. How strange."

"Not that strange," Anthony said. "Oarswomen are common enough on the Scilly Islands."

"I don't mean that, my lord. It's this—" Vincent

lowered the spyglass, looking baffled. "There seems to be a small radius around her boat that is immune to the storm."

"What?" Disbelieving, Anthony pried the spyglass from Vincent's huge hands. "Let me see."

He narrowed his eyes. From a distance it did appear as if the waves she encountered fell calm while the sea behind her small boat boiled white and angry.

"It is an illusion of light upon the water," he said at last. "Look, the rain has stopped. The wind is dying."

"Is that an illusion up there too?" Vincent gestured skyward to the perfect rainbow that had just materialized from the bruised clouds above Morwenna's boat.

On the causeway below, the servants were clapping and hugging one another in wonder.

Anthony shook his head. "One would think they had never seen a rainbow in their lives."

"There are other rather unusual phenomena associated with the young woman, my lord."

"Aside from her predilection for besieging castles?"

"It seems the rare lady's-fan lily, so highly prized by botanists and flower vendors on the mainland, is in bloom for the first time in more than a decade."

"You, Vincent, believing this balderdash?"

"Not really, my lord."

The two men stood in silence until the rainbow faded from the sky. Miss Halliwell's boat had also disappeared behind the cliffs.

"I have wasted enough time today," Anthony said. "Camelbourne intends to take possession of the island at the end of the month, and I have only begun to pack Ethan's personal possessions."

"The staff is afraid they'll be let go when the marquess arrives, my lord."

Anthony frowned. "I suppose we might try to place them on the mainland."

"But not the entire island," Vincent added as Anthony took a step toward the tower door. "That was why she came here today."

"Excuse me, Vincent. Did you want to add something to the annals of the remarkable Miss Halliwell? Did she rise from a seashell while my back was turned?"

The burly manservant looked embarrassed. "Not that I noticed. However, I did neglect to warn you about the raven that has been seen haunting the cliffs since her return."

"A raven?"

"It appears only to alert the islanders of impending danger," Vincent said. "The bird has led a mother to a child stranded on the rocks at high tide, and warned a fishing boat away from one of the lethal undertows that encircle the isle."

"Coincidence."

"The islanders believe it is the spirit of King Arthur in the form of the raven, appearing to save Abandon from a dire fate."

Anthony laughed. "The dire fate appearing in the form of me, I presume."

Vincent smoothed his sideburns. "The natives claim that Miss Halliwell's entire family is endowed with mystical power."

"Ravens," Anthony said. "Rainbows, rare lilies. Send the housekeeper into the library with a pot of strong coffee. The sooner we leave this island, the better. I do not like the influence it has had on you."

2

Although it was still early in the afternoon, candle-light glowed throughout the spacious granite farm-house, a snug haven from the frequent storms that struck Abandon. Morwenna settled into the huge horsehair sofa between the half-dozen cats that had started mysteriously appearing at her door the week of her return.

She saw nothing odd in this; the life of Morwenna and her two sisters had been highlighted with so many inexplicable events that the three of them had almost come to terms with their peculiarity. After all, their mother, dead thirteen years ago, had been renowned on the island for her healing powers. As for Morwenna's father, well, one had only to look around this house to see evidence of a dedicated eccentric.

The housemaid could barely dust for all the arti-facts and bits of ancient relics her father had col-lected. The talking stones by the door that, in

Morwenna's memory, had never said a word. The shrunken head of the Malay shaman above the kitchen sink that gave everyone a fright. The crystal-encrusted circlet that was believed to have belonged to Morgan le Fay and to which Morwenna had formed a close attachment; she couldn't bear to part with any of Papa's treasures, not with him gone only fourteen months, now. She missed him too much.

No Halliwell had ever fit well into society, which was why after one year of living in London with Uncle Dunstan, the pair of them had escaped back to Cornwall. They both pretended that the research needed to finish Papa's book was what had lured them home. The truth was, they had been *dying* in London, friendless and without funds.

For the first time since her return, Morwenna wondered if she had made a mistake. She thumped her stockinged feet on the tapestried footstool and stared out at the misty coastline.

From a practical standpoint, the island supported more than one hundred and sixty people who depended on fishing and flower growing for their existence. This Eden would all come to an end when the marquess took possession. He had already ordered plots of land cleared for the hunting lodge he planned to build. Precious bulbs had been trampled by the carts of uncaring workmen.

All of which the Earl of Pentargon could stop with a snap of his elegant fingers. Yet he chose not to.

"There wasn't an ounce of chivalry in the monster. Not one quality one would hope for in a knight." She wiggled her toes for emphasis. "I don't know why you asked to sketch him, Elliott, you traitor."

The young artist smiled faintly, his dark head bent

over his sketchbook. He sat by the window to catch the dying light of the afternoon. His fingers moved nimbly even as he spoke. "He had the most magnificent face, Morwenna. That jaw could have been carved from granite."

"His heart as well," she said slowly.

"I could almost see the suppressed passion running in his veins."

"That was ice water beneath a frozen pond," she said.

"And the emotions smoldering in his eyes," Elliott said, shaking his head in admiration.

"Greed?" Morwenna suggested. "Impatience? Oh." She gently dislodged a cat from her lap, rising from the sofa. "What on earth are you drawing now?"

He smiled, not looking up.

Morwenna had known Elliott for almost eight years now. She remembered the very day he'd approached Papa in the street, a milliner's sweep-up boy, and had begged for a chance to illustrate Sir Roland's book on the origins of King Arthur.

At first, Papa had laughed. But Elliott had persisted, pushing his pictures under their door, following them to parties. And in the end, Papa had been impressed by his talent and how seriously Elliott took his own art—even to the point of practically abandoning his young bride of only a year to finish this last book. At times Morwenna almost felt sorry for the poor woman. Elliott had been enthralled with his bride at first, drawing endless sketches of her, but now he hardly mentioned her name.

Then he had lost the commission for the fresco painting at the palace of Westminster. Papa died, and

Elliott, in a moody depression that worried Morwenna, had insisted on coming to Abandon to help her finish this last work.

"Your father befriended me," he told her. "I must return the favor."

She gasped now as she peered over his shoulder. He was working on a rough sketch of a maiden in medieval garb embracing a fallen warrior. The drawing itself was lovely, and she was accustomed to Elliott using her as a model for his work. But the horror of it was that he had depicted Pentargon as the wounded knight.

She felt an unexpected shock of pleasure at seeing herself locked in Pentargon's passionate embrace. For a heady moment she experienced all the intense emotions Elliott had managed to convey between the maiden and the wounded knight. Strong flurries of sensation burst inside her, weakening her before she pulled away.

Yes, Pentargon was handsome in that dark way so dangerous to women, but how fanciful of Elliott to sketch him with that look of loyal gratitude.

"That is the most awful thing you have ever done, Elliott. Atrocious. What were you thinking?"

He shrugged. "I liked the look of him. I'm going to use him as the inspiration for Sir Gawain and the Green Knight."

"Are you mad?" she said in disbelief. "Bad enough that you played toady to Pentargon this morning, but to turn around and paint him a hero while he's selling Abandon as an aristocrat's playground—"

"You might have tried a more tactful approach and a little flattery yourself," her uncle said from his corner chair. "How many times have I told you that most gentlemen do not appreciate total honesty in a young woman?"

"Elliott," she said, ignoring her uncle's remark, "I absolutely forbid you to use that picture in Papa's book."

"Roland allowed me artistic license, Morwenna," he said curtly.

"License. Not lunacy."

"It's Pentargon you're angry with, anyway," her uncle pointed out. "Not Elliott."

"Oh, I give up." She sank back down onto the sofa, tugging a handful of pins from her hair so it fell in a tumult of dark gold to her waist. The cats started to play with it, pulling the waving ends until she shook herself free.

"You can't give up, miss," a worried voice said from the door. "You're the island's good luck charm."

The speaker was Emily Jenkins, Sir Dunstan's housekeeper, bringing in a tray of tea and scones.

Together with nearly everyone else on Abandon, Emily's great-grandmother, Annie Jenkins, believed that Morwenna's return was preordained to save the island. No one understood that she had come home only to finish her father's book on Arthurian legend. Still, she couldn't sit by and watch her childhood friends evicted from their homes.

Morwenna and her two sisters had lived on Abandon with their parents until Papa had taken it into his head to travel the world on a quest for mystical secrets. Scotland, Wales, the Far East. The girls had received quite an education until their mother, Mildred, insisted it was time to return to England.

Of course, Mildred had been the one the islanders had turned to for help in troubled times; from the letters Morwenna received from her sisters, both residing with elderly aunts, all three of them had apparently inherited Mildred's penchant for taking up lost causes.

"I failed miserably," she said, shaking her head. "The man's mind is made up."

"But his brother was such a gentle soul," Emily said as she cleared the table to make room for her tray. "He adored the island."

Morwenna sighed. "He and Pentargon could not be more unlike, it seems. I don't know what to do."

"Everyone is counting on you, miss," Emily whispered. "The pellar is offering to help, but at a price no one can pay, so we're all believing in you. Many's the folk only alive today because of your mother's power."

Morwenna stared into the fire, her thoughts in turmoil. The most evil man she knew, possibly next to Pentargon, was Pasco Illugan, the island's pellar, a self-proclaimed warlock who took Morwenna's return as a personal threat to his power. Pasco sold abortives and ill wishes for a living; according to local lore, he had appeared on Abandon the day of her mother's death, like a toadstool that sprang up when the sun vanished behind the clouds.

"If the people turn to the pellar," Emily said softly, "there's no telling what evil the man will wreak upon us. You're going to have to take him on, miss, both him and Lord Heart of Stone, if this island is to be saved."

Less than three hours later, Morwenna was bracing herself for another battle with evil. The pellar lived on the dark side of the island on Cape Skulla, where lilies never grew and ships were wrecked on the rigid spine of rocks submerged beneath the sea.

Plants of evil association such as henbane, rue, and hemlock flourished in his garden. A one-eyed crow sat on the cottage windowsill, watching Morwenna's approach with malice. She paused, wondering why she of all people had been chosen to take up the island's cause. She didn't feel brave or hopeful of a good outcome against the all-powerful Pentargon.

She felt desperate.

"Come on," she whispered over her shoulder to the white cat that had followed her, but the animal refused to come any farther. Morwenna could see the creature pacing before the gate, its back arched in displeasure. Her pony waited in the shadows of the wind-stunted yew woods.

"At least keep me company," she whispered to the cat.

"You desire company, Morwenna? Dear child, you need only to ask—to link your untapped powers with mine. Well, we could conquer the world."

She grimaced at the ingratiating voice in her ear.

Turning slowly, she looked up into Pasco Illugan's grinning face and felt a chill go down her spine. His prematurely white hair sprouted like wings from his head. Mystical symbols embroidered in red silk adorned his short purple cape, and he wore a moonstone pendant with a matching ring. He played the part of a warlock to the hilt.

He brought her hand to his mouth. "To what do I owe this honor, young enchantress?"

She snatched her hand away as his lips brushed her skin. Morwenna despised his dealings with darkness; the atmosphere of evil even in his garden made her soul cringe. "Isn't it obvious? I am desperate."

He stroked a tuft of hair on his chin, guiding her down the garden path to a stone bench. "You did not charm the beast Pentargon?"

She sat as far away from him as possible. "You know?"

"My dear, I know everything, which is, of course, why you have come to me today. You need my supernatural wisdom."

"It is your island too, Pasco. You have as much to lose as the others."

He glanced at his crude granite cottage. "Do you think so?"

"Surely you don't believe the marquess will allow a ninnyhammer warlock to squat on his land?"

Pasco's high forehead wrinkled in a frown. "I had thought I might become his personal adviser. I—"

"Don't be an idiot," she said. "A man of his position isn't going to associate with a lowly nodcock like you."

"Insults will hardly buy my assistance, Morgan." He blinked. "Morwenna, I meant. Ever since that illustration of you as the enchantress, I cannot help thinking of you as she."

Morwenna sighed. Elliott had immortalized her with his illustrations, and her dubious fame as an ancient sorceress had hardly helped her find a respectable place in society. "What am I going to do, Pasco? Pentargon is the coldest man I've ever met."

"Go back to him in person."

"No—he was hideously rude, to all of us. He wouldn't receive me anyway."

His pale eyes glinted as he drew a black velvet

pouch from his pocket. "Burn this in his presence, and his mind will be open to whatever you suggest."

She stared down at the pouch in distaste. "What is it, or shouldn't I ask?"

"That is my secret. Know only that it is powerful enough to make him yours."

"Make him mine?" she said in horror. "I don't want Pentargon—I want him to leave Abandon, that's all."

His lips flattened in irritation. "Charms do not come in specific little packages. Shall we discuss my fee?"

"What fee?"

"You will spend Midsummer Night alone with me in my cottage."

She jumped to her feet. "Oh, Pasco, you are disgusting. As if I would sell my body for a pack of twigs that probably won't work anyway."

He stood beside her. "Did I say it was your body I desired?"

She took a step back, noticing a sleek white shape sitting on the path. The cat had followed her and was sniffing the dank pool at the bottom of the garden.

"Don't drink!" she cried. "The water is probably poisoned."

Pasco grinned. "How thoughtful of you to bring a present, Morwenna. My stock of cat's eyes is almost depleted."

She grabbed the black velvet pouch and threw it in his face. "I should have known better than to come here. You are repugnant, Pasco Illugan."

"Just remember that we need each other," he said, smiling faintly. "Even a rainbow cannot exist without a storm."

3

The following day, Anthony forced himself to go through Ethan's personal effects. After only an hour, he could not bear to continue. As he turned to leave the library, his curiosity was piqued by a gilt-edged book on his brother's desk. It was entitled *Herein Lies Magic*.

The vellum pages felt so sheer that he hesitated at first to turn them. The book was hand-lettered in elegant Gothic script, the calligraphy and illustrations breathtaking. But, strangely, no author or artist took credit. Nor could he find a printing date.

The inscription on the frontispiece read simply:

> *Blessings upon you, Ethan, and welcome to Avalon. May you find the magic you seek in these ancient tales. Your friend,*
> *Roland Halliwell*

"Herein lies magic," Anthony said darkly. "But not enough to save you from falling to your death. You were in no condition to climb cliffs, Ethan. I wish you had never come to this place."

He closed the book as he heard Vincent entering the room, no doubt wondering if the master had lost his mind.

"Just leave the crates in the hall. I haven't the heart to do anything else today. Mrs. Treffry can help the footmen decide what should be packed."

He rubbed his face, and the book broke open again to an illustration of a beautiful medieval woman riding a palfrey. The innocent sensuality on her face brought the picture to life and stole Anthony's breath—until he realized he was staring at the classical features of the girl who was no doubt wishing him in hell at this very moment.

The Maiden Meets the Knight. That was the only thing written beneath the plate.

"Morwenna Halliwell," he said with a soft chuckle. "Of course." And curious to see how the artist depicted her in the rest of the book, he tried to read ahead only to find the pages adhered at the edges, so delicate he could easily tear them.

"Sea air." He glanced up. "What *is* the matter, Vincent? I thought you had gone."

"Actually, my lord, I did not come about the crates. There is a problem on the moor with the mining crew you hired to clear the land for the hunting lodge."

Anthony dropped the book on the desk. "How can there be a problem? The men only arrived last week."

"Yes, well, it's more of a delay. It seems the local pellar has planted himself on the crag and is calling down curses on the men as they work."

"What in God's name is a pellar?"

Vincent shrugged. "A powerful warlock, according to Mrs. Treffry. He put on quite a show, with a one-eyed crow upon his shoulder, a pet goat, and smoke bellowing from various crevices in the crag."

"And the miners, being the most superstitious men on earth, fell for this outrageous display." Anthony snorted. "I suppose I shall have to challenge this force in public to make my point."

"Perhaps not, my lord."

"Vincent?"

"Well, ordinarily I do not eavesdrop, but this morning, with your best interests at heart, I did a bit of espionage and learned that Miss Halliwell was seen visiting this pellar fellow yesterday afternoon."

Anthony's eyes glittered. "Was she, indeed?"

"I'm afraid you may have more of a fight on your hands than you anticipated, my lord. It appears they have made a pact against you."

Anthony was not a man to make idle threats or waste time. For one thing, he had little time— Camelbourne meant to take possession of the island in a month, and his battery of solicitors would descend in a fortnight or so with their binding contract and conditions.

One of which was secrecy. Camelbourne did not object to anyone knowing he had bought Abandon, but he did mind his part of the agreement being made public knowledge.

"If my cronies should find out I am lending your cause support, Pentargon, I shall never hear the end of it."

I have made a bargain, Miss Halliwell.
With the devil, I do not doubt.

Anthony laughed at the absurdity of her accusation as he rode from the ancient castle to the cliff road. Camelbourne might be a self-interested politician, but he was hardly evil. He might not share Anthony's passion for child labor reform, but then few people did. Anthony acknowledged that his concern was probably born of his remembrance of childhood suffering. And three or so years ago, before Camelbourne had lost his beloved wife in an accident, he had actually been a pleasant fellow. Anthony still believed a grain of goodness lay buried beneath his careworn cynicism.

Still, who would not be moved to hear of thirteen-year-old chimney sweeps dying of testicular cancer from their exposure to soot? Who would not feel compelled to action upon learning that women gave birth in coal pits and that underage girls, half-naked and chained, worked the bowels of the earth, raped and beaten by their employers?

Let Miss Halliwell throw a tantrum and lament the loss of her rare flowers. There was too much at stake for Anthony to risk, too many innocent children who needed a powerful protector. While he was not a cruel man, he would not be swayed by the young woman's plea, no matter how beautiful she might be.

He had hired and then transported a crew of seasoned tin miners from Cornwall to begin clearing the ground for the lodge. Unfortunately, the land the marquess had chosen also supported a circle of megalithic stones, which the islanders believed possessed magical healing powers.

When Anthony arrived at the site, only the leader of his crew and two other miners remained. The rest of the workmen had retreated to the sanctuary of Abandon's only tavern, the Seven Stars.

Anthony dismounted, sidestepping the line of shovels and picks where they had been dropped. The foreman of the crew, stocky and sandy-haired, hurried across the mud to greet him. "My lord, we have encountered a problem."

"So I understand," Anthony said grimly.

"It's him. The cunning man."

Anthony glanced up at the crag. Pasco Illugan stood shouting down indecipherable Celtic curses at the ground. His wiry gray-blond hair defied gravity to spike up from his head like the quills of a hedgehog. He wore a purple silk robe, the crow he carried long since gone, but a scrawny goat nosed the tufts of spiderwort at his feet.

Sulphurous fumes and smoke belched intermittently from the crevices of the crag.

"Quite the performer," Anthony said.

"I might even have been able to persuade the men to keep blasting the stones, my lord, but then a white hare ran across Harry's pick, and that's the worst omen to a miner. Then, after the white hare," Carew continued, "the pellar summoned an army of spriggans to attack the men."

"Spriggans?" Anthony said.

"Warrior fairies, my lord, of a particularly vile and vicious nature."

Anthony laid his hand on the man's shoulder. "So, Carew, you're telling me the boys stopped working because of a rabbit and a band of fairies, who, I assume, never did stage the threatened attack?"

Carew flushed. "Actually, it was the woman who stopped us cold."

There was no question of the woman's identity. Anthony could almost feel her mischievous presence in the moorland mist.

"The woman *stopped* you? How?" he demanded. "Did she hold her parasol to your heads?"

"She didn't need to, my lord."

"Her accomplices trained their pistols on you?" Anthony said coldly.

"Accomplice." Carew's voice dropped to a sheepish mumble. "An artist, he was, with pencils, not pistols. He brought the woman to the stones to sketch her, and the men were so smitten, well, it seemed impolite to splatter mud on her pretty gown. Dressed like a medieval princess, she was, my lord."

"Do I pay you to be polite?"

"But they were sketching a picture—to put into a book, my lord. No one wanted to ruin a masterpiece. She was a sight to behold."

Anthony turned on his heel. "I'll tell you what will be a sight to behold—the marquess finding my promise unkept, and you the man responsible for it because of warrior fairies and a woman in a costume. I won't have it, Carew, do you understand? I'm putting a stop to it today."

The entire island knew that the earl was displeased. His brother's barouche had arrived at Morwenna's cottage late that afternoon, and the shamefaced coachman informed her she was thereby summoned to the castle on a private matter.

Not that anything on Abandon remained private for more than a few minutes. Rumors were discharged and dispatched like lightning from cottage to cottage.

A small line of islanders assembled on the cliff road to watch their heroine swept to her dark destiny; no one really believed she would emerge from a "private" encounter with Pentargon in one piece.

On a lighter note, everyone agreed that at least Morwenna looked the part, dressed in a magnificent blue silk gown with an embroidered girdle that emphasized her slender curves.

Actually, Morwenna hadn't had time to change into a decent frock when the arrogant summons arrived. Elliott had insisted on squeezing out the last good light of the day in the garden, and she couldn't very well refuse, as the sketches would grace Papa's final work, the book of his heart.

Elliott was so dedicated to his art that it sometimes frightened Morwenna. Obviously, he wasn't anywhere as dedicated to their friendship because the coward had mysteriously disappeared when the time came for her to go to the castle. And her uncle was off exploring caves on the island, leaving her to handle the matter (or monster) by herself.

Her nervousness was not exactly relieved when a small crowd of islanders slowed the barouche to toss armloads of lilies her way. She felt suddenly like a live corpse on the way to its funeral. *What* could he want of her?

It was almost high tide on this side of the island, that time of day when the castle became as aloof and unapproachable as its lord. Waves attacked the wheels of the barouche as it clattered over the causeway. In another hour, the sea would smother the very foundations of the castle. A sense of isolation engulfed her.

Of course, it was silly to be afraid. There would be

servants swarming about the castle like bees to protect her from Pentargon—oh, what a preposterous thought. He was only a man—an earl, not an ogre—albeit an arrogant tyrant who could decree the fate of her people with a stroke of his pen.

The barouche slowed in the courtyard.

Morwenna felt another chill of foreboding as no one appeared to welcome her. Was it her imagination, or were black clouds massing over her head? What had happened to the fair skies? Why had she not thought to bring Emily for company (protection was what she really meant)?

Would Pentargon eat her alive? Had she offended him with her outburst? Or could he have changed his mind, decided to hear her side of the story?

The thought brightened her a bit. She snatched up her father's portfolio from the seat as Goonie, the middle-aged coachman, hurried down from his perch to help her alight.

"Good luck, my dear," he whispered before unhanding her.

Her heart pounded. Why was she going to need luck? *Was* the almighty Pentargon so angry at her that everyone knew it?

Her fears were confirmed as Mrs. Treffry met her at the door, warped at the hinges from the sea winds. "He knows," the woman said in an undertone. "Prepare your defense."

"Knows what?" Morwenna said in horror. "What did I do that I must defend myself against?"

"Made a pact with the pellar." Mrs. Treffry's voice trembled. "Oh, my lovely girl, what a sacrifice on our behalf. But goodness always wins out in the end, Morwenna. We have faith in your powers."

"Powers?" Overwhelmed, she almost dropped her father's portfolio on the floor. The sky looked practically black through the windows of the mahogany-paneled entrance hall. A shadow moved at the top of the wrought-iron balustraded staircase. She lowered her voice. "What do you mean?"

"The powers you inherited from your mother." Mrs. Treffry turned white as a footstep creaked on the stairs. "Oh, dear heaven, 'tis himself—"

Morwenna stared at the door, contemplating escape, when the dark velvet voice of the devil's henchman said over her shoulder, "How good of you to come on such short notice, Miss Halliwell, and how lucky you must be to miss another dangerous storm."

She turned slowly and stared up into the sardonically handsome face of her enemy, thinking that she hadn't missed danger at all. It was looking her straight in the eye.

"Cat got your tongue, Miss Halliwell? You seemed decidedly more talkative the day we met."

Now she was not merely nervous, she was shaking with terrified anticipation. A pact with the pellar—so that was the rumor that odious Pasco Illugan had spread. As with most gossip, there was enough of a grain of half-truth in it to make it difficult to deny.

Not that she owed Lord Pentargon an explanation. Her personal life was none of his business, even if he did own the earth beneath her feet.

Vincent appeared from the opposite end of the hall to take her shabby cloak and gray kidskin gloves. One of the kittens had chewed a hole in the left thumb, and heat burned her face as she saw Pentargon's too perceptive gaze light upon this flaw.

"You summoned me here for a purpose, my lord?" she asked, with a coolness he surely guessed was feigned.

An amused smile deepened the creases on either side of his cheek. How unfair that the man was so attractive, she thought. She felt scruffy and unpolished in his exalted presence.

He took her elbow, sending an electric shock through her body to scatter her thoughts. "Come into the library, Miss Halliwell, where we may talk in private."

She resisted, sending a beseeching look to the servants peering around various doors down the hall. *Do not leave me alone with him. Help me,* she begged in silence, and in answer to her unspoken plea, Mrs. Treffry bustled right between her and the earl, positioning herself by the card table.

"Now then, let me just lower the lamps."

"The lamps are fine," Pentargon said. "Except for the blasted moths that seem not to recognize day from night."

And as the two women watched in horror, he swooped his hand beneath the globe, capturing a fluttering insect between his fingers only to drop it at the unearthly scream his housekeeper emitted.

"No, my lord! Oh, no!"

"Don't kill it!" Morwenna cried, throwing herself on the other side of the lamp like a warrior.

He stared down at the fuzzy gray wings beating against the glass. "Those are moths, Miss Halliwell. They eat clothing."

"They're not just moths, my lord," the housekeeper explained. "They're fairies, the wee people."

He glanced up gravely. "Spriggans again?"

Morwenna flushed at the mockery dancing in his dark eyes. "Not spriggans. They're evil. These are piskies—the wee people."

"For God's sake," he said.

"Kill a fairy, my lord, and you might just find yourself blinded one day," Mrs. Treffry said with authority.

"You're wasting your breath," Morwenna said quietly. "His lordship does not believe in such things."

"She's quite right," Pentargon said from the Gothic stone fireplace where he had retreated, his arm against the mantel. "I do not believe. Mrs. Treffry, fetch sherry and a few saffron cakes for our"—he stared at Morwenna—"guest. Am I to understand you came here unescorted?"

"Only because you ordered it," she said in disbelief.

He snorted. "The assumption was that you would not come alone. Where is your uncle?"

She flushed again; he made her feel as if she were twelve years old. "Looking for Arthur's cave. As midsummer approaches, our chances are better for finding it. You see, the legend—"

He cut her off in mid-sentence, noting the numerous servants flitting back and forth across the hall. "Come up to the solar drawing room, Miss Halliwell. We'll take our sherry in quiet. I do not desire an audience of domestics for this affair."

"Upstairs?" She clutched the portfolio to her chest. "Alone?"

"Hardly alone. We shall leave the door open and ask Mrs. Treffry to stand guard."

She followed him out of the room, eyeing his tall

figure with trepidation. Elliott, she decided, had been right. Pentargon, at least in appearance, could pose as one of Arthur's knights.

"Pasco Illugan stopped the work I ordered at Wizard Tor," he said in a neutral voice.

She gripped the balustrade until her knuckles whitened. "That was not my doing."

He appeared to ponder her response, then said, "These stairs are torturous. I would think the ascent troubled my brother's leg."

"He used to climb the crags for sport," Morwenna said softly. "I saw him several times."

"I don't know what he found to make him happy here," he said, shaking his head as they reached the long gallery walk. "He could have lived in luxury in Dartmoor. He had a mansion at his disposal. I stayed in London most of the year."

Morwenna exhaled in relief at the sight of Mrs. Treffry climbing toward them. "But Abandon was his."

"He lived here as a virtual recluse."

"And died a hero," Morwenna said, amazed at his refusal to see.

"What?" He turned and stared down at her face, the tension that emanated from him palpable in the shadows. "What did you say?"

She felt faint-headed, aware of his strength, the emotion smoldering in his eyes. He was angry, and she had challenged him. What folly to think a girl of her inexperience could meet him on equal footing. "Surely you know how your brother died?"

"He fell off the blessed rocks to his death. Nothing to make a fairy tale in that."

She almost felt sorry for him, this man with the stone heart. "He was waving a lantern to warn a ship off Cape Skulla. He saved a dozen or so lives. The islanders are eternally grateful."

"A hero." He gazed out the window to the sea, gray and angry as the wind rose. "The poor fool."

"Perhaps death was not his punishment but a reward," she added, not knowing what else to say.

He fixed her with a stare that sent a shiver down to her toes. "Perhaps, Miss Halliwell, for those of your romantic persuasion. The remainder of us mortals, however, treasure our fleeting moments of human existence, which brings us back to earth. I intend to dispose of this cursed island, and you are interfering with my plans."

She was angry now herself. What did she have to lose? "It is *not* a cursed island. Did you know that Merlin the magician caused an earthquake after Arthur's death which submerged the Scilly Islands?"

"Merlin?" He laughed. "There was no such man."

"Actually, Merlin as we know him was introduced by Geoffrey of Monmouth, but there was clearly a basis for his existence in Welsh lore."

"Clearly?"

"There *is* a basis for believing that Abandon is King Arthur's final resting place."

"Only if one believes in King Arthur to begin with," he said with an infuriating smile.

Her anger threatened to erupt at his arrogance. "According to Celtic myth, Avalon is the entrance to the place of the deceased, approachable only by water."

"Meaning what, Miss Halliwell?"

She ached to grasp his broad shoulders and give him a good shake. "Do you fail to see the connection?"

He stroked his chin. "What connection?"

"Avalon. Abandon. A mere three letters of the alphabet—oh, come with me a minute. I want to show you something."

He pretended astonishment as she caught his hand and dragged him past the solar. "In my castle? Now, wait a minute—what of your reputation?"

"I don't have anything to fear from you, do I?" she asked boldly.

"Certainly not."

"Good." Her golden-brown hair was coming undone from its ribbon. "Never mind the refreshments, Mrs. Treffry. Just put them in the solar. I'm showing his lordship the northeast tower."

Mrs. Treffry, at the top of the stairs with a tray, brightened. "The northeast tower. Oh, very good, miss. I had a fire lit earlier while the girls were cleaning. It still might be going. I shall await your call, then, shall I?"

Morwenna smiled slyly. "Yes. Give me some time to show his lordship the magic of Abandon."

4

Magic.

The misguided young woman would hardly be so enthusiastic about luring him to some deserted tower room if she knew how desirable he found her, or what a danger to her innocence such an encounter could prove. It was a damn good thing he exerted an ironclad control over his impulses. Her odd brew of feyness and fire amused him and made him half wish he could do as she asked just to earn her admiration. He had no idea why he was allowing her to lead him about like a pet. In the end, he would only earn her hatred.

She seemed unaware of how beautiful she was, clad in that costume and scuffed boots. But her fingers felt as fine-boned as a bird's, tugging him up some dark slab staircase for heaven only knew what purpose. Her small hand trembled. She was afraid of him, although she had nothing to fear in the physical sense. Yet perhaps she understood that he would destroy her dreams.

The staircase narrowed to an impossible angle. He wanted to escape, suddenly, to have done with this pretense of accord with one he would be forced to disillusion. Abandon could be the Elysian Fields, but it would still belong to the marquess.

"My brother did not manage this climb with his disability," he muttered.

"He managed more than you realize, my lord." She sounded a little breathless. "Anyway, there are worse disabilities than a physical one."

He recognized a barb when it struck him. "Most young women would not think so. My brother came here to mend a broken heart and lost his life in foolish heroics and drink."

"Might it be that he found more than he lost?" she asked.

They stood at the tower door, staring at each other. He said, "Dear God, you are naive, to talk to me in such a disrespectful manner."

Her face went white. "I wonder how it feels to hold the power to enrich or destroy other people's lives."

He thought of the children he hoped to save with his "power" and that he owed this strange girl no explanation. "Quite nice, actually."

She swallowed. "You admit it?"

"You asked me. I answered. Call me heartless but not dishonest." He pushed open the tower door. "Show me this magic. It is getting dark, and you should be on your way back home. I trust you will not interfere in my affairs again."

She followed him into the flagstone-tiled room, dim light filtering through the iron grille of the window. Stormy air charged the atmosphere, and even at this height one could feel the shuddering vibrations of the sea as it cast ton upon ton of water against the castle's cliff foundations.

"I don't know what you mean," she said.

How tempting she was. He gazed from the pulsing beat of a blue-violet vein in her throat to the barely visible swells of her breast. "You deny that you were seen at the home of the island warlock?"

There was a silence. "I went to him, but we came to no agreement. I was unwilling to pay the price for his help."

"Your first-born child in exchange for getting rid of me?"

"Not exactly, my lord."

His gaze moved over her in a way that brought a stain of color to her cheeks. "I see. Then you were right to refuse him. Your virginity is surely worth more than that."

"I never said that was his price."

"You didn't have to." He smiled. "You are so innocent, it is painful to behold. Save your virtue for the man you marry."

She walked away as if she wanted to kick him. "I intend to, with or without your advice."

"And do not meddle in my business again. I am paying a fortune out of my own pocket for those men to work. The marquess *will* have his lodge, whether or not you choose to damage your reputation in a vain attempt to stop me."

"How rude—you *are* a monster."

"Be careful, Miss Halliwell. You are insulting the monster in his own tower. Who can predict what hideous evil you might unleash if you push the beast too far?"

"Do you know that the marquess plans to run a pleasure steamer back and forth from Abandon to Cornwall on a regular basis?" she asked in a trembling voice.

He was amazed the intrepid girl had not allowed his bad behavior to distract her. "That is his affair, my dear. Unlike certain other people, I mind my own business."

She stood her ground. "A pleasure steamer will frighten away the pilchards, and how will the people buy food if they have nothing to eat or no flowers to sell?"

"Pilchards?"

"Yes, fish." She raised her voice. "They come by August and are gone by November. The profits carry the island through the entire year."

"I doubt Lord Camelbourne will let anyone starve," he said unconvincingly, having never really considered the matter before.

"Not that you shall be here to care," she said.

"I believe I have made my point, Miss Halliwell."

"And I see no reason in trying to make mine," she said with a mournful sigh.

"Not to a heartless bastard."

"Your words, my lord." She darted to the chair to collect her portfolio. "I see no reason to stay and show you anything either."

He faced the window, his broad shoulders unyielding as he fought the part of himself that wanted to please her. "No reason at all. As I said before, we are both wasting our time."

He heard her footsteps pounding indignantly against the flagstones. Then the tower door slammed shut with a reverberation that must have taken all of her strength. Grinning at this display of temper, he glanced around to see her staring at the door in stunned disbelief, her portfolio on the floor.

"That is not amusing, my lord," she said, aghast. "You almost caught my hand, and a nasty bruise it would have been."

"I have no idea what you are talking—" He broke off, astonished. "Do you think *I* closed the door from such a distance?"

"It slammed in my face," Morwenna said. "I know that."

He strode toward her. "Then it was the wind."

"A gust of wind with remarkable timing," she said in suspicion as she watched him struggle unsuccessfully to force open the heavy door. "It is stuck."

He put his foot to the wall and pulled the knob until the cords in his throat strained. "I can see that. By damn, the wind did not do this. It is wedged tight."

"Well, open it, please. I do not intend to remain stuck in here all day listening to you insult me."

He gave her a look, taking off his coat and tossing it on the chair. "I suppose Mrs. Treffry thinks she is quite clever, locking the evil lord in the tower until the maiden changes his mind."

Morwenna folded her arms across her midsection. "Mrs. Treffry was not anywhere in sight when that door slammed."

"Oh, come, Miss Halliwell. The next thing I know, you shall ask me to believe that the piskies—or are they spriggans?—have conspired against us."

She stared in curiosity for several moments at his shoulders, then cast an uneasy glance around the room. The sky outside had darkened, sending an eerie black-gold glow through the iron grille of the window. "I think we ought to call for help," she murmured. "It is getting dark, and cold."

Anthony went down on his knees, examining the doorjamb in detail. "When I give the count, try the door again. I believe it is warped from the sea air."

"As you say, my lord."

"One, two, three—" He glanced up in annoyance. "You are pushing, Miss Halliwell, when you must pull." He flicked the hem of her dress from his face. "Once more, please."

"If it is magic, my lord, we are powerless against it."

"Magic? What girlish poppycock. Pull that knob with all your might. I think I see the problem here."

She grasped the knob in both hands and gave a furious tug. Something slipped out from beneath her embroidered girdle. Anthony reached across the floor for it, shaking his head. "It is useless. Here. You dropped this. We shall have to call for help."

Morwenna stared down in horror at the black velvet pouch in his hands. "Put it down, my lord. Drop it immediately. I do not know how it got here, I swear to you. I—I wasn't even wearing this gown."

"What is it, Miss Halliwell?" He chuckled at her grim expression. "A passion potion?"

"It very well could be," she said in utter seriousness, backing away. "It came from Pasco Illugan."

He snorted. "Eye of newt and that sort of nonsense?" Ignoring her warning gasp, he slipped his fingers into the pouch and withdrew a wax figure of a man. Even crudely fashioned, it was obviously meant to be Anthony, the features proud and aristocratic,

the black costume identical to his down to the pearl
buttons on the dark velvet waistcoat.

He suppressed a mocking smile. "If I believed in
such things, I should be very cross with you. What
else is in this pouch—dead leaves?"

"I've no idea. I never looked. I threw it in his
face."

"Ah, well." Then, as she watched in dread, he
casually walked past the chair and tossed both the
effigy and the pouch into the smoldering coals of the
fireplace.

"No!" she cried, darting forward. "*No*—"

Anthony blinked in alarm as a circle of flames
ignited in the glowing coals, hungrily closing around
the waxen effigy. Before he realized her intention,
Morwenna had fallen to her knees and rescued the
wax figure from the fire.

"A noble gesture," he said as she laid the effigy on
the hearthstone, "but quite unnecessary. I do not
fear—"

A shower of sparks and cinder exploded from the
fireplace, landing at their feet. Anthony grasped her
by the shoulders and pulled her to safety before she
could extract the pouch. For several moments, they
stared into the flames and watched the velvet bag
shrivel in a swelter of black smoke. Sweet fumes
filled the air, the acrid scent of burnt herbs.

"Good Lord," Anthony said. "What did you have
in that pouch, gunpowder?"

"It was Pasco's pouch," she said, shaking her head.
"I told you not to touch it. God only knows what evil
you have unlocked."

He stared down at her, aware that his hands still
rested on her shoulders, her frame so delicate he

could probably unbalance her with his little finger. "Do you really believe that plants have the power to influence our behavior?"

"Yes," she admitted. "I do, but I have never personally used one of Pasco's spells."

"I should not think you would need to."

"What do you mean, my lord?"

"A man could almost believe in magic when he looks into your eyes, Miss Halliwell."

"Could—"

He caught her chin in his hand and tilted her face upward. She did not resist. In all honesty, he gave her no time or opportunity to turn away. Astonished, he realized this was the kind of attraction neither of them had encountered before or could have fought anyway. Anthony had had his heart broken twice before, and he didn't want to break hers, which was why he groaned as he felt her soften against him, and the thought flashed through his mind that his fate and future had just been decided, sealed by this one impulsive act.

For her part, Morwenna did not even try to think. Born on Abandon, she had grown up on instinct, taught to follow intuition. Her parents had always given her too much freedom, which was why she had been such a dismal social failure in London, and now, at an age when she ought to be marriage-minded, she was kissing the man who had declared himself her downfall.

But there wasn't much she could do to ignore the eroticism of his mouth. His was practiced seduction, a kiss that entreated and stormed her senses even as it touched her soul. This was nothing like the embarrassed gropings of the island boys. Pentargon was a man, experienced in things she did not yet know of. His lips brushed hers with burning tenderness. So she stood before him in foolish trust and awakening arousal, reeling faintly when he lifted his mouth from hers.

"In future, Miss Halliwell," he said, his voice low, "you must never allow yourself to be caught in another situation like this."

She touched her tenderly ravished mouth, and all he could think was that he ought to take his own damned advice. What was the bloody sense in seducing a defenseless girl who had challenged his authority? Did he hope to prove his power by showing how he could destroy her?

Perhaps *defenseless* was the wrong description.

The blood pounding in his ears had yet to subside, and he felt disoriented, as if he'd fallen off a cliff, as he studied her face in the shadows. He wanted to bury his hands in her golden-brown hair and pull her down onto the floor.

"I apologize," he said gravely.

"For what?"

"For what? You aren't supposed to let a man kiss you like that, Miss Halliwell."

"You do not need to apologize, my lord."

"I most certainly do. If I hadn't regained my control, I might have ended up——" Well, there was no point going into that.

"But it isn't your fault if she's casting a spell over us," she said quietly.

"She?"

"Morgan, the enchantress. After all, this is her island, an otherworldly place. You have to expect the occasional act of magic. I suspect she closed the door."

"Do you know what desire is, Miss Halliwell?" he asked in amusement.

"Certainly. Well, not from personal experience."

"Believe me, it can feel as powerful as any magic potion. I rather think it is to blame for what just happened between us—a human flaw. None of us knows when he will succumb."

She shook her head as if privy to a great secret. "Annie Jenkins predicted this would happen. She said if you could not be persuaded through normal channels to save Abandon from disaster, a supernatural force might be employed."

Anthony paused. He had to admit Miss Halliwell's reaction to his kiss, if rather peculiar, was more refreshing than the usual slapping of his face or bursting into tears.

"I think we should try the door again," he said politely, backing away from her.

"You don't believe me." She walked to the window. "Look at this. It is what I wanted to show you."

He tried the door; it would not open. Nor did anyone respond to his shouts for help. Suddenly, it occurred to him that if they were not rescued before dark, if he and Morwenna ended up spending the night together, he might be morally obligated to marry the girl. He pounded on the door to no avail.

"No one can hear you," Morwenna murmured. "They're afraid of you, anyway."

"I don't know why," he said, turning toward her. "It's not as if I cook small children in a cauldron or put the islanders' heads on the castle pike for display."

"No." She pressed her small nose between the iron grille. "You've only sworn to take the food off their tables, tear down their homes and sacred monuments, and strip them of their dignity and independence."

He arched his brow. There was nothing defenseless about her tongue. He said, "If you happen to see someone on the beach below, perhaps you could call for help. I appear to need rescuing."

"Do you see that spine of rocks beyond the castle?" she asked softly.

He came up behind her. "Yes, but—"

"A long time ago, Morgan le Fay turned a dragon to stone. Its spine is visible sometimes beneath the sea, ensnaring ships that dare to venture too close to the slumbering king. When Arthur is in danger of being disturbed, the dragon awakens, thrashing its tail in what appears to be a storm to ward off intruders."

"Shipwrecks? She doesn't sound like a very nice sorceress to me."

"Oh, you wouldn't want to hurt those she protects. Her vengeance can be deadly. But the evil aspects of her character have been distorted by fiction. Ages ago, she was actually depicted as a healer and a benevolent enchantress."

"Mrs. Treffry told me that you and your uncle are searching for Arthur's cave."

She nodded. "We won't find it without Morgan's blessing. Anyway, only the purest heart can come into the king's presence."

"Are you not pure of heart?"

She tried to ignore him. "Legend has it that the fabled Land of Lyonesse is submerged between Land's

End and the Scilly Islands. A few scholars believe it was the scene of Arthur's last battle. Sometimes you can hear the bells across the sea of more than a hundred sunken church towers."

"Have you heard these bells?" It was obvious to her that he was dying to laugh.

"No," she asked, her back stiff. "Not yet, anyway."

"Then I tell you what, Miss Halliwell. Out of the goodness of my stone heart, I shall guarantee your right to research your father's book even after the island changes hands."

She turned to face him, her mouth curling into a smile. "You miss the point, my lord."

He gave her a beguiling grin. "Which is?"

"The island is *not* to change hands. The enchantress has brought you here for good reason. According to Annie Jenkins, it has been a long time since a warrior has come our way."

Another half hour passed.

Just when Anthony began seriously to worry that he and Morwenna would be accused of improper behavior, Sir Dunstan came to the rescue. By blundering good luck, the baronet managed to open the tower door. Stammering apologies to Anthony, which made it seem that Morwenna trapped men in towers on a regular basis, he ushered her out of the room with comical swiftness.

Anthony remained at the door, their voices echoing up the stone stairwell as they escaped the castle.

"Gracious, child," Sir Dunstan scolded her. "What were you thinking, to come here alone? Did our year with your aunts in London teach you nothing about propriety?"

"Only that it is often an illusion. I did send word earlier today for you to meet me here."

"And I practically flew across the sea when I discovered where you had gone."

"Where were you, anyway? Oh, Uncle Dunstan, you didn't find Arthur's cave?"

"I might have, my dear."

Their voices grew so faint that Anthony had to strain to hear.

"From my description, Elliott said it sounded similar to the dream cave he had sketched, and you know how he has an uncanny sense for these things."

"I shall go looking tomorrow," she said.

A pause, then, "Do you think you managed to convince him, Morwenna?"

Anthony did not wait for her to answer but returned instead to the room. It did not matter what she thought.

The storm had apparently passed, and pale summer light broke through the barred window. The fire had died, but wisps of pungent smoke curled in the air. He walked to the hearth, noting in amusement that his waxen effigy still lay on the blackened stone.

"Thank goodness I am not melted into a helpless lump of wax," he said, chuckling as he bent to the stone.

His hand froze in midair.

There was not one waxen figure on the hearth now but two. The image of himself and a female form clad in a flowing blue robe. Their bodies were fused together from the heat, and the male doll's arms had melted around the woman's shoulders, as if he were trying to shield her from harm.

He stood, the wax effigies still warm in his hand.

Of course, there was a logical explanation. Miss Halliwell had put the other doll there to mock him. There was a logical explanation for every strange occurrence on the island.

Something made a scratching noise at the window.

He turned and saw a large black raven seeking purchase on the parapets beyond the tower. Its dark eyes gleamed at him from beneath the bars, then it was gone.

He strode toward the window and watched the bird take flight into the air. He watched as its black wings soared skyward . . . against the rainbow arched above the clouds.

"There *is* a logical explanation for everything."

"My lord?"

He looked around and saw Vincent at the door, his face puzzled. "You asked me to inform you when Lord Camelbourne's crew had arrived, my lord. They are in the servants' hall, having a snack, and a meaner lot I have never seen."

Anthony nodded. "Then they will get the job done. I trust they understand there is to be no violence."

"I emphasized that point, my lord. By the look of them, however, I am not convinced it was well received."

5

He fell asleep that night with her mischievous face emblazoned on his mind. He couldn't remember when a single kiss had stirred up such a welter of emotion. Certainly not in his recent years. But then, forbidden fruit always tasted sweeter, and even if he had enjoyed antagonizing her, he could not justify luring Abandon's favorite maiden to her ruin.

He also couldn't bring himself to burn the two figures in the fire. Not yet, anyway. They inspired a sort of whimsical apprehension in him, touching and wicked, even slightly erotic. He realized the sexual response they evoked stemmed more from his own attraction to the untamed girl than from any magic, and he also knew if would be far better for them both if he took her in hand instead of to his bed.

Still, if he examined the situation in feudal terms, she was at least superficially under his authority. He supposed he could use that to his advantage, although her heart appeared to be in the right place.

She couldn't help it if her parents had never explained her place in the world. He was doing her a kindness by asserting his position.

The morning passed without incident. No attractive girls stormed the castle. No warlocks threatened to raise the dead. The only sour note in the day was struck by Mrs. Treffry slamming the library door while he was sorting through Ethan's accounts, which were every bit as muddled as he'd expected.

He should have known the peace would not last. Shortly after noon, a man arrived to inform him that there had been trouble at Wizard Tor, a disturbance that had ended in a fight between the men digging.

Anthony left the castle right away, surrendering his hopes for a productive day.

When he arrived at the site, he found Carew in charge and no sign of problems except that it did not look as if much had been accomplished since yesterday.

"Where is everyone, Daniel?" he asked as he dismounted.

"I sent them off to cool their tempers, my lord."

"Then there was a fight?"

"There was, between my men and the crew that come 'ere last night."

"What could there be to fight about in a matter of hours?" Anthony wondered aloud.

"Flowers, my lord."

"What?"

"You heard the man." Morwenna rode her pony alongside them. "He said flowers."

Anthony frowned at her. "I did not pass you on the road."

"I do not take the common path."

"What are you doing here?" he said.

"Taking an innocent ride across the moor."

"Ha."

"Excuse me?"

"It's the *innocent* part of that statement I question, Miss Halliwell."

"I haven't done a thing," she exclaimed.

Anthony stared at her. She did something to him every time he saw her. "What is this nonsense about flowers, Carew?" he demanded.

"Lilies, they were," Carew said, moving respectfully out of Morwenna's path. "They grew overnight in the very spot where we removed one of them standing stones."

Anthony glanced up at Morwenna, catching the fleeting smile that crossed her face. "Then tear the flowers up by the roots."

Carew was starting to perspire, although Anthony could have sworn it was more Morwenna's presence, not his own, that reduced the man to his nervous state. "I did exactly that, my lord."

"Then what in God's name is the problem?" Anthony shouted.

"Perhaps we should call in the authorities," Morwenna said.

Carew sent a meaningful look at Anthony. "That would be him, miss."

"Yes, it would, wouldn't it?" she said, turning to examine Anthony. "Do you have the authority to arrest flowers, my lord?"

He leaned across the pommel, giving her an evil grin. "I'd prefer to arrest the person who planted them."

"Is it actually illegal?" she asked guilelessly.

He took a breath before redirecting his annoyance at Carew. "Why don't you resume digging?"

"Well, we would have, my lord," Carew mumbled, "except that when the men returned from dumping those flowers into the sea, a new crop had already started to grow."

Anthony's jaw tightened. "Within hours? Someone is playing tricks on you, Carew."

Carew lowered his voice. "So I said, but the trouble is, I assigned three men to stand guard over the site."

Anthony looked up slowly at Morwenna. "Well, Miss Halliwell, I shall be direct. Did you plant those flowers?"

She pretended to study the scuffed toe of her ankle boot. "I did not."

"Did Pasco plant them?"

She glanced at him. "Bog thistles and toadstools are more his style."

Anthony vented a sigh. "Flowers notwithstanding, Carew, this hardly seems reason enough to cause a fight amongst your men."

"No, my lord." Carew hesitated. "You're aware the men are sleeping in makeshift huts on the moor until our work is done?"

"Yes," Anthony said impatiently. "If such a day should ever come. What are you trying to tell me?"

"Well, one of the men got up at midnight to answer nature's call and heard queer noises."

"The wind," Anthony said. "I heard it myself last night."

"What they heard wasn't the wind, my lord," Carew said. "'Twas the sound of hoofbeats and the clanking of men in armor."

Morwenna shook her head. "Blame me for that too."

"The wind," Anthony said again, biting off the words like a thread between his teeth. But he missed Carew's reply because Morwenna chose that moment to depart the scene of the crime, guiding the pony back onto the crag path through the pass to the sea.

"And so, my lord," Carew was finishing, "you see my problem."

Anthony turned his attention from Miss Halliwell's receding figure to the foreman. "No, I don't see your problem, unless it is that you do not wish to be paid for this work, and the handsome price we agreed upon. What kind of control do you wield if your men are fighting after only a few days on the job?"

Carew looked up at the crag. "It was because of her, if the truth be known, my lord."

"Miss Halliwell?" Anthony asked, wondering why he should be surprised. "The men were fighting over her?"

"It was the other foreman, Camelbourne's man, who started it. He's a rough sort, my lord, and he wanted to teach the young lady a lesson. I said you wouldn't tolerate that sort of thing."

"I would not."

"Well, he took exception to my point of view and made a nasty remark to my cousin. One thing led to another, men being men, and there was a fight."

"Then you did the right thing, Carew, but for God's sake, keep them in line from now on, and don't ever tell me that the work has been delayed because of *flowers*."

"No, my lord."

*　　　*　　　*

Anthony should have let the matter rest at that, but his instincts said that this was not the end of it; the source had not been suppressed, and anyway, he wanted an excuse to see her again.

He found her easily enough, exploring a small cove at the base of the cliffs that began the treacherous curve of beach called Cape Skulla. He spotted her from the top of the path and left his horse beside her pony. For a moment, he simply enjoyed the sight of her chasing a gull away from a crab. He knew she had seen him too, even though she pretended not to notice him until he was standing barely two inches from her.

"Yes. I know. I know." She straightened from the tide pool she was examining, her hands raised in a gesture of surrender. "You have come to scold me for my badly behaved flowers. Well, I didn't plant them. I swear it, although I half expected something like this would happen."

He braced his foot on a rock, noting she had discarded her boots on the beach. "Does this mean your symbolic flower has a habit of interrupting important works?"

She pulled off her bonnet, letting it fall by its ribbon to her shoulders. Her nose was already unfashionably pink from the sun and the sea air. "I do not believe my flowers have ever created such a wonderful disturbance before. The butterflies did."

"Butterflies?" he said. "You command an army of them, do you?"

She seemed immune to his mockery. "Not me. My sister Mallory. Or was it Meredyth—yes, it was Merry. You see, this other odious man meant to reopen an old mine where several children had died underground while working. Their poor ghosts are said to haunt the shafts. But on the day the crew was set to begin reconstruction, an army—your word, my lord—of butterflies appeared out of the blue and would not go away."

He said nothing, staring into the sea cave behind them as lacy surf foamed around his boots.

"I suppose you think that is silly," she said. "A man of your measure certainly does not concern himself with the lot of lower-class children, especially dead ones, but Merry was determined to prevent that mine from taking any more young lives."

He turned his head, his expression unfathomable. "So your sister ordered her butterflies to swarm?"

"I'm not sure how it happened. The three of us never know when these things will strike." She shook a wedge of sand from her skirts. "They probably appeared in much the same mysterious way as the lilies and rainbows do."

He stared at her. "Have these peculiar phenomena occurred all your lives?"

Morwenna picked up a periwinkle and gently placed it in a rock pool. "I'm afraid so. It seems to be a family affliction—uncles, aunts, cousins, going back for ages. But as for my sisters, well, Mallory was born on Beltane, Meredyth on Samhain, and I on Midsummer Eve. During an off-season storm."

"I suppose there was a nocturnal rainbow to celebrate your birth?"

"Oh, no." She gave him an impish grin, bending for her boots. "Just a shower of shooting stars—oh, watch out, the tide is coming in."

They clambered up the rocks to the cliff path as a large wave broke on shore. Anthony's stallion had waited obediently where he'd left it. Morwenna's pony had wandered off to nose at a patch of stonewort.

"Supernatural signs aside, Miss Halliwell, I fear you have not accomplished your goal. The healing stones will be removed by nightfall so as not to impede Lord Camelbourne's view of the sea."

She shook her head. "Then something dreadful will happen. Annie Jenkins is certain Morgan placed those stones in that very spot for a purpose. Does the marquess know they possess magical properties?"

"I sincerely doubt it."

"I see. Perhaps someone ought to enlighten him."

"Miss Halliwell, you have a fiendish gleam in your eye. I warn you, Camelbourne would chew up a young thing like you and spit you out without a thought."

"How revolting."

He grinned. "Graphic to prove a point—you will not fare as well with Camelbourne as you have with me."

The wind lifted the ends of her hair; a smile crept across her face. "Have I fared well with you?"

He regarded her with dark humor. "The fact that you have defied me twice and lived to tell of it would set London on its ear."

"Thank you, my lord."

"I am not entirely sure that was meant to be a compliment," Anthony said. "In fact, I am positive of it. There is nothing socially attractive in making a nuisance of oneself, or of prowling castles and caves unescorted. Allow me to see you home to your cottage, where I suggest you stay until morning. I would not want you to get hurt in the work that will be done on the moor."

She gazed at him gravely. "I suggest you do the same."

"What?" he said in astonishment.

"The white fairies of Bucca Guidden, the good power, will manifest some displeasure at your stubborn removal of their stones. I should hide in the castle were I you."

He grasped her arm. "I believe I am capable of protecting myself, even if you leave little dolls about to alarm me."

"Dolls?" She stared at him, her eyes reflecting the sea. "Are you referring to the waxen effigy?"

"Effigies. Do not try to pull the wool over my eyes, Miss Halliwell. I am not Carew to believe in spriggans who pop out of the ground doing nasty deeds."

"Effigies?"

His face amused, he removed a linen handkerchief from his vest pocket and unwrapped it to reveal the two fused figures. "You may as well keep them—as a token of your unwise afternoon in the tower with a beastly man. Perhaps they will serve as a warning against future indiscretions. I doubt you would escape unscathed with another man in the same situation."

She studied the waxen figures, not offering to take them. "This is most peculiar," she said after a silence. "I wonder what it signifies."

"It signifies that an unsupervised girl is playing tricks in order to change a man's mind, and the man is *not* deceived."

"I have never seen that female effigy before."

"All right. Then one of the servants sneaked it in to give me a scare." This, however, seemed highly unlikely as Anthony had only turned his back for a few moments; still, for all he knew, the tower concealed a secret passageway in its walls, and the whole situation had been staged.

"You were carrying the dolls next to your heart," she said in wonder.

"Is that all you can say for yourself, Miss Halliwell? The female figure is clearly you."

"That does rather look like my hair."

"I believe it *is* your hair." He held out the effigies. "Do you want them?"

"Do you?"

He sighed. "I shall keep them in a safe place for a few days, though Lord only knows why."

She seemed relieved when he rewrapped the figures in his handkerchief. "They looked rather happy together, didn't they?"

"Deliriously so," he said dryly.

"I can't imagine where I came from," she said. "The figure of me, that is."

He could think of nothing to say to that, so he grasped her arm again. "I am seeing you home. You do know you caused a fight on the moor this morning?"

"Did I?" She looked pleased.

He frowned. "Yes, and I shall give your uncle a good scolding about your unsupervised escapades on this island."

She laughed; it was a delightful sound like the tinkle of a crystal bell. "Perhaps you should. He's probably lost exploring himself at this very moment."

They walked up the path together. He mounted his stallion; she followed slowly on her pudgy pony. The sight of Pentargon astride the massive horse gave Morwenna's heart an unexpected jolt. What a well-built man he was, as rugged as an ancient knight, his manner chivalrous, discounting the evil fact that he meant to sell the island. For all his coldness, she could not deny he was the most intriguing man she had ever met. She was certain that his kiss yesterday had changed her life in some indefinable way.

For one thing, her bed had been filled with moon-beams all night long, their light so brilliant that nei-ther she nor the cats could sleep. For another, she was certain she had heard the talking stones in the parlor whisper something when she walked past them, but what they'd said she could only guess.

Morwenna is in Pentargon's power. She let him kiss her . . .

She wondered what it would be like to belong to a man like Pentargon, how deeply his passions ran, or whether they ran at all into that heart of stone. She wondered why, at times, he seemed to favor his right leg, ever so slightly, a flaw most people would not notice, but Elliott, artist and sculptor of the human body, had.

Had Pentargon been injured in a duel? He rode his horse with practiced ease, his broad shoulders in per-fect line with his narrow hips. Morwenna imagined he would make a possessive but attentive husband. A woman would probably not mind obeying his orders.

She wondered where in the world that wax figure of herself had come from, if it came from this world at all, and if someone had put an ill wish on her, or perhaps if Pasco was working a spell of mischief because she had insulted him. She wondered so many things that she neglected to notice when Pentargon took the wrong path along the cliff.

She just followed blindly, admiring his shoulders and chiseled profile, so that when the huge raven appeared overhead, she was more startled than he.

The raven circled above Pentargon's shoulders before it descended with determined grace. At first even Morwenna thought the bird meant to attack. Its glossy black wings glistened in the sun; its guttural croaks rose above the crash of the waves against the cliffs.

"What in God's name?" Pentargon shouted as he brought the stallion to an abrupt stop.

The animal, sensing its master was in complete control, did not flinch as the bird of prey beat its wings in the air before soaring out of sight behind the cliff.

But Morwenna's pony, a shy cart animal, panicked, attempting to press back against the wall. Morwenna slid onto the rocky path with a startled cry.

Pentargon was upon her before she could disentangle her skirts from the myrtle bush that bloomed in the crevice of the cliff. "Miss Halliwell, are you hurt?"

She indulged herself in a moment of wicked bliss as he gathered her into his arms. The scent of starched linen and shaving soap enveloped her. Beneath the crisp fabric of his shirt, she felt his heart (he clearly possessed one, cold or not) beating in agitation.

"Miss Halliwell, look at me. Are you injured?"

"I do not think so." She sighed as he released her, lifting her to her feet. "Did you see that, my lord?"

"Yes, that damned bird nearly sent us both off the cliffs." He cast a grim glance at the sheer drop.

"Oh, but you're wrong," she exclaimed. "It saved

us—look, the path is crumbling. The warning sign must have blown away in the storm. Everyone knows not to take this path. I was too distracted by— by—well, I wasn't paying attention, or I would have noticed myself."

Anthony stared at her, silent and forbidding.

"The raven's appearance was no accident," she added. "Do you not see?"

"Not quite," he said crisply. "Not unless the bird is one of Pasco's pets, trained to be a nuisance. That would explain why I caught it watching me from the merlons."

Morwenna's lips parted. "You have seen the raven before?"

"The damn thing perched outside the window right after you left the castle yesterday. Odd coincidence, isn't it?"

"It didn't."

"I just said that it did."

She narrowed her eyes. "I do not believe it."

"Miss Halliwell, it is not something important enough that a man should lie."

"It certainly is."

"What?"

She regarded him with renewed suspicion. "Only a favored few have been deemed worthy of the raven's rescue. You do know who just saved us?"

"I do not recall hearing the blessed bird introduce itself."

She pulled a myrtle leaf from her hair. "It was King Arthur, or so the legend goes."

"I scarcely know what to say."

"Judging by the rather sarcastic look on your face, perhaps that is for the best."

He started to laugh.

Morwenna folded her arms across her chest and frowned. "You are laughing at one of the greatest legends that ever lived."

He shook his head, laughing harder. "No, honestly, I'm not. Vincent tried to explain before, but—but—"

"Hmph."

"Miss Halliwell, please forgive me."

She felt the corners of her mouth began to twitch. "I wouldn't blame the raven if it pecked your arrogant head to a nub."

He struggled to look contrite. "A fate I undoubtedly deserve. Forgive me?"

He stared at her until she too began to laugh. "Only if you forgive my flowers."

"Forgiven." His eyes held hers spellbound. "Are we friends?"

She smiled. "I hope so."

The pony would not be mounted after its fright; Morwenna had to pretend to be disappointed when Pentargon insisted she ride with him on his horse. By the twinkle in his eye, however, she did not seem to have done a good job of pretending.

"On second thought, I am capable of walking," she said.

"I do not doubt it."

She allowed herself to press her cheek briefly against his well-muscled back. The man appeared to be in remarkable physical condition. "It is said that only those chosen for a higher purpose are saved by the raven."

Anthony chuckled.

"You cannot continue to deny the supernatural, Lord Pentargon."

"Of course I can."

"More powerful men than you have challenged the enchantress."

"You speak of knights in make-believe stories." A cool smile touched his lips. "They were not real, my dear, and I am."

She was silent for a moment, staring around his shoulder. She could see the castle, Pentargon's lair, jutting up from a foundation of serpentine rock in the sea. She had always thought the fortress was the crowning jewel of Abandon, which lay just outside the circle of the Scilly Islands.

Once a possession of the church, Abandon had previously belonged to the Duchy of Cornwall but had fallen into private hands during the Civil War, when it sheltered several Royalist families.

Ever since Morwenna could remember, Abandon had been enshrouded in legend and dark mist, linked to megalithic Britain. On her shores, mermaids lured sailors to their ruin and took idiot children under their protection.

On her moor, giants had rolled boulders in a game of bowls, and the enchantress Morgan le Fay had brought a dying King Arthur after his final battle; healing him, she had concealed the king and his knights in a secret cave until the time came for him to rise up and battle again for Britain.

She smiled faintly. "You might regret your arrogance, my lord."

"Oh?"

"Sooner than you think."

Anthony doubted that he would regret his arrogance. It served him well to keep the world at a distance. However, he did suspect he would come to regret his unchaperoned meetings with the girl. He felt a sting of pleasure every time he met her, accompanied by a presentiment of foreboding that he was courting a personal disaster.

He wasn't a superstitious man. Experience warned him that he could not continue these encounters without paying a price, but the truth was, he rather enjoyed her antagonism and intelligence.

"Your uncle needs to keep a sharper eye on you," he thought aloud.

He sensed her draw away from him. He had liked the feeling of her small body pressed close to his, and he was tempted to prolong the ride to keep her nestled against his back.

She said, "Then someone would have to watch over him at the same time. He has no common sense when it comes to his own safety."

Anthony smiled to himself. The horse took the stone-hedged lane to the farmhouse, the pony trotting behind. Swatches of wild roses and honeysuckle brushed against them; the air smelled like a bottled elixir of herbage and sea brine.

"Perhaps your uncle ought to take you to London for a season."

"To find a husband, you mean." She sounded embarrassed. "We tried that, to no success. Most of the men I met hinted that I was a trifle too outspoken for their taste."

"You—outspoken?"

"Yes. Hard to believe, isn't it?"

He grinned. "I am at an absolute loss to explain it."

"My uncle is always telling me a woman should not speak her mind. Do you agree?"

"Not when she has a fascinating mind like yours."

She brightened. "Was that another compliment?"

He cleared his throat. "Actually, it was."

"Goodness. I shall grow quite conceited." She broke into a grin. "Like you."

"Like me? Perhaps you have mistaken confidence for conceit."

They came to an open road where a stone marker showed the way. The sun glinted off bright clumps of gorse and heather. In the distance, a dark shape moved, then evolved into a man riding hard toward them.

"It's Elliott," she said in surprise, twisting her upper body around to see. "Something must have happened—I hope Uncle Dunstan didn't get stranded on the rocks again. I've told him to stay away from Cape Skulla."

Before Anthony could stop her, she had dismounted and broken into a run across the moor, her skirts grasped in her hands. He rode up alongside her. By Elliott's disheveled appearance, he was forced to admit something had to be wrong.

"What happened?" she said as Elliott reined in beside her. "Is it my uncle?"

Elliott glanced over at Pentargon. "No, well, not him directly, thank God, but close enough. It's the farmhouse."

"The house?" She stumbled over a stone in her unlaced boots, steadying herself against the massive shoulder of Pentargon's stallion. "There's soot all over your hands. A fire—no, not Emily. Not the cats."

Elliott rubbed his face, his fingers streaked black. "The farmhouse was vandalized. I think all the cats are fine. Emily is hysterical but unharmed. I gather she had been out at the post office and interrupted the vandals. Your uncle was taking a nap and didn't hear a thing, which is a miracle considering the vicious destruction done."

Anthony dismounted, already in charge of the situation. "What exactly happened? You said there were vandals. Did they set a fire?"

The look Elliott shot him could have hinted at accusation or distress. "There wasn't a fire, Lord Pentargon, but the farmhouse was broken into and considerable malicious damage done. Some of Sir Roland's papers and my sketches were thrown in the parlor fire. I salvaged what I could, but when I realized I did not know where Morwenna was, well, naturally, my main concern was to make sure nothing had happened to her."

"Take me home, Elliott," she said. "I want to count all the cats and assess the damage myself."

"Let Elliott bring your pony," Anthony said, turning her with gentle firmness toward the stallion. "I will take you there."

Anthony knew at once it was no ordinary act of vandalism. He stood in silence in the parlor doorway, hiding his shock at the destruction. The lace curtains and sofa had been slashed with a pair of scissors that protruded from the cushions. Wet sand had been splattered on the wallpaper. Gilt-leafed books lay on their broken spines where they had been hurled, and a pile of papers and sketches smoldered in the coal fire.

Morwenna looked more confused than afraid, surrounded by a half-dozen crying cats. "Oh, Elliott, your drawings of Papa as King Arthur are destroyed. I am so sorry."

He helped her right an armchair. "Never mind. We'll find a new model, or I'll work from memory. They weren't my best work, anyway."

She sank down in front of the fireplace, sifting through the ashes. "Oh, look at this. All his work on the origins of Tintagel, the Middle Dutch interpretations of Tristan. I shall never find another translator in time to finish the book."

Anthony coaxed a frightened kitten out from behind the Sheridan writing desk. "I wonder if whoever left the effigy of you in the castle is responsible for this. If so, they have gone beyond malicious mischief."

She glanced up at him. "This was not an islander—not even Pasco would be this horrible. It could only be one of your gangers, for whom you are responsible."

His face darkened as he deposited the cat on a chair. There were charred papers everywhere— Icelandic sagas, medieval chronicles, a sketch of Merlin commanding the sea from a cliff. "I doubt this was the work of the men I hired."

"How do you know?"

He stared at her, unaccustomed to being challenged. "Because they have been warned that I will discipline anyone who breaks my rules of behavior. Carew has worked for me before. He knows I pay well and punish hard."

She came to her feet, her temper erupting. "Who else would it be, then? Nothing like this ever happened until you came here. Oh, never mind. What is the point in begging your help? I shall handle this myself."

"You are not going to handle anything, Miss

Halliwell, except, I hope, your own composure. I will question the gangers."

"His lordship is right, Morwenna," Sir Dunstan said as he entered the room. "We cannot rush to accuse when we have no proof. The fishing fleet has taken on a few outsiders for the summer."

"A total stranger would have no reason to do this," she said, her gaze locking with Anthony's.

"Where is the housekeeper?" he said quietly.

"Lying down with a vinegar cloth on her head," Elliott said. He was staring at the scorched drawing Morwenna had plucked from the coals. "All my work for nothing," he murmured. "Years of study, effort. It's gone now. I'll never have it back."

Morwenna, throwing Anthony a desolate look, went down on her knees beside Elliott. "You can do it again. You're brilliant."

"Not brilliant enough, I'm afraid. I had my moment of brilliance. But now it's gone." He glanced around at her, forcing a smile. "Listen to me. It's you and your uncle I should be consoling. Whoever did this definitely meant it as some kind of threat."

"That is my feeling exactly." Morwenna rose to face Anthony again, but he had turned to the doorway, focusing his attention on the tearful housekeeper Sir Dunstan had summoned from bed.

"Miss Jenkins," he said, "I know you have been upset." His voice sounded so gentle that Morwenna caught her breath. "I want to ask you a question or two, then you may return to rest. Did you see the men who did this? Could you identify them?"

She shook her head, weepy and fragile. "I came in the kitchen door and saw a figure all in black, my lord. Black hood, black cloak. He was talking to someone in the parlor, I think, but I only caught a glimpse of the one. I gave a scream when I saw him. He turned and threw a chair at me. I think I screamed again. I don't remember anything else."

Sir Dunstan patted her arm. "It was quite a scream to wake me from a nap, my lord. I found the poor woman in a faint on the floor. For a horrible moment, I thought she had been assaulted."

"The gray kitten with the sore paw is missing," Morwenna exclaimed, rising from the floor. "If they've hurt him—"

She was gone before Anthony could say another word. He turned back to Sir Dunstan. The housekeeper had returned to her bed. "I do not believe the men I hired would do this, but you have my word I will look into the matter."

Sir Dunstan lowered his voice, motioning Anthony into the hallway. Elliott was preoccupied with cleaning the mess in the parlor. "I want to show you something else, my lord. I do not know what to make of it. Perhaps you might venture an opinion."

He led Anthony into Morwenna's bedroom, a rather cluttered but charming rose-chintz retreat from the world. Where other girls might collect perfume bottles and fans on the dressing table, she displayed such startling items as an Aborigine mask, polished stones, shells, and a tottering pile of ancient books and Saxon maps. Then he noticed the bed.

"What in God's name—"

In the middle of the feather bed, covering the faded down comforter, were heaped several shovelfuls of mud. Around the dirt, a circle of pale ivory lilies protruded, their fragrance so poignantly evocative that Anthony felt a visceral reaction in his gut.

A disturbing enough sight, but more disturbing was the small stone cross that rose crookedly from the mud. The significance of it escaped him—the feeling of evil it exuded did not.

"What does it mean?" he said in a clipped voice.

Sir Dunstan looked grim. "It's a pagan burial cross from the moor where your men are digging, my lord. It was unearthed only this morning. God knows whose wretched soul has been disturbed, but the lilies are Morwenna's—or, rather the species her mother, Mildred, introduced to the island. The meaning seems horribly clear to me. Someone is threatening my niece's life."

Anthony raised his head to the window as a girlish voice broke the silence of the room. Morwenna ran past, chasing a kitten into the barn. Against his will, he smiled, wondering how he had found himself in her bedroom, suddenly determined to protect her.

He supposed it was possible that a couple of Camelbourne's men had decided to frighten her. Marquess or not, he was still the one they obeyed. He told himself that was the only reason he should become involved. Pray God, let there be nothing more complicated in his feelings for the girl than that.

He could not imagine a romance between them. He an earl, she a hellion. Who in his right mind would desire a wife who ran about in unlaced boots, challenging men in their castles? A public nuisance to bedevil his private life. It was ridiculous to think of courting such an elfling; he grinned at the very notion.

Then, suddenly, he saw her again outside the window, and he knew himself to be a liar. He was drawn to her. He cared about her. He would not be there otherwise.

He caught a glimpse of Sir Dunstan studying him in the mirror. "Do you have any idea who would do this?"

The man's gaze shifted to the floor. Clearly, Sir Dunstan believed Anthony played at least an indirect role in this. "I don't know. There was one unruly lad Morwenna refused to marry, but that was some time ago, before we left for London. He's settled down now."

"What about Pasco Illugan?"

"Capable of anything, I suppose. I always thought he had a soft spot for Morwenna, though. Perhaps it has become an obsession."

Anthony stared at the stone cross. "An odd display of affection."

"If it is Pasco's work." And clearly, Sir Dunstan suspected it was not. "I hate to think of what might have happened had the culprits found Morwenna in this room."

Anthony's mouth tightened. "Perhaps until they are identified, we should not take that risk. I invite you and your household to stay in the castle under my guard. Bring Elliott and your housekeeper. There's room enough in the tower, and a respectable distance between my living quarters to keep the gossips at bay."

"In your castle?" Sir Dunstan looked so pleased at the offer that Anthony had to smile. "Surely my niece and I would be an inconvenience, my lord."

"No more of an inconvenience than you have

already been," Anthony said with good humor. "I trust your niece will not be offended by my offer, or read any impropriety into it."

"Impropriety be damned," Sir Dunstan said. "I value the girl's life above her reputation. Morwenna will do as she is told."

Anthony picked up a crystal pendant from the floor. "The chain has been broken."

"She didn't notice, or she'd be heartsick. It was her mother's. Morwenna was only seven when she lost her."

"It was from illness?"

Dunstan hesitated as Anthony handed him the pendant. "I don't exactly know. No one does."

"What?"

"She vanished into the mist one night. Whether she sank into a bog hole or met with foul play, we never learned. Roland searched for her for an entire year. I think it is why he came back here to die. He hoped he would find her."

Anthony moved to the door. "I will have your rooms prepared."

"Morwenna will be grateful, my lord."

As he rode from the farmhouse, Anthony reflected on the man's parting words. From what he'd seen of Morwenna, the exact opposite appeared to be true. But then, he did not know her . . . not as well as he intended to.

He did not waste a minute making his anger known. He cantered across the moor until he reached the slags of broken turf and granite of the construction site.

A man with a battered face and barely veiled insolence stood watching him approach. "Where is Carew?" Anthony demanded as he dismounted.

"Carew's gone." The Cornish man spat a stream of spittle over to shoulder. "My name is John Hawkey. I'm foreman now."

"Gone?" Anthony looked around in disbelief. "He was here an hour ago."

"I sent him off, my lord. He didn't have the nerve for the job."

"Who the bloody hell gave you the right to order my men about?" Anthony said indignantly. "You work for me."

The man leaned against his pick. He had a stocky, bullish build and reeked of liquor and sweat, and Anthony wouldn't have hired him to burn a rubbish heap. "Actually, my lord, I work for the marquess. His lordship was impatient to have his lodge built and sent me here to see there was no nonsense."

Anthony could barely control his fury. "Camelbourne sent you to see there was no nonsense. Does that include attacking a housekeeper and damaging a young girl's home?"

Hawkey didn't bat an eye. "It might. If they got in the way of my work. Camelbourne gave me carte blanche, my lord."

"Did you or your men ransack the farmhouse this afternoon?"

Hawkey's face darkened. "I can account for every minute I've been on this island. The same for my men. Ask around if you don't believe me."

"I intend to."

A small crowd of islanders had gathered on the sacred carn above the site. Anthony saw the outrage on their faces, but it didn't match his own. "Listen to me, John Hawkey. If you hurt anyone on this island, under Camelbourne's orders or not, you'll be on your way to Bodmin gaol so fast you'll swear you sprouted wings. Until the deed passes hands, I own this island, and its people are under my protection. Do you understand?"

Anger against authority flared briefly in the man's eyes. "I understand."

"Good. I'd hate to have to explain myself in a more physical way."

He felt the man's coal-black eyes burning into his back as he returned to his horse and rode away. The people—farmers and fisherfolk, the island school-mistress and her young charges—watched him with apprehension, as if he were one of the conquerors believed to have invaded this land in ancient times.

Suddenly, he wheeled and cantered in the opposite direction, knowing there was one stone left unturned. It took him a full hour to reach Pasco Illugan's home, a granite cottage in an overgrown hollow of a cliff.

He stalked through the garden, crushing hemlock and henbane under his boots. A man's high-pitched giggle stopped him on the pathway.

"And so the giant Thunderbore stalked the land, destroying all minor creatures who stumbled underfoot. Welcome to my humble home, Lord Pentargon."

Anthony stared at him in disbelief and unbridled fury. "Miss Halliwell's house was broken into this morning. Was it your work?"

Pasco smiled at him. "I cannot take credit for every evil act that occurs on Abandon, as much as I would like to. No, it wasn't me."

"Can you prove you were otherwise occupied at the time?"

Pasco's smile faded. "I was working a spell on Black Carn. The forces I summoned could hardly be called upon in a court of law."

Anthony reached into his coat. "Did you or your forces put these in the tower?"

Pasco looked down at the two joined figures, his gaze widening. "Morwenna made you a mate of wax. I had no idea she was so attracted to you. Forgive me, my lord, I believed her when she said she hated you. That certainly wasn't the spell she asked for."

"She asked for a spell—to be used against me?"

"That is confidential information." Pasco lowered his voice. "I'd never divulge the secrets of my clients. In fact, I've said too much already."

"Someone placed a grave marker on her bed. Could you guess why?"

"A grave marker? How positively morbid, and delicious."

"Her uncle thought it might be you," Anthony said in a cold voice.

"Really? Well, I see my fame is growing."

"You are an ugly little slug, Pasco."

Pasco pretended to look hurt. "Does this mean you will not come in and share a pot of crab stew with me, my lord?"

"One false step, and it's the bottom of the sea for you, Pasco. I might have you watched."

Pasco giggled. "Shall I leave the curtains open? I dance in the nude, you know."

Anthony pivoted, barely aware that he was still holding the waxen figures in his hand. Before he took a step on the path, a shower of sparks shot out around his feet, and a cloud of sulphurous smoke erupted from the gateposts like miniature geysers. Pasco shrieked in delight, clapping his hands like a child.

Anthony continued walking to his horse. "Cheap theatrics, Pasco. I've seen better tricks onstage at a traveling fair."

"Smug bastard," Pasco whispered, standing in the wisps of dying smoke. "She was mine before you came here. I'm not going to let her go."

Morwenna wept when she walked into her bedroom. It wasn't only that she was frightened to find a funeral marker on her mattress. She felt sick to her stomach.

But she was furious too. For one thing, her sweet gray kitten had a bruised rib, no doubt from being kicked by the intruder; and the same evil men had ruined her mother's silk counterpane. She had so few memories of Mama to treasure. The red moorland mud would never wash out.

To top it all off, Pentargon had lorded over the whole affair with an arrogance she found not only aggravating but reassuring. Elliott was too emotional by nature to handle a crisis; he'd never recovered from losing the royal commission to paint the queen's robing room. And her uncle was too old to go challenging a gang of miners on the moor.

She believed Pentargon's crew had done this. She'd never encountered trouble before on Abandon, except one spring when one of the Beltane revelers had thrown a fireball in the yard, which was the sort of drunken mischief one expected from time to time. And lately, she suspected Pasco had paid his pack of orphaned boys to leave dead toads on the doorstep as a sort of twisted courtship offering.

But she couldn't remember anything of this vile and personal nature, and how would she recover the pages of her papa's burnt manuscript when the book was due in a few short months?

Her uncle put his hand on her shoulder; she was sitting at the dressing table, forlornly attempting to piece together scorched pieces of a Welsh Myrddin poem. "Lord Pentargon has offered us the protection of his castle until the culprits are found. I thought it wise to accept before your temper made him change his mind. Pack a few necessities, my dear."

She raised her head, her face ghostly pale. "You accepted—oh, Uncle Dunstan, how awful, how humiliating, encamping with the enemy."

"Now, Morwenna—"

She shot to her feet. "Do you know what he tried to do to me in the tower?"

His mouth opened, but no sound emerged. Morwenna threw him a scornful look. "No. Not *that*, but enough of a prelude that if I had an ounce of sense, I would be mortified."

"I will not tolerate any inappropriate conduct toward you, earl or not. Your father's dying wish was that I protect you."

She sighed. "Thank you, Uncle Dunstan."

"However, it seems for now I must choose between the lesser of two evils. I would rather sacrifice your name than your life."

"I won't go, Uncle Dunstan."

"Yes, Morwenna, you will. Gather your things."

"The only things I'll be gathering are my cats. In

fact, I'm taking the gray one to Annie Jenkins for a poultice."

"A poultice? For a stray cat?" He scratched his bald head, looking at a loss. "You are your mother's daughter, in ways that begin to alarm me."

She stared resolutely at the stone cross. "I know. Sometimes I alarm myself."

Anthony stood at the tower window, waiting for the barouche bearing Morwenna to arrive. His anticipation amused him. What had happened that he looked forward to a heated encounter with a girl who resorted to magic spells to get rid of him?

Yet she had responded to his kiss. She'd fit against his body as if made for him alone. He would never let it happen again, of course. Except for the obligatory dinner he had planned that night, merely to be polite, he would retire to his own quarters.

"They're coming, my lord!" Vincent shouted in excitement from the battlements; he had been stationed there to alert the earl the minute the barouche reached the cliff road to the castle.

"All right." Anthony stepped away from the window, not wishing to be seen. "There is no need to inform the entire world."

He strode down the stairs and through the labyrinth of unlit passageways to the entrance hall.

He did not want to appear overanxious to greet Morwenna, but it would seem rude not to meet her in the courtyard. Mrs. Treffry nearly collided with him at the door.

"They have arrived, my lord. Shall I serve sherry and biscuits in the drawing room?"

"No. Yes. Good Lord, one would think the queen herself has come for all the fuss throughout this castle." Vases of fragrant spring flowers adorned every bare surface, and the floor was polished to a blinding gleam. Not even a dust mite danced in the air.

He glanced at his reflection in the hall-stand mirror. Freshly shaven, hair brushed back on his scalp, black broadcloth suit that emphasized his large frame, but did he have to look so broodingly intense, so smug and condescending?

He was going to frighten the girl away with that arrogant smirk, which was probably all for the good, but couldn't he at least greet her with a less intimidating look?

No, he couldn't. Not when the sight of her made his blood pulse in anticipation. Not when he had already undressed, seduced, and mated with her in his mind at least a hundred times. And what delicious matings those imaginary encounters had been, for both of them, of course. Anthony might not be the most handsome young buck in London, but he knew how to please a woman. The arrogant smirk returned to his face.

"Here, my lord." His fantasy dissolved as Mrs. Treffry thrust a bouquet of lilies into his arms. The scent was heady. "For Miss Halliwell."

He frowned. "Do you think—"

"Oh, yes, my lord. A lovely gesture of conciliation, to show her how sorry you are."

He sighed. The only thing he was sorry about at the moment was that his seduction of Miss Halliwell would have to remain a fantasy. He did not intend to touch her again. Not so much as shake her hand. God forbid he should end up on the wrong side of a church altar wedded to the girl.

Feeling idiotic, he went down the steps with the flowers to meet the barouche as it slowed to a stop on the freshly swept cobbles. Sir Dunstan gave him a rather grim look, and Miss Halliwell, or what he could see of her lower half, appeared to be on the floor of the vehicle with her rather sizable bottom in the air, engaged in what task he could not tell. The sight gave Anthony pause. He'd thought her a bit more slender than that.

Strange mewing cries broke the silence. He glanced up, wondering if the castle was beset by sea-gulls, before he realized that the plaintive sounds came from a crate inside the barouche. And that the sizable bottom belonged not to Miss Halliwell but to her housekeeper, Emily Jenkins.

Morwenna had not come. His mouth curled into a small smile. Did the girl not realize that he had swallowed his own pride to protect her? That he had weakened his position of power by offering her shelter? Did she think he was the kind of man who gave up his privacy to just anyone?

He stood in annoyed silence as Dunstan climbed down to meet him. "What is the meaning of this?" he demanded. "Where is your niece?"

"She refused to come, my lord." The man looked mortified at the admission.

"I see."

"She said to thank you in person for your kind

offer of protection and has sent her cats and house-keeper instead."

"I see that too." A glimmer of reluctant amusement lit Anthony's eyes. "Are you staying with them?"

"Of course not, my lord." Sir Dunstan stared at the ground. "I suppose you want me to take the cats back."

Anthony sighed. "The cats may stay."

Anthony rode to the farmhouse early the next morning. From the gate, he saw Elliott sketching her in the garden. He watched them for a few minutes before making his presence known.

Elliott appeared to be unmoved by Morwenna's charm. Or if it affected him, he concealed it well beneath a veneer of professional detachment. Such a feat seemed difficult to Anthony. He found himself increasingly attracted to her.

The breeze almost caressed her, molding the sheer blue silk of the gown to her lithesome body. From the distance, she looked like a virgin goddess, unattainable, heartbreaking in her beauty because she was unaware of it. In fact, at the same instant that Anthony admired her in amused silence, she opened her mouth to give an unladylike yawn.

"Morwenna." Elliott threw down his pencil in frustration. "What is the matter with you?"

She grinned ruefully and tugged the silver circlet from her forehead. "I didn't sleep at all, and I feel so odd, hot one minute and cold—"

She looked up and saw Anthony leaning on his horse outside the gate. Their gazes locked, and he felt a charge of electricity and emotion immobilize him. She put her hand to her heart, whether from surprise or something else, he did not know.

He did know she ought to fear him. He was angry enough to shake her senseless, if he could trust himself even to touch her.

He pushed open the gate and strode through the garden, a veritable paradise where lilies, lupines, and roses grew in a delight to the senses.

"Lord Pentargon." Elliott gave Morwenna a puzzled look, possibly just realizing what had transformed her grin into a scowl. "Don't tell me you have come to let me sketch you. Morwenna, find your father's sword and helmet for his lordship. Do we still have that suit of armor?"

Anthony glanced at her. "Never mind, Miss Halliwell. I'm not here to stand as a model."

Elliott, evidently not wanting to waste a potential artistic moment, ran toward the farmhouse to fetch the required costume. Anthony released a sigh, frowning at Morwenna.

"You do know why I'm here, Miss Halliwell," he said in a forbidding voice.

She turned her back on him, to hide a sly smile, he suspected. Clearly, his stern demeanor wasn't having enough of an effect.

"Your cats have overrun the castle." He kept his tone austere, circling her slowly. "One cannot take a step without treading on a tail. I woke up this morning with one of the creatures in my bed."

Which was where, at this point, he had secretly hoped their mistress would end up; of course, it was fortunate matters had not progressed that far.

"Nibbling on my toes," he added.

She laughed at that, half turning to look at him. "Thank you for taking care of them."

"I had meant to take care of you."

Her eyes widened. The words had escaped him before he could stop himself. "What I meant was, well, I cannot be positive that I am not indirectly responsible for what happened here yesterday."

She looked incredulous. "Your men admitted—"

"They admitted nothing. However, the new foreman is openly insolent, and if he is not guilty, he does not seem appropriately shocked at being accused of the crime. Nor does Pasco."

"Pasco?" She wrinkled her nose. "Well, I suppose it could have been him, as revenge for my refusing to meet his price."

He raised his brow. "The price for getting rid of me?"

She gave him a wistful smile. "I'm afraid so. It does seem silly now."

He glanced away, wondering what had happened. He had come here to scold her, not to be caught in her spell again. He forced another frown to his face.

"What seems silly," he said sternly, "is that you have refused my offer of a place to stay until the culprits who ransacked your house are found."

"But what if they are never found?"

His jaw tightened. "What matters is that you are not in danger."

She leaned back against a trellis of roses. He was fascinated by how much of her breasts the silk garment revealed, and resentful that Elliott, not he, had been privileged to enjoy the sight all morning.

"It may sound foolish, my lord," she said, "but I don't think anything truly bad could happen to me on Abandon."

He felt an almost unbearable need to kiss her, to draw her down and take her on a bed of flowers. Where had the impulse come from? It was insane, here in full view of the house, but all of a sudden, the scent of lilies drenched the air; she had lured him into a plot of them, watching as he drowned in their perfume and damned himself for desiring her.

"Are you all right, Lord Pentargon?" she asked, looking a little afraid of him again.

He realized the dark confusion of his thoughts had shown on his face. "Yes, I'm—it does sound foolish, what you just said, and it makes me angry. My brother died on this damn island. Don't ask me to believe nothing bad ever happens here."

"You don't have to believe anything I ask you. You only have to tell the marquess you've changed your mind."

"But I haven't."

She dropped the snapdragon she'd picked and turned on her heel. "Then go away."

"As soon as I'm finished here." He followed her, sidestepping the flower she had discarded. "Obviously, what I have to do has made me an unpopular man on the island."

"Obviously, my lord."

"I don't care what people think of me."

"That is obvious, too."

"I don't care about most people, that is."

She bit her lip. "How fortunate for the few who are included in the elite circle of those you care about."

He grinned. "I am a loyal friend if nothing else."

"To those fortunate few."

"I believe that the circle has grown wider," he said in a low voice. "By one."

Anticipation thrummed in her blood, sudden and almost painful. She stood against a wall of lupines and the barrier of his body. Did she imagine the touch of his hand on her shoulder? Was it female instinct that warned her, *Do not give in, or your soul will be lost to him?* There was power in his eyes, his voice, a power that spoke to some secret part of her.

"I tell you again, Miss Halliwell, I did not order my men to intimidate you, but the work must continue. For my peace of mind, I offer you the safety of the castle. A young woman needs someone to protect her, even here."

"Well, my uncle—"

He narrowed his eyes as she turned. "Hardly in his prime."

His arrogant gaze swept over her, making her all too aware that he, unlike her uncle, was a man at the peak of his virility, capable of defending the entire island if he chose. Why did he pretend to offer her kindness? To assuage his guilt or prove a point? To amuse himself until he discarded Abandon and returned to his world?

"I shall never come to the castle again, my lord."

His gaze pierced her. "Why not? Ah, the kiss. I assure you, it will not be repeated, until, of course, you wish for it."

"What a thing to say," she exclaimed.

His eyes glittered with good humor. "I await the word."

"You shall wait quite a long time, then."

"It might be worth it—depending on what the word is, of course."

Elliott returned to the garden at that moment, staggering under the weight of the suit of armor and knightly accoutrements he deposited with a clatter at Anthony's feet. Morwenna burst into laughter at Anthony's startled expression, relieving the terrible tension between them.

"Your armor, my lord," Elliott said in a breathless voice.

Anthony recovered from his shock and started laughing himself. "No."

"No?" Elliott shook his head in disappointment.

Morwenna picked up the tarnished shield. "Lord Pentargon isn't about to be anyone's hero, not in life, not in art, and he isn't going to fight any battles that do not benefit him either." She directed a challenging look at Anthony. "Am I right, my lord?"

"I don't know." The anger that had brought him there had transmuted into a far more subtle and dangerous blend of emotions. "It depends. Will you reconsider my offer of the castle?"

"Never." She stood in her garden of flowers holding the shield like a warrior queen. Determination glittered in her green eyes. "I will never set foot in the castle again, unless *you* reconsider your position."

He bowed, then backed away. When he reached his horse, he heard Elliott say, "Damn it, Morwenna, you might have coaxed him into posing, if only for the sake of the book. Anyone can see the unfortunate man desires you."

Her heart in her throat, she watched Anthony ride away from the farmhouse, and half of her wanted to follow while the other half clung to her abhorrence of what he intended to do to the people and place she loved. How could she be so attracted to a man like him? Yet she was. Even now, she shook at the memory of his blue-gray eyes branding her, arrogance and need in their depths. *Come to the castle*, he had said, when he might have meant, *Come to my bed.*

"Perhaps you should have gone with him," Elliott said in an amused voice.

She started, unaware that her conflicted emotions were so obvious. "To push him off a cliff, you mean."

"To protect you." He stared at the shield clasped to her breast. "You do like him, Morwenna."

"I most certainly do not, and I don't need him to protect me either."

"But think of that handsome face and rugged physique."

"You think of it, Elliott, if you admire it so much."

He smiled slightly. "A knight who does not even need armor to defend you."

"Against what?"

"Obviously, someone wants you dead."

The statement chilled her to the bone. "What do you mean?"

He frowned. "The stone marker on your bed—did you miss the significance? My God, Morwenna, I took the meaning clear enough. Your father is gone. You ought to be frightened."

"Of course I am, but I won't let a scare stop me. Whoever left that marker wants me to be frightened. Anyway, I have you and Uncle Dunstan to take care of me, don't I?"

"For all the good it did." He glanced up grimly at the sky. "Another day's work wasted. Oh, well, I might as well look for that cave. I'm going out in the boat this time and don't expect me home until I find it."

"I don't think you should go, Elliott. Not today."

He gave her a wistful smile. "But neither of us can take advice, can we?"

Anthony threw down his gloves on the library table, aware that an audience of at least four cats watched his every move. He guessed the creatures preferred this room because it was private and warm with the coal fire burning in the Gothic fireplace. It did not cross his mind that the cats liked *him* and craved his company.

He went to sit in his chair, then stopped, noticing Ethan's book on the seat. The firelight imparted a blood-red glow to the heavy brocade curtains. His shadow looked enormous against the flocked wallpaper, distorted, alone.

Open me.

Read me.

He frowned, rubbing his face. No more fairy tales for him tonight. No more rescuing maidens or confronting would-be wizards. He wanted a bottle of brandy and the mind-numbing bliss it would bring.

Open me.

Read me.

Know your fate, young lord.

Dear God, he was tired and lonely and . . . aggravated. He missed his friends, his home. How had Ethan stood living here without a wife or mistress? Why had *he* gone to Morwenna's farmhouse again today when she had made a fool of him, sending all these damn cats, one of whom had slyly insinuated itself beside him on the chair? He wondered suddenly if she and Elliott were secret lovers. Was her innocence an act? Not that he would interfere. Her private life had nothing to do with him.

Open me.
Read me . . .

He grunted, pushing the book to the floor, and reached for the decanter of brandy as thunder rumbled over the sea. Another storm was about to break over Abandon, and he hoped to be comfortably drunk when it did.

7

Morwenna pounded at the castle door until her knuckles ached, her earlier vow a mocking refrain in her brain. *Never, never, never. I will never set foot in the castle again . . .*

And only eight hours after refusing the devil's challenge, here she stood begging entrance to his den, at Pentargon's mercy, needing his help.

Who else could she ask? His quiet strength beckoned her like a beacon in the storm that raged across the island. She wanted his confidence, his guidance, even though it made no sense. Even though she expected him to laugh in her face and ask why he should do anything for her after the way she'd spoken to him.

Elliott had never returned from his search for Arthur's cave. After his conversation in the garden with Morwenna, he had taken a boat out to look for the hidden sea cave Dunstan had glimpsed on Cape Skulla, a death trap in rough waters.

Worried when he did not appear at supper, Morwenna and several islanders had combed the public house, the few shops, the vicarage, the cottages in which Elliott might have sheltered from the storm.

Then a fisherman had brought devastating news.

Elliott's capsized boat had been sighted in an inaccessible inlet known as the Dragon's Jaw. From what the searchers could see from the cliffs, Elliott had not been caught between the rocks, and no one could attempt that climb in the rain. Until the sea calmed, they could not venture close enough in their boats to right Elliott's craft, to see if he were trapped beneath, or dead.

Don't let him be dead.

She raised her voice above the rain and beat at the castle door in frustration, refusing to believe the worst.

Pentargon.

He was the first person to enter her mind for help, the last man on earth she ought to ask. He would gloat at the victory, and she didn't care. Why did he not answer the door? Where were the servants? The castle sat in bleak darkness, battered by wind and rain. Where had everyone gone? She clenched her chattering teeth, soaked to her underclothes, so upset that the sting of rain no longer penetrated.

"Lord Pentargon!" She slammed her fists on the black oak door, her voice raw from calling him. "Anthony, please, please, answer the door!"

He should have been drunk by now. He meant to be drunk on Ethan's expensive cognac. He slumped lower in the chair, fascinated by the dying embers of the fire. He would have given everything he owned to have his brother sitting opposite him. They had not talked in years, and now it was too late.

He would have given everything to have *her* there. She *would* come to him. He wished it. He willed it. Then, in the next instant, he buried his face in his hands and laughed at himself. How could he desire such a frustrating, incorrigible female? How could he take advantage of her inexperience when he would be gone in a month?

Rain washed against the mullioned windows. There was a peculiar violence to this storm. He doubted that even Morwenna could produce one of her darling rainbows when the air cleared. Waves pounded the roots of the castle, and in his half-inebriated trance of self-pity, he imagined hearing her voice.

A huge figure loomed in the doorway. "My lord, excuse me."

"I gave everyone the night off, Vincent. Isn't there some sort of celebration going on in the servants' hall? Gunther's birthday?"

"Yes, my lord, but that young woman is at the door."

He sat up slowly. "That—woman?"

Vincent glanced at the half-empty bottle on the table. "I do believe you should come immediately."

"Is there something wrong?"

"I fear so, my lord."

A myriad appealing scenarios rushed through his mind when he saw her standing in the darkness. More than anything, he wanted to take her by the hand and lead her upstairs to make love to her, teasing her about her dramatic timing. At the height of a storm. Braving the elements all by herself to come to him. He sobered at the thought of what dangers her impulsive behavior could attract.

"Miss Halliwell, may I help you?"

She took a breath. "Yes, my lord, you have won. I am here, and I do need your help."

He smiled faintly as she stood before him in silent misery, bedraggled, anticipating an act of revenge. How easy to throw her words back in her face. *I will never set foot in the castle again.* But he held his tongue, looking her over with more concern than satisfaction.

"Go ahead," she said, sighing. "You may gloat. I saw that smile."

He stared at her. She stood in a dripping puddle of muddy water, and her face was as wan as candle wax. "You are only partially right, Morwenna. I smiled because you are here, but perhaps not for the reason you suspect. Let me take your cloak."

She closed her eyes, unwillingly relaxing as he divested her of her sodden garment. She had driven her trap until the road washed out, and then, leaving the ponies at a cottage, she had run the rest of the way. Now she was exhausted, so aware of his strength and presence that her knees almost buckled. "Why do you smile, then?"

"Because you knew you could come to me. Because you knew I would not refuse to help you. That implies a depth of trust that often takes a lifetime to build."

"And will there be a price?" she asked quietly, remembering what he had said about Pasco, about men in general.

"Perhaps." He reached for her, engulfing her slender-boned fingers in his hand. "But perhaps you will be more than willing to pay it when the time comes—perhaps it will not even be what you expect."

When they reached the library, where he hoped to put her at ease, the fire blazed so brightly in the hearth that Anthony stopped in his tracks. He stared at the cheerful flames for a moment, taken aback. He could swear he had passed no servants sneaking upstairs from their party to stoke the dying embers.

"Sit down, Morwenna, and tell me why you are here. You're blue with cold. A glass of brandy—"

He turned, his gaze arrested on the table where his crystal decanter sat, and beside it two glasses. *Two.* Damn it—ah, Vincent, of course, taking it upon himself to prepare the room for her comfort. Anthony poured the glass for her.

"Let us get you out of those boots and stockings."

"It's Elliott," she said in a broken voice. "He disappeared in his boat while looking for Arthur's cave. The storm came up so suddenly. I fear for his life."

He frowned and knelt before her. "Where is the boat?"

"Snagged in the rocks off Cape Skulla." He began to unlace her half-boots. "Oh, goodness, I'm going to get mud all over you."

His frown deepened. "I have a feeling I'll suffer worse before the night is over."

She leaned forward in the chair to help. "Please, my lord, I don't feel right having you wait on me like a servant."

But the boots were already unlaced and on the floor. She sat back, transfixed as she felt his powerful hands peeling off her stockings.

"There." He had not removed his hand from her knee. "You are half frozen, elf. I will call the housekeeper to take you to bed."

"Bed?" she said in astonishment. "I can't go to bed until Elliott—I can't go to bed here at all."

"You will not leave this castle in the middle of the night with the roads awash in mud. Is that clear?"

"But Elliott—"

"Risking your own life will not bring him back if he is gone."

"How hard you are, my lord."

"Fortune doesn't favor the tender, does it?"

"I came here to ask you to help me find Elliott," she said in distress.

"Which I will do only when I am satisfied that you are safe."

She stared up at his unsmiling face. "I do not feel safe," she whispered.

His fingers tightened around her ankle, sending tingles of pleasure along every nerve ending. For a moment, she could not breathe, watching his eyes darken as he studied her, seeing deeper than any other man had dared.

In a low, rough voice, he said, "Hand me my jacket, so I may at least make an attempt at honor by joining the search for your friend."

She rose and lifted the black broadcloth jacket from the back of his chair. Scarcely had she handed it to him than she heard her uncle's voice in the hall. She turned as Dunstan practically burst into the room, Vincent at his heels.

"My lord, forgive the intrusion, but my niece—oh, there you are, Morwenna. You had me wild with worry."

"His lordship is going to join the search." She glanced involuntarily at Anthony, unable to suppress the catch in her voice. "My lord, I suggest you wear heavier clothing. An oilcloth coat, perhaps."

Amusement flickered across his chiseled face. "Thank you, Miss Halliwell."

He left her, nodding politely as he passed Sir Dunstan at the door. The older man turned to follow, but not before he glanced significantly at Morwenna and the two brandy glasses on the table.

"We shall talk about this later, my girl."

She sighed. "There is nothing to talk about."

He looked at her, hair disheveled, eyes bright, feet bare, her stockings on the floor. "I fear there is."

8

Anthony gathered a group of gangers and fishermen to form another search party. In a storm this violent, Elliott's body could have been washed out to sea or snagged in an inaccessible cave or crevice. With safety ropes around their waists, the rescue crew lowered themselves by lantern light from the cliff at Cape Skulla. In the black cauldron of water below, Elliott's boat banged up against the rocks until Anthony and three young fishermen drew it ashore. There was no one inside.

The rescuers thanked Anthony for his efforts, then left abruptly; they might respect his authority, but clearly no one pretended to trust him. On the walk back across the cliffs in rain and darkness, he saw Pasco standing alone. Anthony stared at him, then resumed walking, too wet and exhausted to confront the dangerous fool.

"You did not find him?" Pasco shouted into the dying wind.

He tensed, half turning. "Do you know something?"

"Happy to take the credit." Pasco giggled, raising his cloaked arms to the wind. "But not the blame."

Anthony hesitated. He dreaded his return to the castle. Undoubtedly Morwenna would be waiting, and he, the messenger with bad news, would have to report her beloved island had claimed another life. She would resent him all the more.

"Look at this, Lord Pentargon." Pasco's shrill cry of excitement set his teeth on edge. He struggled not to push the idiot away when he sprinted up behind him.

"I found this beneath a myrtle hedge, my lord. What do you make of it?"

Anthony looked down at the white length of cloth, a man's cravat, stained with blood. The same neckcloth Elliott had been wearing in the garden yesterday morning. "I'll take it," he said curtly. "Show me where you found it."

"Oh, there's nothing else," Pasco said excitedly. "But that's blood, don't you see? Blood from a fatal struggle, perhaps."

"It could mean anything," Anthony told Morwenna and her uncle an hour later as they stood in the predawn darkness at the bottom of the stairs. "He might have fallen on the rocks, cut his hand, and used the cravat to bind it."

Morwenna nodded. "That makes perfect sense. If Elliott cut his sketching hand, he would not care about ruining his costume."

"Still," Sir Dunstan said, placing his hand on her shoulder, "he has not been found, my dear."

"He will be. He isn't dead." She looked up, her eyes dark with emotion. "I think he's discovered the cave and is sketching in a fit of inspiration. He took supplies for a day or two, and light. You do not know Elliott, my lord. When he begins a work, he loses track of time."

Sir Dunstan released a sigh. "He becomes quite mad, quite obsessed. Not unlike my late brother. These artistic types, they tend to be peculiar. It does not occur to them that they cause the rest of us such worry."

"I know we'll find him," Morwenna said. "I feel in my heart that he's safe—I think he found the cave and is afraid to leave it."

Anthony looked away. "Perhaps, Miss Halliwell. We shall certainly know in a week or so. Now I suggest we all go to bed. Your rooms have been prepared."

Sir Dunstan glanced at the bloodied cravat before meeting Anthony's gaze. "Your hospitality is appreciated, my lord."

As is your protection. The words might not have been spoken, but their meaning was implied.

Twenty minutes before dawn, Anthony was awakened by faint strains of music coming from the east tower. Annoyed, determined to confront the castle troublemaker, he made his way quietly up the stairs and through the drafty passageway. The sea winds had extinguished most of the flames in the ancient brass moldings on the wall—he thought it strange that anyone should think to light them up there, anyway.

From the half-opened door, he saw a rather shapely female posterior positioned on the floor, and this time there was no doubt about its owner.

Mrs. Treffry boasted a much larger backside. Morwenna's curves were more enticingly sculpted. He entered the room, kneeling beside her.

"What are we looking for, Miss Halliwell? Hidden treasure or more waxen dolls?"

She gave a start, swinging around to stare at him. A slender taper burned in a saucer beside her. "Oh, my heavens, it's you."

"What are you looking for at this ungodly hour, elf?"

"Holes," she muttered, chestnut-gold hair falling in her face. "I noticed they were plugged with dust when I brought you here, but I became distracted when you . . ."

"When I?—"

She gestured vaguely with her hand. "When you and I—oh, goodness, we just talked about it in the garden. You must remember."

"I most certainly do."

"It isn't the sort of thing one forgets, is it?" she whispered.

"Indeed not. In fact, I have spent an inordinate amount of time thinking about that afternoon."

"Did you come to any conclusion?" she asked hesitantly.

"Not that I care to reveal at this time."

"Oh. I see."

"Do you?"

She swallowed. "I couldn't sleep. I keep thinking about Elliott."

"The search is not over yet."

She met his gaze. "But you believe he's gone, don't you?"

"I lost a brother to this island," he said in a subdued voice. "Yet I suppose one cannot give up hope. I shall look myself again tomorrow afternoon."

She glanced away. She appeared to be wearing one of the maidservants' serviceable night rails, a heavy flannel gown that made her seem impossibly small and appealing when it should have had the opposite effect.

"Holes, you said." He sat back, annoyed that he had lost his original thread of thought. "As in mouse holes?"

"No. As in piskie holes. The little people. I suspect the dark energy that afflicts this castle is because something has blocked their entrance."

He cleared his throat. "Well, thank God. I thought it was me. The dark energy, that is."

She regarded him steadily. "That is still a possibility."

"Go back to your room, Morwenna. Your music disturbed me from a deep sleep."

"Music?"

"A harp, wasn't it?" He glanced around the shadowed room. "Where have you hidden it?"

She widened her eyes. "You—*you* heard the music?"

"There is nothing wrong with my hearing."

"Then it was *her*, the enchantress, but no one of my generation has ever heard the harp." She drew away from him in suspicion. "Are you trying to mock me again? Has one of the servants told you about the legend?"

He stared at her, sitting on her knees in the dark. Her long hair curled around the undersides of her breasts, and his blood quickened as he thought of putting his hand under that unflattering gown and touching her. She had no idea how little he cared for legends at the moment. He was interested in far more earthly matters.

"All I know of Camelot is what I was forced to read in school," he said.

"Not Camelot," she said. "My father found no reference to its existence before the medieval French writer of romances Chrétien de Troyes. It is a later invention."

He leaned even farther toward her until her small frame was forced against the wall. "Do you know what I remember most about the tales of King Arthur?"

"I have a feeling I do not wish to have that question answered."

His grin made her heart skip a beat. "They were a lusty lot, those knights and their ladies. Adventurous, brutal, vulnerable to temptation—as I recall."

"That is the human condition, my lord."

His voice dropped to a teasing whisper. "I'm feeling incredibly human myself right now."

Her lips tightened in an attempt not to smile. "You will also remember, from your schoolboy lessons, that the sins of the most valiant knight usually did not go unpunished."

"Sometimes resisting temptation is punishment enough."

She tried not to stare at him, even though he continued to study her in unabashed amusement, more handsome than any man had a right to be. His dark vitality fascinated her, as did his physical attributes, all hard angles and muscled power in a white linen shirt and expensive black trousers. He smelled so delicious, like brandy and male and starched linen, and she hated herself for admiring him.

She turned back to the wall. "Oh, dear. That explains it."

He was right behind her, leaning over her shoulder. She gave a shiver as his shoulder bumped hers; in the dark, his presence seemed more irresistible than ever. His rich voice brushed her ear. "You have made a grim discovery, Morwenna?"

"A fairy wing," she said sadly.

He glanced down at the iridescent shred in her palm. He did not have the heart to tell her it was the wing from an ordinary housefly.

She looked up then, her eyes meeting his. "What is it? Is something wrong?"

He said softly, "There will be if you don't leave this room this very instant."

She rose swiftly, sidestepping the candle. He stood and brought his hands to the silken ties at her throat. The night rail fell away, and he was cupping her breasts, kissing them and losing the war with himself for control. Soft flesh, her flesh, the pink tips hardening against his tongue. A girl so undefiled that she brought rainbows to the sky, and the things he wanted to do to her—

"Oh, my God, Morwenna," he said in a broken voice. "At least pretend to resist. Do not make this easy for me."

She was so lightheaded, she couldn't move. She grew weak, awash in warmth, flooded with powerful feelings, and when he kissed her, his mouth devouring hers with a sensual expertise that made her bones dissolve, she doubted she could stumble to the door.

He walked her into the wall, his body wedged against hers so tightly that she could barely exhale. His hands caressed her buttocks through the flannel gown. He drew a ragged breath at the thought of rendering her helpless and naked in this room.

She said nothing, only moaned, and he knew the power was his, to seduce, conquer, mate, but a lifetime ago a boy had made a vow, and the man that boy had become cursed the memory of it. He didn't want to think of honor and principles. He wanted *her*. He slid his hand across her belly, so soft, untouched.

The music saved her. Faintly at first, he heard the haunting song, the faraway strains of a harp. Then nearer and nearer until he felt the vibrations in the room.

He drew away from her. "Do you hear it?"

"Hear what?" she said, opening her eyes, trembling.

He pulled the night rail back over her shoulders and retied the laces, his face dark, intense. "It was nothing. Only the sea. Go back to bed."

"You heard the music again, my lord?" she said softly, more curious than afraid.

"It was the sea. Listen."

There was silence, the sound of the waves, then footsteps from the depth of the stairwell, coming closer until the door behind them opened. Suddenly Morwenna's elusive white cat appeared, brushing against Anthony's leg.

"Oh," Morwenna said, starting to laugh in relief with her hand on her heart. "I thought it was—"

She caught the warning look Anthony sent her a second before the door opened wider and her uncle walked into the room.

"Morwenna." Sir Dunstan looked at her in anger and disappointment. "I followed the cat up the stairs when I checked your room and found it empty. What is the meaning of this?"

Anthony straightened his angular frame, an unconscious gesture to protect the girl. It occurred to him that he should have stepped away, but her uncle sounded angry enough to punish her. Rather than move, he held his ground, ready to intervene if Dunstan lifted a hand to strike her for a sin she had not invited.

"I was looking for piskie holes," she said, more steadily than Anthony expected.

"Good Lord, Morwenna," Dunstan said in dismay. "At this hour in the morning?"

"I deemed it an emergency, Uncle Dunstan, especially after what has happened to Elliott."

"And you, my lord?" he asked. "Were you looking for fairies too?"

Anthony felt preposterous. "I thought I heard music. Harp music, but it—it was the sea."

"*Her* music," Morwenna said, edging around his towering figure. "Can you believe it?"

"Go to your room, Morwenna," Dunstan said. "I want a word with his lordship."

She hesitated, then shrugged, plucking the cat from Anthony's ankles before escaping the tense atmosphere in the room.

Sir Dunstan shook his head as she slipped out into the hall. "I am not upset to find my niece hunting for piskie holes in the middle of the night. What distresses me is to find her with a man."

"Yes."

"Do I have reason for distress, my lord?"

"Do I look like a despoiler of maidens, sir?"

"I do not know what such a man would look like, my lord. Depravity comes in many forms, some quite attractive. Morwenna is not accustomed to clever courtships or experienced suitors. She was an abysmal failure among the *ton.*"

Anthony brushed the fly wing off his shirt. "I find that hard to believe."

"Is there something I should know about your intentions toward my niece?"

"Know that I am a man of honor." Anthony gave him a direct look. "Will you accept my offer to stay?"

"Do you think we are in danger, my lord?"

And Anthony knew the question had a double meaning. *Is Morwenna safe from you?* He shook his head. "As long as you remain here, neither of you is in danger."

It was the first vow he had ever made that he hoped he could fulfill.

Anthony found Ethan's strange book sitting on the nightstand when he returned to his bed a few minutes later. A freshly lit taper burned beside it, and since Vincent had gone to bed an hour ago, Anthony could only assume the castle troublemaker was playing tricks again.

He sat down on the bed, taking the book with him. "A message from beyond the grave, brother?" he mused softly. "How could you believe this nonsense?"

He opened the book to the frontispiece, and a chill crawled down his nape. In a bold masculine hand was the inscription:

> *To Anthony*
> *Always do right, young lord. Defend the weak. Protect the innocent.*
>
> *One Who Wishes You Well*

There was a logical explanation, of course. Anthony had probably told Ethan about their governess's strange command years ago and had forgotten he had done so. Presumably, Ethan had asked Sir Roland to sign another edition, intending to give it to Anthony at a later date. One of the servants must have found it and put it here, hoping the inscription would prick Anthony's conscience.

He stuffed the book under the bed and blew out the taper, leaning back against the pillow. He was in no mood to look at pictures of pretty young maidens who reminded him of Morwenna when he would be thinking of her all night, anyway, and how close he had come to committing an irrevocable act.

If this nonsense continued, he would have to talk with the staff about their unsubtle attempts to persuade him not to sell Abandon. If Morwenna Halliwell in all her alluring sensuality could not sway him, then no earthly power could.

The storm continued into the next afternoon, then tapered off by nightfall in uncertain calm. On the second day of Elliott's disappearance, the young artist's sketchpad was found on the beach. His final drawing depicted the mouth of a magnificent cave; the geographic composition of hornblende, feldspar, and granite was not one that even the most experienced fisherfolk could identify as anything seen before on Abandon.

Morwenna and her uncle kept to their tower apartments, distressed over their friend's disappearance. Anthony and a crew of fishermen continued to comb the local seas for a sign of Elliott and returned silent and discouraged.

On the morning of the third day, Sir Dunstan sought out Anthony in the library where Morwenna's entourage of cats had taken up residence on the bookshelves. Anthony, reviewing the child labor reform proposal he intended to present to the marquess, looked up from his desk.

"You are engaged, my lord," Sir Dunstan said, "and I apologize for the intrusion, but I suspect she's gone out searching for Elliot. One of the castle boats is missing. Ordinarily, I would not bother. The girl rows like a young Amazon, but it is the matter of that trouble at the cottage, and Elliott's cravat. The blood, my lord. There was something not quite right."

Anthony reached behind him for his cloak, his face grave. "I should not admit it, but I share your concern. In fact, I meant to row out myself in another hour. But does your niece always go about with such disregard to convention and safety?"

Sir Dunstan nodded. "Her father traveled the world with the girls and paid little attention to their social upbringing. At one point, he even employed a headhunter as a sort of nursemaid. I confess I was never so relieved in my life as when he decided to limit his research to the British Isles."

"I should think so."

Dunstan followed him out the door. "My lord, do you suppose I should notify Elliott's wife? She lives in St. Ives."

Anthony did not stop to answer, consumed by an irrational sense of anxiety to find Morwenna and end her dangerous explorations once and for all. "Wait a few more days. If the news is bad, you are obliged to deliver it to her in person."

*   *   *

He rowed to Cape Skulla, surprised at how strong the undercurrents proved to be on such a mild day. Sir Dunstan had returned to the farmhouse to see if Morwenna had gone back for her books or was visiting her many friends. Anthony's instinct told him she was still hoping to find Elliott. He didn't know why, but he was haunted by the image of her trapped inside a cave, betrayed by the island she loved so well.

After three hours, he almost gave up. The fishermen claimed to have seen her earlier, and she had waved at them from her rowboat, appearing to be perfectly fine. Anthony wondered if he were merely chasing her around in circles. By now she might even be back at the castle.

The light on this side of the island was poor on the fairest day, and suddenly he realized that the current had caught hold of his boat. No matter how hard he strained at the oarlocks, he could not turn or fight the invisible tug of water. He could only let it take him where it would and row straight to shore when the undertow released him. On such a calm day, death did not seem a possibility.

Yet this might have been what had happened to Elliott Winleigh.

The current carried him around the cove, not out to sea but into a channel of fang-toothed rocks. He braced himself for a collision, then found he was borne toward a sea cave that could not be seen until one stared practically into its mouth. He saw a woman in a pale gown standing within its shadows. Morwenna, he thought in anger and relief. She turned to him, and he caught a glimpse of her face. Older than Morwenna, but pretty still. He would have called to her, but suddenly she vanished, apparently into the cave.

Only when he reached the shore did he realize he might have stumbled upon *the* elusive cave, glittering with the multicolored veins that ran through it. But it was already half filled with sea water. Could Morwenna and that woman be inside? Had they located Elliott and were unable to move him?

He waded into the cave until the water reached his chest. There was no sign of the woman or of Elliott—perhaps she had run back along the beach when he secured his boat. Nor did he see Morwenna.

At the very end of the cave's high ceiling, an otherworldly light glowed—he thought it was some phosphorescence from the sea on the walls. But it gave a weird effect, almost luring one to explore the mystery of its hidden crevices. He wondered what he would find if the tide allowed him to continue. Even here, the current proved strong.

He pulled himself up onto a shelving ledge and climbed the rocky entrance to return to his boat. Boyish adventures could wait until after he'd found Morwenna and explained to her in no uncertain terms that as long as he owned Abandon, she would not take risks with her life.

He found her on the other side of the island, sitting in the sand. She jumped up when she saw his boat and ran toward him, her skirts encrusted with salt. With a practiced grace that made him smile, she climbed over the rocks to secure his craft.

She scanned his face. Her own was flushed from the sun and wind, her bonnet forgotten somewhere on the beach. "Did you find Elliott?" she asked anxiously.

He'd forgotten he had meant to be angry. "No, but I looked."

"Oh." She turned away, crestfallen. "Thank you for trying."

"I might have found the cave, though."

"The cave?" She took his arm, too excited to care that she was half dragging him back to the boat. "Could you find it again?"

He paused. "Actually, it found me, although, yes, I suppose I could find it again, though not today, not at high tide."

"Tomorrow, then?"

"I—perhaps." He scowled at her. "What are you doing here alone, anyway?"

"Looking for Elliott. Pasco's apprentice said he saw something unusual from the cliffs late the night Elliott disappeared."

She was still holding his arm. Her fingers felt warm and fragile but not without strength. He imagined how it would feel if she touched his bare body, and a visceral pleasure gripped him before he shook the image away. "You should not be talking to Pasco's apprentice—you should have come to me."

The breeze rose, lifting her long hair so that the ends danced over his wrist. "I thought you would tell me to stay at the castle."

"Yes." She had the softest mouth he had ever seen. "I would have."

"But I saw something myself." She released him to splash through a tidal pool. "Out there—where that projection of rocks is. There's something caught, something white."

He turned, seeing immediately the unidentifiable

pale object that bobbed in the water. "Do you have a pair of field glasses?"

"No." She was dancing up and down with impatience. "I was waiting for the fishing fleet to come in to help me."

He frowned. "I shall row out."

"You can't. I couldn't either. There is a formidable whirlpool."

"I warrant I am a little stronger than you, Miss Halliwell."

Her mouth curved into a smile that made him want to eat her up from head to toe. "I warrant you are, but that water is stronger than us both."

He stripped off his cloak. "Stay here."

"I want to come."

"Stay here, elf."

He pushed the boat back into the waves and leaned into the oars, propelling himself toward the islet of rocks. If it killed him, he would show her what a monument of power he was. The current presented a challenge, but nothing like the undertow of Cape Skulla. This he could handle. He felt in control, until he glanced back and saw Morwenna rowing out in her boat toward him.

"Hellfire and damnation!" he roared. "Did you not hear what I said?"

She shrugged, feigning ignorance. Her small face was screwed up with effort as she struggled to catch him. "I was afraid you might have an accident and need my help!" she shouted back.

"Accident, my—" He ground his teeth and leaned forward; he had circumvented the current by rowing past the rocks from the other side. Morwenna followed his lead, bumping against his hull with her boat.

"We made it," she said, grinning in triumph.

He glared at her. "I do not like being disobeyed."

Her grin faded. "I don't think you would like being drowned, either."

"Do I look as if I were in danger of drowning?" he demanded in a furious voice.

She eyed his strong neck and the powerful chest visible beneath his damp linen shirt. "Nooo," she admitted slowly.

"And did you hear what I said to you on the beach?"

She pulled a strand of hair from her eyes. "About finding Arthur's cave? Yes, indeed, my lord, every word."

He wanted to shake her, the infuriating brat. "Except the phrase 'Stay here.' You did not hear that?"

"It seems to me you said, 'You *should* stay here,' implying an element of choice in the statement."

"There are no choices when I give an order, do you understand me?"

"I don't know."

He raised his voice. "And what must I do to make myself understood?"

"Perhaps you ought not to shout."

"Shall I give my orders in a more physical way?"

"I beg your pardon?"

"Have you ever played charades, Miss Halliwell?"

"Not in a boat."

The waves bumped their boats together; then Morwenna's craft began to drift away. Afraid she was about to be swept out to sea, Anthony reached over and hauled her by her arms into his boat.

"Oh, my heavens!" she exclaimed.

He plunked her down on the bottom of the boat, scowling into her startled face. "Did you understand that?"

"That was a barbarous act," she said breathlessly, scrambling onto the thwarts. "An act of piracy. Something a Viking would do."

"Have I made my point, Miss Halliwell?"

She squeezed a stream of salt water from the hem of her petticoats. "Yes. You are a barbarian, my lord. A veritable Norseman, to judge by that violent act upon my person."

"That was hardly a violent act."

A seagull swooped down on the rocks behind them.

"That was an act of frustration against a stubborn-minded female," he added.

"Well." She huffed out a breath. "I should not like to be the victim of one of your violent acts, that's all I can say."

He smiled darkly. "Indeed, you would not. Now, listen to me. Two people we cared for have drowned on this island."

"Two?" she said, her face distressed. "We don't know that Elliott is dead. Don't say that."

He was sorry for upsetting her, but she needed to realize that she could not continue her behavior without sooner or later paying a consequence.

"I fear the anchor is not holding, Miss Halliwell. I am going to attempt to climb the rocks and reach around the other side to dislodge whatever is caught there."

She gasped. "That is a dangerous quest. What if you slip?"

"If we wait for the fishing fleet to come in, the white object might wash back out to sea."

"Do you suppose—"

She couldn't finish the thought. She could not bring herself to ask if it might be Elliott they'd seen trapped in the rocks. It was an unspeakable possibility, even though everyone else presumed him dead.

"Do not fall, my lord," she called after him as he took the first leap from the boat.

Her shout so startled him that he almost missed his footing. "I shall try not to," he said wryly, vanishing from her view.

The rocks were abrasive but without much foothold, making it difficult to climb to the other side. He was forced to work off his boots, then socks, to keep from slipping. One arm hooked around the thinnest peak of granite, he pulled himself inch by inch around.

Morwenna soon lost sight of him. "Are you still there, my lord?"

"No, Miss Halliwell. I am in North Devon. Where the deuce do you think I am?"

"Well," she said, "I cannot see you."

"I cannot see you either, but I can certainly hear you, and you are disturbing my powers of concentration."

"Oh." She sank back down onto her bottom. "I shan't say anything again then, shall I?"

Silence. She took the oars, trying to maneuver around the massive tower of granite to catch a glimpse of him.

"Damnation," he said, and there was a plop.

She turned white. "Oh, my goodness. Are you in the water?"

"One of my boots fell off the rocks."

"Oh, no."

"Oh, yes."

"Was it a good one?" she asked. "Oh, oh, *oh—*"

"What is it?" Anthony said in alarm, nearly falling off the rock himself. "Morwenna, answer me. What is wrong?"

"My boat is floating away."

"Is that all?" he said in exasperation.

"Is that all? You were upset enough to lose a silly boot. A boat certainly ranks above a boot in importance."

Another silence, then a loud splash that made her jump. Morwenna crossed her arms over her chest, shivering as the sky suddenly turned violet-gray. Minutes passed without a sound from him, too many minutes for her liking. The sea grew rougher. She felt the boat's anchor battling the water, although they sat not all that far out to sea.

"Lord Pentargon?" she whispered when she could not stand the suspense another second. "I know you shall shout at me, but I must know if you are all right."

Just when she had decided she would be forced to climb after him, he swung around the rocks and dropped into the boat. He was soaked, his hair slicked back on his scalp. Blood flowed from a fresh gash in his forearm.

She leaned forward in concern. "What did you do?"

"Caught my arm on the rocks when I was reaching for what we saw. It was only a piece of an old sail."

He gave her a grim smile as he tried to stanch the blood with his sock. "Razor-sharp, those rocks."

"Dragon's teeth," she said unthinkingly. "Dear me, that does look bad. Let me use my sleeve."

"Don't tear your dress—"

"Nonsense." She tugged the stitches loose before he could stop her. For a moment, he was transfixed by the pleasure of seeing her bare arm. Her skin was brown, the muscles firm from rowing.

"You've ruined your gown."

"Do hold still," she muttered as she wound the muslin around the injury. "There. That should do. Does it still hurt?"

"It never did," he lied.

"I'll help you row."

"You will not."

She did, and the only reason he let her was that he enjoyed the experience of watching her strong young body working in harmony with his. The unexpected intimacy of it almost made up for losing his boot, ruining his shirt and trousers, and injuring his arm.

She collapsed on her knees in the sand when they reached the shore. "That was terrifying. For a time, I was certain the current had taken you."

He stared down at her small form. The sun had disappeared behind a bank of sullen clouds, and his cloak was stranded on a solitary rock as the tide rose. He felt a keen sense of foreboding. "You look utterly disgraced, Miss Halliwell."

She examined her gown. "Yes, I do, don't I?"

He reached his hand down to help her to her feet. "I think we shall have to walk home and explain the situation to your uncle."

Her eyes met his. "It was innocent enough."

"Was it?"

"Well—"

"Until now, perhaps."

Time stopped in that moment. Just looking at him made her shiver, that sensual mouth, those heavy-lidded eyes that glittered with sensual awareness. His wet shirt and trousers adhered to the hard contours of his body, highlighting his flat belly and lean hips. She grew warm as she stood in the icy surf, his hand gripping hers. She thought of how it would feel to be held against all that strength, and then the fantasy dissolved.

It became real.

He drew her down on the sand, groaning as the gulls cried overhead, kissing her into breathless silence. Her lips opened at the sweet invasion of his tongue, allowing him to plunder her mouth. She barely noticed when a wavelet splashed her shoulder, but when he put his hand under her skirt, she gasped, and when he buried his face between the cleft of her breasts, she felt herself dissolving into the sea.

"Anthony, we can't," she whispered as she battled the part of her that silently begged him to continue. "We shouldn't."

He pressed kisses on the peaks of her breasts through her gown until flames of pleasure burned in her belly. "This is what I've wanted to do since that day in the tower," he said softly.

"The waves are going to smother us," she said, a more forceful protest beyond her dazed state of mind. How on earth could she explain the instinct that urged her to submit to him?

"I want to pound you into the sand, Morwenna," he said, kissing her throat. "I want to put my face between your legs and do things to you I cannot even say."

Another gasp caught in her throat. "For heaven's sake, then, don't say them."

"I dream about you," he said in a wickedly sweet voice.

"Pleasant dreams?" she whispered.

He grinned. "I dream about tying you naked to the bedposts and licking you all over."

"Dreaming is one thing, my lord, but—" Bound to his bed, a prisoner of his desires. Oh, God. She began to shake, her imagination taking a wild turn. "That— that's shameful."

"Oh, I know, and you'd love every naughty thing I did to you, little virgin."

"You have the most devastating effect on me," she said in a whisper.

"As you do on me," he said, closing his eyes, fighting a battle with himself for control, until slowly he came to his senses. She was sweet and succulent, ripe for the plucking. She was also trembling violently, overwhelmed by what had happened, and he couldn't explain it, either, but he knew he had never felt like this about anyone before. His body was so aroused, he wondered if he would ever recover, and yet he would not bring dishonor upon her.

His strong arms encircled her waist, lifting her to her feet. He looked away in regret as she shook out her skirts. "Take my advice, Morwenna," he said in a low voice. "Do not allow yourself to be alone with me again. Hide from me until I am gone. Run if you should see me, or I will surely take your virtue the next time. Protect yourself from me before it is too late."

"It is too late," she whispered, her hand frozen on the tangled mass of her hair.

"No, my dear, you do not understand—that's what I mean," he said with a wistful sigh. "You are so pitifully innocent. What has happened between us is our secret, and no one need ever know. I keep my word."

She drew her hand to her side and swallowed hard. "I think it is you who do not understand."

He raised his head, following the direction of her gaze to the cliffs above, where a small group of onlookers watched their every move. Sir Dunstan, the Reverend Miles Trecombe, even Vincent, and several island folk.

"Witnesses to the act," he said under his breath.

"Do you think they saw us?" she said in panic.

He gave a laugh rich with irony. "I don't think we can convince them we were digging for clams."

She started to swing around, evidently hoping to escape their outraged audience. He clamped his hands down on her shoulders and held her fast; the gesture could have been interpreted as either arrogant or possessive by those who watched.

"Let me go, my lord," she said indignantly. "My uncle is coming down the path toward us, and he looks fit to kill."

"Yes, I can see that perfectly well, which is why I am holding you here."

Her eyes widened. "To use as a shield?"

He laughed again. There was a dangerous look in Anthony's eye, a gleam of defiance she had never seen before. She had no idea what he intended to do.

"Don't—don't do anything you will regret, my lord."

He looked down at her in amusement. "Too late for that, sweetheart."

She did not care at all for the fatalism in his tone. "Let me go," she demanded again.

"Too late for that too, I'm afraid."

And it was.

Sir Dunstan strode through the sand like a bull-dog; his body was so rigid with fury that it was a wonder the man could walk at all. The vicar and Vincent followed close at his heels. Vincent obviously hoped to reach his master before Morwenna's uncle went on the attack. And Morwenna stood, a morti-fied and strangely fascinated observer whose life appeared to have taken an unexpected twist.

"And for that," Anthony murmured as Sir Dunstan drew back his hand and hit him on the face. "Too late again. Damn, that hurt."

His cheekbone reddening, Anthony maneuvered Morwenna behind him, but he made no other move to protect himself should Sir Dunstan strike him again.

"Shall I take care of him, my lord?" Vincent asked, rolling up his sleeves.

Sir Dunstan stared at Anthony, contempt in his eyes. "I trusted you. You gave your word you would protect her."

Morwenna had wriggled away; Anthony reached around and caught her hands, dragging her back firmly to his side. "No escape from this for either of us," he said in a sardonic undertone. "Stay put, Morwenna. We will stand or fall together."

The vicar was staring at him in embarrassed con-demnation, and no small measure of sympathy.

"You ought to hit him back, my lord," Vincent said under his breath. "There's a red mark on your face."

Anthony sighed. "One does not fight with family."

"Family?" It was Morwenna who took his meaning first. She pulled her hand free and faced him, her gaze stark with shocked disbelief. "What are you saying?"

He smiled at her and found, to his amazement, that what he had feared he now confronted with almost wicked anticipation. "Morwenna has agreed to be my wife."

Sir Dunstan blinked, the news apparently more than he could digest. "But then—what have you done to her dress?"

The vicar shook Anthony's hand. "Congratulations, Lord Pentargon. It will be an honor to officiate, unless, of course, you prefer a more elaborate ceremony on the mainland."

Anthony glanced at Morwenna in sly amusement. "What does my betrothed prefer—that is the question."

Morwenna looked around the beach in bewilderment. At least a half-dozen fishermen, friends who had known her since birth, offered their hesitant congratulations, but she could see the question in their eyes: Had she converted the enemy, or had he converted her? She did not know. The future of Abandon might be at stake, but so was *her* life, and it had just been snatched out of her control by a man who had not even asked her opinion on the subject.

Not "Will you marry me, Morwenna?" Or "I think we ought to get married. It is the honorable thing to do." Or even "Please marry me, Morwenna. I don't want your uncle to murder me."

Not a word. Just "Morwenna has agreed to be my wife."

She felt overwhelmed by the prospect and a

begrudging admiration for his cool arrogance in the matter. Yet she could not deny her share of the blame. She could have refused to respond to him, and now they would both have to pay. The Wheel of Fortune had taken a turn for the worse, or was it really bad? Something deep in her rebellious heart rejoiced that he had chosen her. Something in her woman's soul wanted to surrender to his strength.

"Oh," she said, because a more intelligent reply was beyond her, "what are you thinking?"

His smile was positively forbidding, for what he had been thinking at that precise moment he could not reveal in public. Certainly not in front of her uncle or the vicar.

He was thinking that in a fortnight or so, she would belong to him. She would be morally ensconced in his bed, missing more than the sleeve of her gown. Her nude body would be his playground, his to enjoy, and not for love or money would he be deterred from pursuing the wicked pleasures he had planned for his wife.

His *wife*. Dear Jesus, what had they done? He ought to be swimming for his life toward the mainland instead of standing at her side, calmly committing the rest of his life to the elf.

He flashed her a beguiling grin. "I suggest a small wedding on the island, sweeting. But if your little heart desires something grander, I'm sure it could be arranged."

She gave him a glacial stare, realizing the rogue had left her no choice in the matter. "My little heart desires a long engagement—how does fifty years sound, my lord?"

Anthony slid his arm around her waist, imprisoning her in an inescapable grip. "Too long to be deprived of your enchanting company."

"Absence makes the heart grow fonder." She pushed down on his forearm, frowning as muscles of steel met her feeble effort. "Have you ever heard that quote?"

His smile was devilish. "Absence from whom we love is worse than death. I do not believe in long engagements."

Sir Dunstan smiled at her without humor. "Nor do I." He was staring at her dress again, then at Anthony's bandaged arm, as if he had just made some sort of connection and was not happy about it. "I do wish, however, that you had chosen a more appropriate place to make this announcement. I became frantic when neither of you returned to the castle. One of the fishermen spotted Morwenna's empty boat at sea and rushed to fetch us. For a while, we feared another tragedy had occurred."

The vicar grinned. "Little did we guess a marriage proposal was in the offing."

"Little did any of us guess," Anthony murmured, gazing down amusedly into Morwenna's face.

She refused to smile back, which cast a sudden silence over the small gathering, as if everyone suspected something was not quite right between the betrothed couple. But no one said anything. After all, Pentargon owned the island. The obvious hope was that his rainbow bride would persuade him to stay.

"Morwenna." He gave her a little shake, realizing that she had been stunned by his proposal. Did she think he had planned for this to happen? Was he any less terrified by the prospect of marriage? The difference, perhaps, was his age. He had courted enough women to know what he wanted and didn't want in a wife. And he wanted her. He wanted her enough at the moment for both of them, and what did it matter that he had been forced to acknowledge the truth? He was a grown man, responsible for and aware of his own actions. Better to make her his bride than to leave her there and live with regrets for the rest of his life.

"We will make the best of this," he said in a quiet voice no one else could overhear.

"How?" she asked, rather bleakly for a woman about to take the bridal walk.

"Worse matches have been made."

"When?" she whispered. "During the reign of Henry the Eighth?"

"It is the right thing to do," he said, chuckling at her expression.

She glanced at her uncle, watching their every move. "It is the *only* thing, I'm afraid, but yes, you are right. We will make the best of it."

With Elliott missing, Anthony deemed it inappropriate to make a huge fuss over the betrothal; it *was* a little embarrassing to admit how his engagement had all come about. Vincent, however, took it upon himself to suggest a small dinner party that same night to celebrate the happy event. Mrs. Treffry agreed to handle the arrangements, grinning in delight, but Anthony was not deceived. The housekeeper was only being nice to him in the hope that his bride-to-be would change his mind about selling Abandon.

But he could not. He would honor his legal and moral obligations, and Morwenna, as his wife, would have to accept that. In time, she might come to forgive him. If not, she would still have to obey her husband.

A challenge, that.

She had not looked at him once since they had returned to the castle a few hours ago. Yet when he announced their betrothal to the staff and kissed her, he had felt a softening beneath her resistance. Her attraction to him was a definite advantage, and he would use it to forge a bond between them.

His friends in Town would laugh slyly and ask how in hell he'd allowed himself to get leg-shackled to a girl with no background or wealth. And then they would meet Morwenna and understand. Their amusement would become envy.

He dressed for dinner, although Morwenna had not sent word that she would be down to join him. In fact, she had disappeared like a puff of smoke the instant he released her, her small figure vanishing from his sight.

"Am I a monster, Vincent?" he asked as his valet brought him a pressed black jacket.

"Not to me, my lord."

"My future wife is avoiding me."

"Bridal nerves, my lord."

"Bridal nerves." Anthony grunted. "Does Miss Halliwell strike you as the highly strung type?"

"Indeed not." Vincent whisked a brush over Anthony's wide shoulders. "Lady Pentargon is most delightful, my lord, her skill with a parasol notwithstanding."

"She isn't lady anything yet. She still could change her mind. As could I. Who was the young woman I met at Finley's fox hunt last year?"

"Her name eludes me, my lord."

"Nobody's name eludes you."

"She was rather plain, as I recall."

Anthony smiled. "Compared with Morwenna, you mean."

"Will that be all, my lord?"

"No." Anthony turned from the mirror. "I need a special license—I have a cousin in the office of the Archbishop of Canterbury who will hasten the procedure."

"I shall leave in the morning on the mail packet."

"No. I have a feeling I will need you here. Send Gunther instead. Tell him to contact my jeweler on his way back and have a necklace and wedding ring made for my wife. Something simple but elegant."

Anthony extinguished the candles and glanced once around the smoky room as the valet disappeared. His gaze fell on the bed, to the heavy book propped against the pillow. The chambermaid must have moved it while she was cleaning.

For a moment, he was tempted to glance through it again. But Morwenna was somewhere in the castle; she could not avoid him forever. They would have to make up. And in that bed he would never read again. Not with her as his wife beside him. He would be too engrossed in staging the most tender seduction imaginable. They would do many things in that bed before they left the island. But reading would not be one of them.

His future bride became a little tipsy during dinner. Unaccustomed to the potent brandy Ethan and Anthony preferred, she began the meal in silence, only to erupt into a fit of giggles the moment he suggested a toast in her honor.

His betrothed was scared to death of him, he thought, hiding a smile. She was too young to understand the joys he had in store for her. Yet she was not a child. She was a woman grown, all too alluring in a simple apple-green silk frock that put the elaborate fashions of the *ton* to shame. Yes, his friends would envy him, and he would take care never to leave her alone with any of the rogues.

He fingered the stem of his fluted glass. "You are uneasy, Morwenna," he said gently. "What is it you fear?"

She gazed at him around the huge Gothic epergne that sat on the table. Her giggles had subsided into a silence. They were momentarily alone—the vicar had departed to write his sermon, and Sir Dunstan had excused himself to fetch his dyspepsia pills.

"I fear . . . " She touched the tip of her tongue to her lower lip. Why *had* she drunk that brandy, to chase away the delicious memory of his kiss? Her head felt horribly fuzzy, and his gentle patience was stripping away all her defenses. She wanted to escape before he broke through her final guard. She could feel herself drawn to him more and more.

"You fear . . . ?" he prompted, leaning forward to admire her in the candlelight. He could covet her openly now, and he did, his gaze dark with desire. "Be honest, my dear."

"I fear," her eyes met his, shy and shining with innocent fear—"that I am about to marry the devil."

He sat back, a smile curving his chiseled lips. "I do not know if I should be insulted or amused. The devil, well, being that evil carries enormous responsibilities and privileges. Are you serious?"

Her head was swimming. She blinked to clear her

blurred vision—and the disturbing illusion of the
epergne's branched candlesticks rising from his tem-
ples like a pair of horns. A devil, yes, so beautiful and
masculine that her attraction to him must derive
from some unearthly force; she trembled in terrified
anticipation of how, as her husband, he could use his
power over her.

"You do possess some unholy power," she said
musingly. "How else could you have heard the magical harp and found Arthur's cave? Why has the raven
appeared to you twice in a week when decades could
pass without anyone seeing it?"

He shrugged his broad shoulders. "I don't know
how to explain it."

She watched the idle tapping of his long fingers
against the table. She could not explain why, but the
sight aroused her—images flooded her brain, of his
strong hands unhooking her gown, cupping her
breasts, touching her in the most private places.
Releasing a sigh, she closed her eyes as her body
began to tingle all over. It was too horrible, too wonderful to guess what he would do to her.

"Are you falling asleep on me, my dear?" he whispered in her ear. "Do you need more . . . stimula-
tion?"

Now her body did not merely tingle. It shivered as
if every nerve ending were exposed to naked flame.
She had not heard him leave his chair, but he was
suddenly bending over her, his mouth finding a vulnerable spot behind her left ear. He pressed a kiss to
her flesh that sent her pulses into chaos.

"I guarantee you will not doze when you are in
my bed."

She sat bolt upright in her chair a mere second

before Dunstan returned to the room. The older man glanced from his beautiful young niece to the earl who watched her in brooding silence. The atmosphere between the two of them was thick as fog, but Dunstan did not remark on it. Their attraction to each other seemed as clear to the casual observer as was their enmity. They would bring great passion to their marriage bed, along with problems.

Even Dunstan could not predict the outcome. A moral man, he knew only that he would not see Morwenna used and discarded, disgraced for the world to see. Pentargon would right the wrong he had committed—indeed, he'd accepted his responsibility like a gentleman. Pray God he would not use his power and arrogant will to crush the girl in retaliation.

"Do you feel better, Uncle Dunstan?"

Morwenna's voice cut into his thoughts. Anxiety etched a frown on her face, but there was strength too, untested perhaps, and even deeper still, a magical quality, an inborn power that placed her on more than equal footing with her future husband. Dunstan took comfort in that. Morwenna would not go into this marriage unarmed. Pentargon, if he were as intelligent as he appeared, could more than handle her.

It was not each other these two strong-willed people had to fear. Dunstan looked up at the window, the sky violet-black above the sea. *A greater enemy would confront them*, and he didn't know what had spawned the thought, probably this sad business with Elliott. With each passing day, the young man's death became harder to deny.

"I feel much better, thank you," he said heavily, the words a lie.

Morwenna directed her gaze at Pentargon. "I want to move back into the farmhouse until the wedding. It is only proper, and I desperately need to work on Papa's manuscript. There are too many distractions here."

Dunstan tensed as if he expected the earl to refuse. But Pentargon only nodded and said, "I thought you might. Vincent will stay with you and your uncle, as both servant and bodyguard."

Her face darkened. "Vincent, the—"

"—giant slayer." Pentargon's eyes glittered amusedly in obvious memory of the day he'd first met her. "You may leave in the morning. The barouche will take you back to the cottage, weather permitting."

She rose from the table. "And does my gaoler also give me leave to retire?"

Her uncle almost choked on his pills. "Morwenna, child, your lack of manners embarrasses me."

She threw him an annoyed look. "One hardly needs manners when dealing with a—a wolf."

Pentargon laughed, waving his elegant hand in dismissal. "Go to bed. Let sleep sweeten that temper. Matters always look more favorable in the morning."

She shook her head. "Or worse, unless I wake up tomorrow to find this is all a bad dream."

His face registered a flash of black humor. "You injure me, beloved."

"Do not tempt me, my lord," she said sweetly.

Dunstan covered his face in his hands as Pentargon stood up, overshadowing the girl who challenged him.

"Would you like to take a candlestick to bed, my pet?" he asked in amusement.

"I should like to take one to your head, my lord."

"A lantern, then, my little bride-to-be?"

She smiled reluctantly, acknowledging defeat.

"Thank you, no. I shall find my own way through the darkness."

She whirled around, her small shoulders set as three cats appeared from under the table to follow with their tails held high. Anthony watched in enjoyment as the dignified procession marched to the door. There Morwenna shot him a look fraught with emotion before she led her feline entourage off to bed.

"Remember," he said softly, "we are going to make the best of this."

She turned, muttering to herself, "The best of it. I *am* going to make the best of it."

"Do not fall on the stairs, darling," he called after her, chuckling at the unintelligible retort that came from the hallway, a curse by the sound of it.

"Could I fall any lower, my lord?"

That was clear enough. He turned, sighing, and met Sir Dunstan's worried gaze. "I apologize, my lord, the girl is not herself."

"But she is herself," Anthony said, "and that is why I like her." He stared past the older man into the fire. "Very, very much."

"Is your valet a trustworthy man, my lord?"

The question startled Anthony. He sat down in his chair. "Absolutely. He will guard my girl, and you, with his life."

"Naturally, I do not doubt your judgment," Dunstan said. "It is just that I thought, well, I will have to go to St. Ives to give Elliott's wife the bad news. I do not wish to leave Morwenna alone until the marriage."

Nor do I wish to leave her with you.

The unspoken statement hung implicitly in the silence.

Anthony smiled. "I shall send Vincent *and* Mrs. Treffry to guard her. Of course, I shall keep an eye on her myself." *Like a hawk. She will not leave that farmhouse without my watching her every move.*

"Very well, my lord."

"The license should arrive by the time you are back," Anthony added.

Dunstan raised his brow. "A midsummer marriage? The superstitious would say you tempt fate."

"Or it tempts me." Anthony's smile cut deep creases of cynicism into his cheeks. "All things considered, I do not think this wedding can wait."

The sea washed around the waves of the castle throughout the night, capable in one moment of the most sublime gentleness, of violence in the next. On the other side of the island, in a deep cavern guarded by a dragon's tail, an ancient power stirred. According to legend, King Arthur and his knights awakened every Midsummer Eve for the Wild Hunt. Few people were allowed to witness the ghostly reenactment. Those who did were said never to be the same again.

Morwenna lay in bed and listened to the sea, but her mind was too conflicted to hear the secret it would whisper in warning. She could not think of anything but the man who had claimed her heart.

Beware.

Another life will be taken before the month ends.

Anthony saw the book on the bed as he took off his vest. It had been opened to another illustration when he knew he had left it closed.

Annoyed, he strode forward to push it to the floor,

when he recognized the two figures in medieval dress who knelt before a stone altar.

The Knight Takes the Maiden to Wife.

He stared at the beautifully detailed picture, his profile and Morwenna's. Their devotion to each other leaped from the illustration, rendered the couple so alive that he could feel the knight's desire for his young bride.

Coincidence? A trick? No one could illustrate and print these pages in a matter of hours. And yet—

He rifled through Ethan's chest of drawers and found a letter opener; with painstaking care, he tried to pry the sealed pages apart. When that did not work, he ran downstairs to the kitchen and demanded that Mrs. Treffry boil a kettle.

The housekeeper, putting a saucer of milk on the floor for the cats, stared at him in alarm, as if he had taken leave of his senses. "I-I'll make a n-nice pot of tea and bring it to the library, my lord."

"I don't want tea, woman," he said. The fear on her face made him realize he did present an alarming appearance, the shirt hanging out of his trousers, half buttoned. The castle groom, Barnabas, stood in the doorway with a pitchfork, drawn by the commotion. A pair of sleepy-eyed kitchen maids peered over the man's shoulder.

"No tea?" Mrs. Treffry bumped up against the stove. "Coffee, then, my lord? Hot chocolate? Water for a wash?"

"I want steam, woman, don't you understand? *Steam.*"

Barnabas put down his pitchfork and entered the kitchen, nudging the housekeeper away from the stove. "His lordship wants *steam,* Tillie." He gave

Anthony a sly wink. "For your steamship, isn't it, my lord? Could you not wait until the morning to set sail?"

"We could launch it in the garden pond," one of the maids suggested timidly.

"Crack open a bottle of champagne for her maiden voyage," added the other one.

Anthony stared at them all, realizing they thought him mad or drunk, or both. "I do not wish to set sail, moron. I want to steam open a book—" He stabbed his finger under the housekeeper's nose. "The same blasted book that someone, most probably you, keeps changing and moving around this accursed castle to influence my decision. But it isn't going to work, do you hear me?"

"Everyone from here to Penzance can hear you, my lord," Morwenna said from the doorway. "What on earth are you fussing about?"

Mrs. Treffry bit her lower lip, close to tears. "Steam—a book."

"Ethan's book," Anthony said between his teeth. "The one given to him by your father. The illustrations keep changing. Do you understand what I am saying?"

Morwenna glanced accusingly at the housekeeper. "Did you serve his lordship strong drink after supper?"

"I am not drunk." Anthony grabbed her arm. "Look. Follow me. I left the damn book on the bottom of the stairs. Come. I shall show you what I mean."

Morwenna glanced over her shoulder at the housekeeper and groom, her face bemused. "I think we should humor him," she said in a resigned whisper, then gasped as he practically dragged her through the door.

The book had vanished. Anthony stared at the darkened step in angry disbelief. The servants followed, watching in silence from the doorway. "It was there, I tell you. Sitting right next to that white cat of yours, Morwenna."

She shook her head. "I do not have a white cat, my lord. She belongs to herself."

"I swear to you, the cat was here."

"Lord help us," Goonie muttered under his breath. "First he's seeing steamships, now cats. What next, I ask you?"

Anthony rounded on the small group with a black scowl that made the kitchen maids clutch each other in apprehension. "I will have every nook and cranny of this castle searched tomorrow, and that book *will* be found."

The gathering dispersed; Anthony stood alone with Morwenna at the bottom of the stairs. "What was it in that book that so upset you, my lord?" she asked in concern.

He stared down at her face, remembering the maiden bride and the medieval illustration. Would Morwenna ever look upon him with such devotion? When would the distrust melt from her eyes? "The illustrations seem to mark the events of my life," he said slowly. "And yet it cannot be so. Was Elliott the book's artist?"

"No. It was an old friend of my mother's."

"You have seen the book. You do not remember thinking the illustrations unusual?"

Morwenna smiled. "Everything associated with my mother was unusual, or so it is said." She covered a yawn behind her palm. "We'll look at it together in the morning, shall we? I couldn't read my own name

tonight, I'm that tired. So much has happened today.
I apologize for being rude to you at dinner. It was the
shock, I think."

"Then you are not unhappy about our engagement?"

"Are you?"

"I asked you first."

She lowered her voice to a whisper. "All right. I
admit it. I am not unhappy."

"Is it a secret that you cannot say it aloud?" he
asked in amusement, leaning down toward her.

She caught her breath.

"If you laugh at me, it is."

"Oh, Morwenna, I'm not laughing at you. In fact, I
am quite enamored."

"Of me?" She put her hand to her heart. "Are you
saying that to make me feel better about our marriage?"

"Does it?"

"Only if you are not just saying it to make me feel
better."

He began to laugh.

She grinned up at him. "There. I knew it. You're
making fun of me."

She turned to climb the staircase, and he was
tempted to follow until her uncle appeared on the
landing. "You were not in your room, Morwenna.
What mischief are you chasing now?"

Anthony smiled at her annoyed expression, then
glanced around as something moved in his peripheral
vision.

The white cat.

It darted between his legs, almost unbalancing
him before it disappeared into the gloomy corridors
of the servants' hall. He entertained the fleeting

notion that if he followed it, if he could catch the creature, he might solve a mystery or two. But he'd be damned if anyone was going to see him chasing a cat and asking it to help him find a book. Everyone seemed to think he was half cracked, anyway, and there was no point in proving them right.

Still, tomorrow he was going to find that book and show Morwenna what he meant.

Instead of returning to his room, he decided to take a calming glass of sherry in the library; he needed to draft the letter that Gunther would need in the morning to obtain the special marriage license.

The marquess should put in an appearance sometime in the next fortnight. With any luck, the license would arrive before then, and Anthony would be spared the embarrassment of explaining how he had been brought to the parson's mousetrap by Morwenna. Camelbourne was a rather tragic figure, a man who so grieved his late wife that he went through women like boxes of sweetmeats, tossing them away when his appetite had been sated.

"Why go to the trouble of marrying her?" Camelbourne would say. "She doesn't have any money. You are perfectly capable of luring her into your bed. Set her up as your mistress for a time."

But Anthony knew what he wanted; he'd waited long enough to find it, and nobody, political ally or not, could stop him from marrying her. Marriage—it meant children, commitment, companionship, and growing old together, sharing secrets, and, of course, a sexual intensity that would take them to the stars.

Smiling at the thought, he turned the corner to the library. He'd left the room in a shambles; he and

Vincent had boxed up most of Ethan's books and personal belongings.

He opened the door.

And found everything exactly in place as it was the first day he had come to the castle. Every book, every letter, every pen and inkpot arranged where Ethan had left it.

The curtains were drawn back, and a sea breeze wafted through the open window. The white cat lay curled up in his chair. "God," he said, not moving from the doorway. "Oh, God."

9

In the morning, he reminded himself there had to be a rational explanation for everything. Mrs. Treffry (not as innocent as her pretty face implied) had replaced Ethan's possessions in an attempt to bedevil him. The same logic applied to the book, which he had not yet found. For all he knew, ten of the blasted volumes had been hidden around the castle. For all he knew, the servants operated a printing press in the dungeon. Let them play. They could not win.

The cat, well, the cat was a cat, unpredictable and elusive, and the lot of them had taken command of the castle. Even Morwenna was heard to utter a few colorful curses as she collected her coven to take back to the farmhouse.

Anthony and Vincent spent three hours chasing the creatures across the battlements, up and down the stairs, in and out of the guard room.

"My lord," Vincent said, huffing for breath as they

passed each other in the long gallery, "I am exhausted."

Anthony laughed, scooping a kitten out from behind the bronze umbrella stand. "And I was going to ask you to ride with me to the moor. Hawkey promised to have the ground cleared by today."

Vincent did not answer. His rugged face had taken on a look of warning; Anthony straightened and saw Morwenna trudging down the hall with her tapestry bag.

"I believe she overheard you, my lord," Vincent said in a sad voice.

"Well, what if she did?" Anthony felt like shouting his frustration. Here he stood, a cat squirming under each arm, about to take a bride who expected him to hand her an entire island as a wedding gift. What had happened to his power, not to mention dignity? How had this imp of a woman so shaken his world?

"Vincent, do not look at me like that. You know perfectly well what must happen."

"Yes, my lord." The servant turned away. "That is why I am looking like this."

Anthony's words echoed after her as she wandered through the castle like a wraith. Pentargon's bride, his wife, the mother of his children. Soon it would be true. She would marry the man even though she had failed to soften his heart. Betrayed by her own behavior, she would belong to him.

She found herself in the library, inhaling the manly scents of smoke, leather, and brandy with an undertone of beeswax. She touched the studded armchair where he liked to sit, imagining his stern face with a shiver of pleasure.

She picked up the black leather gloves from his desk and brought them to her cheek, remembering the wicked delight of his hands on her body. Soon he would have the right to touch her as he pleased. She would fall asleep and awaken in his arms.

He would belong to her, too. The thought slipped unbidden into her heavy mood, a stab of anticipation she did not expect. He would be hers, and yet she would refuse to give him her entire heart. Not a man who valued a business obligation over human lives.

Part of her would despise him every day of their life together if he allowed her home to be turned into a hunting ground for the rich and idle. But another part of her had already been won over by this man she barely knew. She was confused by his contradictions; could his kindness to her all be a ruse?

Cruel or kind, she would be his.

She had dreamed of marriage, of course. She had dreamed of a husband, a knight in shining armor to appear out of the mists. But there had been no heroes for her in London, only bored young bucks who mocked her countrified innocence and intellect. The island boys admired her; one or two of the bolder ones had pursued her, but it had always been an unspoken rule that Morwenna Halliwell was in a class apart from the others. And now Pentargon had claimed her, obeying no laws but his own. She would obey him too.

She looked up to see him in the doorway, watching her, and the sweet confusion started again, her heart hammering at the mere sight of him. "I am ready to go," she said, her throat aching.

He came toward her and took the bag from her hand. His mouth grazed her temple, the kiss of a man who knew what he wanted, whose passions smoldered beneath the surface. "Not an escape," he said softly, "but a reprieve. I will send for you when the license comes, unless, of course, you cannot stay away."

Her breath caught. Had she not backed into the chair, her knees would have buckled. She was so aware of him that her body tingled. "I can stay away."

"Can you?" he said in dark amusement. "Yes, I'll warrant you can, if only out of stubbornness. Still, when the license comes, it will not matter—you will be my wife."

She kicked off her shoes and sat on the bare dirt floor of the fisherman's cottage. She had hoped to feel more at home here among old friends than at Pentargon's castle. But the transformation into countess had already begun. Ashamed of herself, she took note of the threadbare curtains, the reek of drying fish, the flower crates that served as chairs, and compared it with the quiet elegance of the refined world she would soon embrace.

The Lanreath family gathered around her, Matthew, his wife Rose, their three children, and their aunt Jane, Matthew's sister, who held a black-haired baby to her breast but wore no wedding ring. Jane would not name the boy's father, but everyone on the island knew, had seen her sneaking to and from the castle before Ethan died.

Salt of the earth, hardworking, proud, and independent. These people would give their lives for Morwenna, and in her heart she had betrayed them.

"We heard such an awful thing, Morwenna." Rose pushed a bowl of steaming mutton stew toward her and passed her a horn spoon.

A horn spoon. The cutlery at Pentargon's stable had been the finest silver, crested with acanthus leaves. She despised herself for having been impressed. To atone for her guilt, she decided she would have to impoverish her new husband by giving away all his possessions to the people she loved. One by one, she would sneak every costly piece of silverware, every candlestick—

"It isn't true, Morwenna?" Rose said again, this time horror as well as anxiety deepening in her voice. "You aren't going to marry the man?"

"It's true." It wasn't Rose who spoke this time but Jane, her beautiful black-haired sister-in-law. "Am I not holding evidence of the Hartstone charm in my own arms? Look at poor Morwenna, she is already lost to the man."

Morwenna jumped up. "Don't say such a thing. It isn't as if either of us exactly had a choice in the matter."

Matthew looked up from his meal. "We can smuggle you to the mainland if you like. There's no need to be sacrificing yourself to save us."

She turned to the window, avoiding his eyes. How could she explain that even by marrying Anthony, she would not be able to save her friends? How could she make them understand her betrayal when she didn't understand it herself? She could never explain the things he made her feel.

"There's no good offering to smuggle her away," Rose said quietly, inclining her head to the window.

Morwenna drew back the curtain to reveal a man astride a white stallion on the rise of the road. Pentargon, dressed in black, his angular profile cut like a silhouette against the sky. She fought the urge to run outside to meet him. "He's waiting for her, afraid to let her out of his sight. I do believe he loves you, Morwenna," she added in wonder.

"Then there's hope yet," Matthew said, breaking into a grin. "Jane, your boy is going to grow up on Abandon just as you hoped, and mayhap his lordship will even set you up in your own home when he learns he has a nephew. It won't be all bad, eh, Morwenna?"

Morwenna swallowed as Anthony caught sight of her through the window, lifting his hand to her in a sardonic salute. She smiled before she could stop herself, a tingle of pleasure going down her spine. Her heart tightened as she whispered, "No. It won't be all bad."

10

$\mathcal{T}$hey were married a little over a week later in the Norman church of St. Geraint on the hill, the day before the summer solstice. Anthony wore an elegantly tailored Bond Street suit, a blue cutaway coat and bow tie with a white ruffled shirt, vest, and straight-legged black trousers. White gloves completed his elegant attire.

He had never looked more darkly handsome or forbidding to Morwenna. Vincent had shaved him so closely that the bones of Anthony's face seemed to be carved from stone. In fact, his frown intimidated Morwenna enough that she nearly turned on her satin heel to run back outside. But then he saw her, and the angular lines softened into what she could only describe as a smirk of arrogant satisfaction—and relief?

Had he really been afraid she would run away? Did she imagine that streak of vulnerability in him? Could he have come to care for her? The hope of winning his heart drew her toward him. "You look beautiful," he said, his eyes dark with triumph.

She stood before him at the Jacobean altar in her mother's dress, heavy ivory lace with pearl-buttoned sleeves that draped her small body to perfection. Her bridal wreath of pink-tinged lilies filled the church with their fragrance, and Anthony remembered that their scent had made him think of a wedding the first day he met her.

Even then he must have known, as he knew now, that she was the only one for him.

As he stopped at the altar, her uncle said, "I hand you to this man with both relief and trepidation. But I am forced to do so. You have brought this thing upon yourselves."

Anthony laid a white-gloved hand at her waist, whispering to her, "I am not sure if that was a blessing or a curse."

Her heart raced at the prospect of what lay ahead, days and nights of private pleasures, sharing thoughts. Already he touched her in the intimate manner of a husband. "Nor am I, my lord."

No one attended the small private ceremony except for the castle staff and the vicar's family. Morwenna's friends stayed away as if they mourned the loss of the island's magical daughter, and her heart was saddened that she had failed them, even though there had been no other way.

It was raining lightly when they began to exchange vows. At the end, sunshine broke through the triple lancet windows. By the time they signed the wedding register, a rainbow had appeared over the sea.

*　　*　　*

The barouche awaited them outside the church. Sir Dunstan walked with them to the gate, his manner subdued.

"Are you sure you will not come back to the castle for cake and champagne?" Morwenna asked him, so anxious that Anthony had to smile.

"No. No." Dunstan fingered the rim of his black silk hat. "I have delayed going to St. Ives to face Elliott's wife. I tried to believe he would turn up before it came to this. I think he might have wanted to sketch your wedding."

"Perhaps he'll surprise us yet," she said quietly. "Perhaps he'll even bring me a drawing of Arthur's cave as a wedding gift."

He looked away, clearly not in agreement. Everyone except Morwenna had given up all hope of finding Elliott alive. "Perhaps."

Then Anthony's hand was at her waist again, his manner patient and protective. Their eyes met as they took their seats in the vehicle. She glanced away, seeking an escape from the mordant humor on his face. But she could not escape that resonant voice. It made her shiver all over, and she bit her lip, knowing her fate lay in his hands.

"Lady Pentargon, I find I am looking forward to this night."

"Oh." What else could she say? Her heart in her throat, she waved at her uncle as the barouche took off.

"Morwenna." Anthony caught her chin in his hand and kissed her, bringing his other hand to her breast to stroke the underside. Even through her gown, his fingers roused sweet fire. Sensation danced across her skin. "Do you come to my bed a reluctant bride?"

She drew a breath, daring another glance at him. His fingers closed around her other breast, his thumbs teasing the nipple, and she could feel her blood stir in response. "In the barouche, Anthony," she said, moaning involuntarily.

"Shall I pull down the top?" he asked teasingly.

"Don't you dare—not with everyone watching."

"Everyone?" He grinned, glancing over her shoulder at the road. "There's no one around for a mile, except our driver and the men working on Wizard Tor, and they're too busy to care what their employer is doing with his wife."

She twisted around, shivering suddenly with something darker than desire. "But I felt someone watching—I *felt* it."

He looked around again. "Perhaps what you sensed was the cat running after us. It will be our children next, I'll wager."

He stood unseen in the fissure of the crag, watching the wedding party leave the church. The rainbow was the perfect touch. The bride was so beautiful, radiant almost, and the groom towered above her with the arrogance of all the aristocrats who thought they owned the world.

See how the smitten husband took her elbow and led her away. See how she followed, submitting to his power already. By tonight, she would no longer be a maiden, and her blood would stain the earl's sheets.

Blood.

He glanced down at the hare he had just killed. Blood dripped from its throat, running down the rocks. The bride deserved a more refined death, he decided as his hand tightened around the handle of the pick. Something prolonged and appropriate for her punishment.

Morwenna went through the motions of celebrating their marriage like a sleepwalker, although Anthony did everything in his power to put her at ease. The champagne helped. She couldn't take a bite of the cake. But when the staff stood waiting like a line of soldiers in the hall to congratulate her, she lost control and started to laugh. Laughter born of nerves and an appreciation of life's absurdities.

Mrs. Treffry had held her in her arms when Morwenna's mother disappeared. Goonie had rescued her from a bramble bush when she was seven, carrying her scratched little self all the way home. Davy and Travis, the footmen, had helped repair the farmhouse roof only last month.

How could she even pretend to give these people orders? They were her family, her dear friends. She felt like an impostor, calling herself their mistress, and she would fight tooth and nail to see them protected when the island changed hands.

"Come, Morwenna. There is a fire and more champagne upstairs."

Her husband's voice. She stared at him in awe, a thrill of anticipation rippling down her spine. It was he who would give the orders, and everyone hastened to obey, including her.

He took her hand, and she suppressed a wicked impulse to tell him they would not need a fire. She went up in flames whenever he touched her. But the champagne would help.

11

He closed the bedchamber door and took her into his arms. "You have not eaten anything for hours." His voice was gentle. "Will my wife waste away before my eyes?"

"I drank champagne," she said weakly.

He stared down into her face, trying not to smile. "To fortify yourself against the monster?"

He kissed her before she could give an intelligent answer. His hands found the hooks at the back of her wedding dress, and suddenly she was drowning in the eroticism of his mouth, melting into the hard male body that pinned her to the door while he casually disrobed her.

Almost a stranger, and yet he was her husband, a man whose clever hands had already unfastened her corset and chemise, exposing her breasts for his pleasure. She closed her eyes, in panic and enjoyment, not knowing what to expect next.

"Do you love me even a little, Morwenna?"

He cupped her breasts, gently tasting the pink crests until the nerve endings quivered in the sweetest pain she had ever known. The question had startled her.

"Do you love me?" he said again, his hands gripping her arms, the answer more important to him than anything he had ever asked.

The quiet intensity of his voice broke the spell he had cast over her senses. Her heart stopped as she opened her eyes and saw the solemn hope on his handsome face. "You own me, my lord," she whispered. "You own the very air I breathe. Is that not enough?"

A smile of self-mockery curved his mouth. "For most men, perhaps that would be enough, but no, I want more. I want everything from you, Morwenna. Your devotion and your trust."

"Do you love me, my lord?"

His gaze burned her like a brand. "I know that I have never felt this way about a woman before. Damn it, yes, I love you. Isn't it obvious?"

"Will you reconsider selling the island?" she whispered.

His face hardened. "Oh, Morwenna, ask me for anything but that."

"But why? Why?"

"When the bargain is assured, I will tell you. You will understand. I am sworn to secrecy until then."

"Bargain?" Her voice broke in anguish. "Is the marquess the devil? What power does he hold over you? Is it blackmail, my lord?"

He caught her to him, the buttons of his vest abrading her breasts. "No power that I have not given him, and if I could go to him and take it back, I would."

"And how can I go back downstairs to face those people, knowing I have failed them?" she cried.

Anger and hurt flared in his eyes. "I would prefer my bride to view our wedding bed as something other than a sacrificial altar. It is me you have to please. Trust me on my own terms, Morwenna."

"I don't see how I can."

An awful silence fell. Morwenna realized she had hurt him, and she told herself he deserved it. He was a hard man. Yet the truth was that she stood half naked in his arms, not of his manipulations but of her own volition, and despite everything, she believed in him, or she would never have spoken the wedding vows. She meant to make a life with this man.

He saw the softening on her face and wanted her badly enough to exploit it. "Come to me willingly, Morwenna," he said. "Tell me you want me, and all will be well between us."

He bent his head to kiss the distended areolas of her breasts again. She wrapped her arms around his neck, surrendering to his seduction. He went down on his knees, his hands around her waist. She didn't realize he was untying her petticoats until they fell around her feet with her wedding gown. He pulled down her drawers, groaning as the delicate perfection of her body was finally revealed.

She gasped and belatedly crossed her hands over her lower torso. Her husband chuckled at this modest but useless gesture as he grasped her bottom and brought her to his face.

"Anthony!"

"Hmmm?"

His warm breath tickled her belly, and she wriggled away only to find herself held more firmly in place. Then his face disappeared between her thighs; she was so mortified, she could barely choke out a cry as he licked and nibbled at her, his tongue penetrating the most private places, until she fell silent in shame, and then shame turned into the most sinful pleasure she had ever known. The soft curls of her sex were soon soaked with her arousal.

"Do you come to my bed willingly?" He raised his face, his gaze dark with desire, and gave her a beguiling smile that would have melted a stone.

Their eyes locked in a primal battle.

He nuzzled the pink folds of her femininity. Morwenna was lost.

Her back arched, giving him deeper access. She groaned, her head falling back against the door. His fingers had joined his mouth to drive her wild, and the tension built inside her, tighter and tighter, coiled into a knot, until her knees buckled, and she collapsed with him on the carpet.

"My God, Morwenna." His mouth, his hands touched her everywhere, searing her, adoring and disarming her of every weapon she possessed.

His voice came from a dreamlike distance. She could not control her movements, could not control *him*.

"I don't think"—he unbuttoned his expensive jacket, vest, and shirt—"that we will even make it to the bed, bride."

She started to laugh, curling up into a ball. She had drunk too much champagne; no, she hadn't drunk enough. Did people actually do this on the floor? It was a far cry from her girlhood fantasies of a fairy-tale marriage—but somehow—she was kissing him back—it was sweeter than anything she could have imagined. She would honor her vows to this man even as he broke her heart.

Her artless kisses excited him. He laughed, a low, deep sound of triumph that told her to expect trouble. Winding a hank of her hair around her waist, he brought her gently back to her knees. He couldn't kiss her deeply enough. He wanted to hammer her on the carpet, spread her legs, and love her until they both fell unconscious.

"My wife." His voice sounded uneven as he pulled off his clothes with one hand, the other caressing her face. "I have never desired anyone like this. Do you want a pillow for your head?"

She closed her eyes. *"Anthony."*

"No." He stood, bringing her with him. "Not on the floor for your first time."

"Well, thank heaven."

"Perhaps the second. Or the third."

He cradled her against his naked chest as if she were weightless. The power of his body overwhelmed her. As he lowered her to the bed, she realized he was bare below, too. Her gaze dropped shyly. He was the most beautiful male, fully aroused, sculpted muscle and sinew.

He slid down her body, molding himself to her in the most indecent way. She couldn't stop shaking; the friction of his shaft as it teased the swollen folds of her womanhood tempted her, made her want to open her legs wider and take him inside her.

He kissed her from head to toe. His talented fingers played with her and gently tormented the peaks of her breasts until she quivered in anticipation, sensitized to his touch. He was her husband. She let him do things to her she had never dreamed a man and a woman could do. The heavy-lidded enjoyment in his eyes told her that her acquiescence pleased him. She was helpless against his power.

The room seemed to grow smaller as he straddled her. The thick knob of his manhood probed her, easing into her sheath. When he lifted her legs over his shoulders, the candle flame on the nightstand beside them blurred into one radiant ball of light.

"My wife," he said, watching her, "I am going to win your love no matter how long you resist me."

He took her virginity in a deep thrust, touching her face with the intensity of emotion that rushed through him. He felt her tremble at the invasion, at the loss of innocence, and he found himself overcome by what she meant to him. She was truly his now, to protect and cherish.

She gave a soft cry of shock as he began to move. "What are you doing?"

"What do you think I'm doing?" he asked tenderly, smiling down at her. "I'm trying to fit all the way inside you."

She lay perfectly still, her face embarrassed. "I don't believe it will fit."

"I believe it will." He rotated his hips, groaning in heartfelt pleasure as he proved himself to be a man of his word.

"But I can hardly breathe."

"Then I am not deep enough, or you would not breathe at all."

Beneath the pain and embarrassment, she began to feel a deep flush of pleasure again. He was so big, she still could not imagine her body would hold him. She made a subtle attempt to wriggle away. He gripped her to him with such a frown of displeasure that she gasped, captive beneath him.

"I didn't give you permission to move," he whispered, his gaze impaling her.

"I *can't* move," she said in protest.

He lowered his head and kissed her, withdrawing his shaft from her passage only to plunge back even deeper inside. "Let me give you pleasure, Morwenna." He groaned against her throat. "Trust me at least for this one night."

"I will try, my lord," she whispered, stifling a moan.

He flexed his hips, arousing sensations that made her arch upward. He was pumping into her faster now, his handsome face intense. She grasped his waist, anchoring herself to him, as her body caught his rhythm. "Better?" he whispered, knowing perfectly well it was.

"More," she answered in a wanton voice that could not be her own. "Harder. Oh, more, Anthony, *more.*"

"Anything my bride wants."

She ran her fingers over his powerful hips. "I want you. Inside. Deeper." She couldn't believe what she was saying. *"Now."*

"With pleasure." He drove her down into the mattress, his shoulder muscles straining.

The bed hit the nightstand. The crystal brandy decanter fell to the floor and spilled. Morwenna lifted her head in horror. "You will disturb the servants, Anthony."

"Do you think I care?"

He thrust into her with such renewed vigor that the bed frame bounced across the floor. "Obviously not!"

The intensity of his lovemaking made her heart stop. She arched her back, certain she would die beneath him. He caught her wrists in his hand and held them over her head, ravishing her mouth with deep kisses. Small cries of surrender broke in her throat as she closed her eyes. He seemed to revel in pleasuring her, proving his domination. The pulsing in her belly was unbearable, building, building until even her bones seemed to melt into his magic.

He gripped her face in his hand. "Look at me when you come. Remember you are mine, and that I love you."

As if she could forget. She opened her eyes to stare up at his dark face, mesmerized, watching his mouth curl in pleasure as she shattered in climax. "You are so incredibly beautiful," he said, and gave himself up to an experience so powerful that their souls bonded together for all time.

He did not move for so long that Morwenna wondered if he had fallen asleep. She felt a tenderness toward him that surprised her, considering the storm they had just weathered. Never had she felt this close to anyone in her life. She stroked his shoulder in a tentative caress, admiring the beauty of his male body. He fell slowly to the side of the bed, pulling her against him, still embedded in her body.

She attempted to edge away; he reached out and drew her back beside him. "Where do you think you're going?"

"I was going to bring you a cool towel. You look in need of a restorative."

"I look in need of nothing but you." He opened his eyes and gave her a lazy smile. He noticed she wore nothing but his wedding ring. He liked that very much.

"What sort of marriage will we have, my lord?" she wondered aloud after several moments of silence.

He grunted in amusement. "A vigorous one, to judge by our first encounter."

She snuggled into his chest. "And fidelity?"

"Do not doubt it, Morwenna." He sounded angry that she would even ask. "I am not one to take my vows lightly. I go into a commitment with my whole being."

She examined his finely muscled body from the corner of her eye. She could certainly attest to the truth of that statement.

"Anthony, if this is to be typical of your fervor, I suggest we take a few precautions in future."

His dark brows drew into a frown. "Precautions?"

"Such as bolting the bed to the floor and extinguishing the candles before we retire."

He glanced around at the nightstand, grinning slowly. "I never even noticed. I was too lost in loving you."

His grin became entirely too seductive. She felt a tingle of anticipation dance over her skin. "There is something I ought to tell you, Anthony." She drew a safe distance away from him. "Actually, I should have told you before you married me."

"A wedding-night confession. I am intrigued, as long as it does not concern another man."

"Actually, it concerns a town full of them."

"What?" he said, startled enough to bring his head off the pillow.

"And women."

"Now I am intrigued."

"I speak of society, in its entirety." She took a deep breath. "I don't know what my uncle told you of my miserable attempt at a debut. I assume he painted a rather flattering picture of my visit to London to encourage you to honor your proposal."

Anthony waited several heartbeats to reply. It seemed impolite to point out Dunstan had warned him that Morwenna had been a lost sheep among wolves.

"I do not recall his exact words," he lied. "But they were flattering."

She shook her head. "Then the old dear fibbed to impress you. Socially speaking, I was a soufflé."

"A what?"

"A soufflé." She sighed at the memory of her humiliation. "A fallen one. So full of high hopes that I collapsed at the first slight. Do you know what I mean?"

He lowered his head, tugging her back toward him. "I haven't a clue. What are we talking about?"

"I don't know how to be the wife of an earl, Anthony. I don't have an inkling how to charm— well, let us say, the Spanish ambassador, should he come to dinner at our house."

"As I have never met him, it seems highly unlikely you should have to worry, Morwenna." He wrapped his arms around her, chuckling softly. "Anyway, you charmed me easily enough."

"Did I?"

"Completely."

She felt a flutter in her stomach as he pressed his forehead to hers. "Do you think we can be contented together?"

What a question. All he wanted to do was rest for

a few minutes, then take her again. "I am as contented as I have ever been." Which, he realized in surprise, wasn't quite true. He could not ever remember this sense of rightness and hope for the future. "And you, are you contented with the husband fate has forced upon you?"

She was silent for a moment as she studied his face, the seductive blue-gray eyes, strong bones, and clefted chin. The face she would awaken to every morning for the rest of her life.

"Yes, Anthony. I am, except for the one matter that stands between us."

"In time, I hope you will come to understand," he said. "It would be hard to continue hating the father of your children."

"Children?"

His arms tightened around her slender waist. "If tonight is any example, we will raise a large family."

"It is difficult to imagine," she murmured.

"Until I met you, I would have agreed, but now, Morwenna, well, suddenly the impossible not only seems possible, it has become a probability."

She sat up, her hair in wild tumult around her shoulders. "Still, you could have chosen a better bride from society. Some men would be furious at being trapped into marriage."

"Not after what we just did." He sighed in satisfaction. "Most men would kill for that."

"Really?"

"Take my word on it."

She had no idea how desirable she was, he thought. Isolated on this island, immersed in her father's lost worlds and legends, she had no inkling of her worth.

"I am a man grown, Morwenna. If I was stupid enough to half seduce you on a beach in public view, I could hardly complain about the consequences. In fact—" He broke off, turning his head to the window. "Did you hear that?"

She frowned. "Did I hear what?"

"It sounded like bells."

She looked up at the window in disbelief. "You heard bells—*the* bells? The bells of Lyonesse? My heavens, it might mean that Arthur is about to arise."

"To hell with him." He gave her a devilish grin. "*I* am already risen."

"But—the bells might also ring in warning. Or they might ring to—"

He forced her down beneath him and captured her mouth in a kiss. He cupped the soft globes of her backside, tracing his fingers between the cleft. She subsided into a daze of sensual anticipation.

"They might mean—oh, goodness, that feels positively naughty, Anthony. The bells might be trying to summon you."

"I shall bear that in mind, Morwenna." He couldn't hear the damned bells anymore, and now he wondered if he ever had. In fact, he couldn't even remember what they had been discussing two seconds ago.

Nor, for that matter, could she.

12

The young women Morwenna had grown up with crowded into the farmhouse parlor to see her the morning after her wedding. Like a ghost haunting its former home, she craved a return to all she had left behind. She had experienced such a flood of emotions upon awakening in Anthony's bed that she'd felt compelled to escape the castle before he stirred. *Remember you are mine.*

She gazed in awe at his nude body for a full minute from the doorway. His well-muscled limbs sprawled across the entire bed. The grainy light of morning exaggerated the symmetrical angles of his face. Even in sleep he exuded an aura of male authority and latent strength, and yet last night *she* had enchanted him.

"You are mine too," she whispered, hugging herself. "And the answer is yes, I do love you."

Dressing quickly, she crept barefoot from the room. She wouldn't have been surprised to find him waiting at the bottom of the stairs. As if he could appear by magic.

Even when she reached the castle door, she could see his handsome face in her mind, could feel his hands and mouth on her body; she could breathe his musky scent in her hair. She was entirely captivated by her husband.

Then she ran outside into the sunshine, as if the sea air could purge her soul of him.

Now she stood in the farmhouse, the haven that only yesterday had been her home. But in the familiar surroundings, she felt like a stranger. She felt like an exhibit at the museum, gawked at, whispered over, examined in lurid detail.

"We never thought you'd come out of the castle again, Morwenna."

"Did you think he would wall me up in the tower?" she said indignantly.

"Pasco Illugan said Pentargon is a warlock, that he bewitched you, and now you will betray us."

"A warlock." A shiver went down her spine. "What a load of rubbish. He's but a man."

"See, you're defending him already, Morwenna. He has you in his power."

"He does not," she said, thumping down onto the hard horsehair-stuffed sofa. "I'm here, am I not?"

"Is his male thing a magic wand?" one of them whispered. "Did he wave it in the air?"

"Stop it, all of you!" she cried, biting her lip against the urge to giggle at the ridiculous image of Anthony they evoked.

They gathered around her, more like a gaggle of stupid geese than the girls she called her best friends.

"Then you've made him change his mind? The island won't be sold?"

"Idiots, I've only been married to him for a day."

And it was Midsummer Day, which would explain the mystical undercurrents in the air.

Jane sat down beside her, the only female present who regarded her with understanding because she too had fallen under the former castle lord's spell. "The vicar and his wife are giving a wedding feast tonight in your honor. Will you and your husband come?"

"I don't know." Morwenna sighed when she thought of what had occupied her time last night.

"And the festival on the moor afterward?" Vivian Wescott asked. "Pasco is taking bets in the tavern that your husband will forbid you to come. A countess cannot dance like a commoner, he said."

Morwenna's eyes flashed. "Of course I'll be there. Have I ever missed it? Even when I lived on the mainland, I came home for Midsummer Eve. That isn't going to change. Tonight is—"

She broke off as a young girl of about five or six burst into the cottage, her face streaked with tears. "He t-took my dog! He's going to train it to hurt people. I h-hate him."

Morwenna stood, pushing through her audience to the door. "Who took your dog, Sarah?"

Vivian answered in a grim voice. "It's Pasco again. He's been threatening to steal pets to use as familiars."

"And no one is stopping him?" Morwenna asked in disbelief.

"Darren Sennen tried last year," Jane said. "He thrashed Pasco half to death, and the next thing

Darren knew, his wife had a miscarriage in her fifth month. Now everyone's afraid to stop him."

"Pasco didn't cause her to miscarry," Morwenna said with certainty. "She lost the baby because she caught the measles."

"Pasco claims he made her sick as punishment. Darren found a doll with red spots on his doorstep the night the baby died."

Morwenna grabbed her straw hat from the table and the old muddied half-boots she'd left by the hearth. "Where are you going?" Jane called after her.

"To fetch her husband," one of the girls whispered. "There's going to be a battle of warlocks on the moor."

"Is that where Pasco is?" Morwenna jammed on her boots. She had thought to have come back to the cottage for her father's manuscript, a work she had woefully abandoned since meeting Anthony. It seemed she would have to neglect it for yet another crisis. Still, the theft of a young girl's dog was not a sin she could overlook.

"Be careful," Sarah's older sister said as Morwenna marched to the door. "Pasco has a big carving knife."

"He was brewing a potion in the stone cauldron at Wizard Tor during your wedding ceremony yesterday," one of the girls said in distaste. "I wish the wind would come up and blow him into the sea. He's promised to do something vile and nasty tonight to show his scorn for Lord Pentargon."

Jane drew aside the curtains and watched Morwenna lead one of the ponies from the barn. "If Pentargon's bride doesn't show him first. Oh, do be careful, Morwenna," she whispered, putting her hand to her mouth. "Pasco has sold his soul to the devil, and he's always been obsessed with mastering you."

She was so angry that she couldn't even speak when she found him, squatting amongst wax-splattered stones on the flat boulder high above the moor. The puppy banged in panic against the slats of a wooden cage; she opened the door to release it before Pasco even realized she had climbed up behind him.

But the dog could not escape; Morwenna's hands trembled so badly that she almost could not untie the strings he had wound around its muzzle. In panic, the puppy clawed at her arms and throat as she bent over it. She had barely unwound the string when Pasco saw her.

"Run!" She stomped her foot, and the puppy scampered down the hillside, barking joyously at its freedom.

Pasco jumped up and down, his spiky hair giving him the look of a demented hedgehog. "I needed that damn dog, you interfering little twit!"

The puppy had reached the bottom of the hill, only to race back up again to Morwenna's side. Pasco made a lunge for it, cursing as Morwenna scooped up a handful of rocks to hurl at his head.

"That is going too far," he shouted, almost comical in his efforts to recapture the liberated dog. His face turning purple, he started to run after it only to fall as Morwenna stuck out her foot to trip him. Pasco was thirty-two, but sometimes he acted like a child.

He turned over on his back like the slug he was, staring up at her in naked fury. Spittle ran down the side of his mouth. "You will be so sorry you did this," he said softly.

"I'm only sorry I can't lock you away in a cage with a string around your mouth."

"You don't mean that."

"Oh, yes, I do."

"Deep in your heart, you have always been attracted to me. We could make such wicked magic together, you and I."

She took a step back, a gust of wind blowing her skirts around her knees. "I could kill you right now, Pasco, that's how much I love you."

"Don't move, Morwenna." He levered himself up on his elbow, his pointed face suddenly intense. "Do not take another step."

"Why?" She pushed her hair from her eyes, straining to look down at the ground.

A lewd grin broke across his foxlike features. "Because I can see right up your dress to your drawers. It's a beautiful view."

She picked up a heavy rock and dropped it on his stomach. He howled in pain, then sprang to his feet, his small cape billowing out like a bat's wings. "You'd better run, witch, because if I catch you, I'm going to drag you into a cave and teach you the meaning of submission."

She backed away, her face taunting. "You're a child, Pasco. You can't catch anything except helpless creatures."

"I'd like to see you helpless, Morwenna. I'll warrant you wouldn't be so brave if I got you alone."

She grabbed her skirts in her hands. "You're a pathetic worm!" she cried, then she whirled and ran.

"Child, am I? A worm? I'll show you what a child can do."

He chased her and the dog down the hill and

through a narrow lane where Sarah and her friends waited to rescue the puppy. With the other girls watching in horror, he pursued Morwenna until they broke into the open moor, and she stopped abruptly, stunned by the site of the scarred earth, the absence of the magical stones the workmen had rolled into the sea.

Pasco grabbed her by the shoulder, but she shook him off; they were both too unsettled to continue their fight. They were shocked at the rape of the virgin moor, trenches dug into ancient burial barrows, sacred stones replaced by stacks of hand-hewn beams and slate quarried on the mainland. The marquess had imported Scandinavian wood, and everywhere she looked she saw buckets, hammers, pipes, and sacks of lime.

"They're really going to build the lodge." Her voice was hushed, a funeral knell. The death of all she cherished.

He gave her a sullen look. "Your husband is. You married our executioner."

Her husband. She suppressed a stab of guilty longing at the thought of Anthony abandoned in their bridal bed. No doubt he wondered where she had gone, and she wished she had not left him. How could he break her heart like this? It unsettled her to realize she wanted to find any excuse to forgive him.

"This is private property." John Hawkey strode toward them in a leather jerkin and muddied boots. "Move off, the pair of you. The wood and pipes ain't for taking."

Pasco sneered at him. "Do you know who she is?"

"I know you're the island idiot." He acknowledged Morwenna with a bow of mock respect, her dirty skirts and disheveled hair. "And can this be the lovely Lady Pentargon? Don't tell me the bloom is already off the blushing bride?"

"If her husband hears you address her in such an insolent tone, you great lummox, you won't be blooming much longer yourself," Pasco said grimly.

But Morwenna wasn't even listening. She wandered around the huge scar in the earth where the Wishing Stone had stood, hugging herself against a hurt so deep she could not cry. In a year, it would all be gone.

Pasco and Hawkey began trading insults. With any luck, she thought they might end up killing each other.

"I suppose you won't grace us tonight with your glittering presence at the Midsummer revels?" Pasco shouted after her. "I suppose your high and mighty husband has other plans for you after the feast?"

She ignored his taunts and walked away. With every step, she could feel Hawkey staring after her, making her skin prickle unpleasantly. She found her pony waiting where she had left it. Her mind numb, she let the animal amble at its pace. She was so disheartened that she scarcely noticed the magnificent yacht anchored off the cove or stopped to think what it might mean.

She only knew she had been right when she had accused Anthony of making a pact with the devil for possession of Abandon.

She never expected to find the devil himself waiting at the castle.

13

Anthony was puzzled and a little panicked when he woke up to find his wife gone. Missing her, he dressed and searched the adjoining room. He told himself she was hiding like one of the castle cats, shy after the night of passion they had shared. But they had made a beautiful start, he and his rainbow bride, and he could not wait to begin another day with her.

He searched the tower and the lower rooms of the castle. When he went outside, he found Vincent and Mrs. Treffry tiptoeing about the walled garden, uncupping their hands at various intervals, then flapping their fingers in the air.

"Good God," Anthony said. "There are two lunatics in my garden, one of whom closely resembles my valet."

Vincent glanced up, pressing his index finger to his lips.

Anthony put his hands on his hips. "Are you shushing me?"

"You'll frighten them away, my lord." Vincent waved his hand over the flowers—flowers that Anthony would swear on his brother's grave had not been growing yesterday morning.

He looked up in the air. "Frighten who or what away?"

"The ladybirds, my lord. Lady Pentargon's friend, old Annie Jenkins, brought them in a jar this morning as a wedding present to protect the flowers. The wee people inhabit their bodies."

What flowers? Anthony would have asked only twenty-four hours ago, but now, before his very eyes, healthy blossoms were sprouting from every available inch of soil. He stared up at the wild honeysuckle entwined around the base of the stone fountain. The castle looked like a hothouse and smelled like a French parfumerie.

"Where is my dear wife anyway? It is her birthday, and I have a gift for her."

Mrs. Treffry coaxed a ladybird off her nose. "She mentioned something about a manuscript at the farmhouse, my lord."

Anthony frowned. "And who escorted her ladyship across the island? Vincent?"

Vincent looked apologetic. "She must have been gone before I even arose, my lord. Until this very moment, I assumed that you and she were still, well, sleeping."

Anthony's frown deepened. "I am going upstairs to change. Kindly have my horse saddled so I may at least see her home safely."

"Yes, my lord."

When he came back downstairs a few minutes later, he decided he would have to talk to Morwenna about curbing her independence. Yes, she was probably fine, enjoying the morning air, but the incident at the farmhouse had made him uneasy enough that he worried about her. Despite Anthony's persistent questioning and surprise visits to the moor, he had found no evidence to attach blame for the vandalism to the miners.

Vincent, a ladybird still attached to his sleeve, stopped him at the foot of the stairs to announce a visitor.

"Whoever it is will have to wait," Anthony said. "Make up some excuse why I am not available."

"It's *him*, my lord," Vincent said in an undertone. "The servants have spotted him on the causeway."

"Him—not Camelbourne?"

"I'm afraid so."

Time came to an inconvenient stop whenever the Marquess of Camelbourne chose to stage a visit. Minor personages were expected to revolve around him, to contort their lives to fit his schedule. Anthony did not enjoy playing toady to the pompous tyrant, but he couldn't afford to offend him either. And, at times, he actually liked the man.

"He's a week early," he said in a clipped voice.

"Yes, my lord," Vincent said mournfully.

Anthony gave him a look. "What is the matter with you? Did you lose your ladybirds?"

"You probably do not wish for me to tell you, my lord."

"You're probably right."

"It's just—oh, never mind."

"Say it, Vincent, before I shake you."

"It's just a shame, my lord, that you are going to give away this enchanted island. A terrible shame."

Then the marquess appeared in the hall with his valet, his secretary, and a pair of footmen. Anthony greeted the man with appropriate courtesy and ordered Vincent to give him a tour of the castle. But the whole time, as Camelbourne discussed hunting and masonry, Anthony kept glancing at the grandfather clock in the corner, and when it struck two, he knew he had to find Morwenna whether the marquess took offense or not.

He strode from the library at the same moment Camelbourne descended the stairs from his "tour." He was puzzled by the look of amusement on the man's face until he realized what had caught his attention.

Then he turned and stared, stunned at the vision before him.

There, in the middle of the hall, stood Morwenna, his bride, island hoyden, child of Abandon, with muddy boots, snarled hair, her dress torn and stained.

He moved forward to grasp her arm, Camelbourne completely forgotten in his shocked concern. "My God, Morwenna, are you hurt? What happened to you? Tell me who did this."

Camelbourne had pulled down one of the ornamental lances from the dark paneling. "A fight over a serving girl. I like this place, Anthony. I rarely see this sort of excitement at home. Let's go, girl. Show me the miscreant so Pentargon and I may slice him into ribbons to thread in your hair."

She was white and shaking, certain she would collapse if Anthony hadn't retained such a possessive grip on her. "It was Pasco."

"Pasco." Anthony stepped away from her, nodding grimly. "Then he is dead."

"No." She caught his wrist. "*I* attacked him, to be perfectly fair."

Camelbourne came up before her. "Well, this gets better and better."

"What do you mean, you attacked him?" Anthony said in confusion.

She was a little calmer now, calm enough to suspect that the other man examining her with such interest might be the worst enemy of all. He was unexpectedly good-looking, stockier than Anthony, with gray-streaked black hair and a rugged yet aristocratic face that bespoke importance.

"Pasco had stolen a little girl's dog to use as a familiar, and I—I stopped him."

Anthony drew a breath. "How?"

She shook her head in chagrin. "I don't know—I kicked him and hit him with a rock, I think. Then we ran down the moor in the mud and met that awful man Hawkey."

Camelbourne whistled through his teeth. "A warrior maid. I like this island more and more."

"Not a warrior." Anthony threw him a look. "My wife."

"Your—" For once, the great statesman was speechless, his craggy face frozen in amused disbelief.

"Morwenna." Anthony reclaimed her hands in such a bruising hold that she gasped. "There are scratches on your throat and wrists. There are tears in your dress, and you tell me Pasco did not *touch* you?"

"He didn't have a chance." She wanted to die of mortification, looking like a slattern in front of the two elegant and powerful men. "The puppy clawed me when I untied it and set it free. The poor thing was frightened to death."

Camelbourne laid the lance against the wall. "No wonder you have not answered my last letters," he said to Anthony. "You've been too entertained to bother."

"More entertained than you can imagine," Anthony retorted.

"Indeed." Camelbourne graced Morwenna with a wry smile. "Will you join us for sherry, my dear? I think I would rather enjoy being entertained by you myself."

She did not return his smile. "I would rather drink from a pig trough than with you, if the truth be told."

Anthony closed his eyes.

A muffled chuckle of approval came from behind the library door where Vincent and Mrs. Treffry had last been seen.

"My wife did *not* mean that," Anthony said.

Morwenna looked indignant. "Yes, she did."

He swore under his breath. "She didn't."

She looked the marquess in the eye. "I did."

"Excuse me." Camelbourne put his hand to his heart. "Do I know you—have I done something to earn your malice such as kill your last husband or father in a duel? If so, forgive me, my dear."

"You have killed no one I care for yet," she said steadily. "But as certain as the sun sets, you will."

Camelbourne glanced at Anthony. "Is she mad?"

"No. Just overwrought from her experience." Anthony stared down into her face before he dragged her to the stairs, his tone strained and low. "Have a bath. Change your clothes. I will handle this."

She pulled her hands away. "I saw what they've done to the moor. I saw you have done nothing to stop it."

"Join us for luncheon, Lady Pentargon," Camelbourne said in a cold voice that could not be countermanded. "I wish to learn more of my friend's wife."

"Anthony." There were tears of anger in her eyes. "I cannot bear this."

"You have charm and courage, Lady Pentargon," he said in a quiet voice. "You are an enchantress. Use your talents to influence him instead of your anger. He is not an evil man. Selfish, self-absorbed, yes, and once, believe it or not, I considered him a friend. Now I am in his debt."

"Will you tell me why?" she whispered. "I need to understand. I am your wife."

"Tonight. I promise."

She nodded, then turned to flee up the stairs. Two of her cats streaked passed Camelbourne to follow her. He turned to Anthony.

"Take me to the library, Pentargon. I find I am more intrigued than ever by this island I will soon own."

Anthony stared up the staircase, unable to shake off the sick feeling caused by seeing his wife in such a state. "Our business dealings will have to wait another hour or two, Lloyd. It seems I have a more pressing matter to attend to."

"Do you need my help? I do love a good fight."

"No. This one is mine."

Anthony stared dispassionately at the man he had thrown against the cottage wall. "Listen to me, Pasco."

"How can I listen?" Pasco's voice was a whine of pain. "I'm dead. I'm bleeding from the nose. You've murdered me."

"Not quite, but I would not rule it out as a possibility. There will be no more taunting my wife or any other woman on the island. No more capturing small animals for your spells."

"No pleasure at all," Pasco said, groaning as he lowered himself onto the ancient oak settle. "I suppose you expect me to wave a good-fairy wand for a living? People pay for curses, my lord. Ill wishes are in demand. I could have trained that mongrel to be of use."

Anthony pulled down his shirtsleeves, glancing in distaste around the untidy cottage. A one-eyed crow sat in a cage in the corner. Behind it rose a dusty shelf crammed with phials, potions and nostrums, and a medieval helmet.

Frowning, he moved forward to examine it. "I've seen this helmet before."

"I didn't steal it." Pasco was suddenly defensive, holding a cloth to his nose. "I found it on the beach."

"When?"

"How the hell do I know? Time is meaningless to the metaphysician."

"Perhaps another encounter with my fists will refresh your memory."

Pasco pulled his cape over his head. "Half the homes on this island are filled with treasures gleaned from shipwrecks," he said in a muffled voice. "Two days ago, or three."

"Where?"

"At the cove. I'm not saying the exact spot, or everyone will be there, stealing my finds. I have an instinct—"

He squealed as Anthony yanked the cape from his head. "Where, you fairy-brained fool?"

"At the Dragon's Jaw."

"It belonged to Winleigh," Anthony said.

"Did it? And here I was thinking it was King Arthur's." Pasco lowered the cloth from his nose. "He who finds keeps, he who loses weeps—do you think *I* killed him?"

"Did you?"

"I cannot take credit for every death on Abandon, my lord, as much as I would like to."

Anthony turned to the door, too disgusted to continue the conversation. "I do not think you have the cunning to commit a murder. Just leave my wife alone."

"She's a witch," Pasco said slyly. "Did you know that?"

"You really do not value your life, Pasco."

Pasco stood, unsteady on his feet. "I am only trying to warn you, my lord. Morwenna is not a woman you can hold for very long. She won't be yours forever."

14

He shouldn't have allowed Pasco's warning to bother him, but the words burned into his brain. *She won't be yours forever.* Was she even his now?

He had managed to forget his business with the marquess until he cantered into the castle yard, and then he dismounted, staring up at the tower, feeling a sense of heaviness in the air. Was it his imagination, or had the flowers that bloomed so vibrantly this morning already begun to wilt?

He entered the keep, bracing himself to find Morwenna and Camelbourne locked in a verbal duel. Instead, he caught them alone together in the library on the couch, heads bent together over a book.

He stood in the doorway for several moments before they even noticed him. Morwenna had clearly taken his advice to heart, changing into a rose silk frock and pulling her thick hair into a simple chignon that showed the classic beauty of her features. She was actually laughing, as was Camelbourne, and

Anthony felt a jealousy that was so overpowering, he could not move. He'd never felt such an intense level of emotion before and didn't know how to react. Following his instincts did not seem like a good idea, as he wanted nothing more than to throw the marquess through the window.

Camelbourne possessed a charm that attracted women from every walk of life, an easiness of spirit that Anthony had always secretly envied—but never more so than at this moment, when that charm was turned, with evident success, on his young wife.

He wasn't ready to share her with the world yet. Their marriage was built on too uncertain a foundation to withstand a test. Horrible thoughts filled his head. What if Camelbourne lured her away? What if he could offer her all she desired? The man had been widowed too many years—

He found his voice, managing not to sound like a man in the throes of emotional torture. "I see you've made friends."

Camelbourne looked up, a flicker of irritation on his handsome face before he smiled. "This is quite a fascinating book. Did you know I have an interest in Arthurian lore?"

Ethan's book. Anthony's own interest in the mysterious tome faded into insignificance as he met Morwenna's eyes. "I found it under your chair," she said softly.

He stared at her, taken aback as always by her quiet beauty. In fact, he had almost forgotten Camelbourne's presence until he realized the man was waiting for him to respond. "Arthurian lore. My *wife*"—he emphasized the word—"is quite an expert on the subject."

"Yes." Camelbourne glanced at her in amusement,

and Anthony checked the instinct to add, "She's mine. She's innocent. You can't have her. I found her first."

But then Camelbourne could give her what Anthony could not, unless he reneged on his agreement, and even then the matter could be taken to court. "Have you heard of Sir Roland Halliwell? He was a leading authority on Arthurian legend."

"I've more than heard of him," Camelbourne said. "I have devoured every word he ever wrote."

Morwenna closed the book on the wedding illustration. "Except the one I am working to finish."

"My dear lady, this is an honor," Camelbourne said. "I am a believer to the marrow."

"Then you must be aware of Abandon's links to the legend?" she said in a suddenly serious voice.

"Of course I am. Lyonesse and Morgan le Fay—it isn't every day that a man can buy his own enchanted isle."

"More than legend, my lord," she said. "Abandon is home to almost two hundred people."

Anthony settled into his chair, recognizing the militant gleam in his wife's eye. Well, another battle was about to be fought in King Arthur's honor, and lost, no doubt. Camelbourne was a ruthless businessman, and Anthony didn't know where all this nonsense about believing in Arthurian lore came in unless it was to impress Morwenna, which did not exactly impress *him*. Still, if anyone could change the marquess's mind, it would be his bluestocking sorceress.

"I have no intention of destroying the island's natural beauty," Camelbourne was saying.

"But you already have," Morwenna replied. "A circle of standing stones—sacred monuments—were cast into the sea."

"Then they will be uncast," Camelbourne said simply.

Morwenna glanced at Anthony. He arched his brow, acknowledging her victory. Few men could claim that honor. Camelbourne was not known for his willingness to yield.

"The stones are one thing, my lord," she continued, "the welfare of the people another."

"Are we casting citizens into the sea too?" he asked in mock horror.

She did not smile. "You might as well be. Where will they go when their homes and means of employment are taken from them?"

He shrugged his shoulders. "I'll provide work, naturally. The lodge will need gamekeepers and gardeners."

"Nearly two hundred people, my lord. Can you employ them all?"

He was saved from making a commitment by the sudden appearance of his secretary at the door. Anthony could not help feeling that somehow the interruption was staged, that the man had been standing out in the hall, waiting for the right minute to intervene and rescue Camelbourne from an awkward moment.

"It's seven o'clock, my lord," the secretary said. "If you mean to make breakfast in Penzance with the architects tomorrow, we should set sail."

The marquess rose, and all of a sudden, the mood in the library changed.

Camelbourne was transformed back into the impersonal statesman. "It was a delight to meet you, Lady Pentargon. In future, I shall insist that my men seek you out first before they remove any standing rocks—"

"The foreman's name is John Hawkey," she said quickly, "and he is insufferably rude."

Camelbourne glanced at his secretary. "Send Davies to the moor and tell Hawkey that he is permanently dismissed." He smiled politely at Morwenna. "Perhaps you'll grace the lodge with your presence when it is completed. Of course, you and Anthony are welcome to remain in the castle for as long as you wish. I don't care much for castles myself. I spent too many dreary years in them as a boy."

He picked up his gloves from the table. Morwenna stood, the heavy book held to her heart. Anthony could see the agony in her eyes, and it was almost more than he could bear. If he had met her even three months earlier, then he would never have agreed to this. If Ethan had lived . . . but there was no going back in time for any of them, and when he explained his reasons to her, he thought she would understand. He would never have hurt her this way, not when he wanted them to build a future together.

"The money will be transferred into your bank at the end of the month," Camelbourne said briskly, oblivious to the despair on Morwenna's face.

She turned to Anthony. "Don't you have to sign the papers first?"

"A wife needn't trouble her mind about such matters. We have a binding agreement, don't we, Pentargon?" Camelbourne glanced at Anthony. "And while you are enjoying your honeymoon with your enchanting bride, I shall be drafting several acts as my part of the bargain."

"Thank you." Anthony's voice was flat.

"I still think it is a waste of time," Camelbourne added. "Keeping these children of yours gainfully employed is no doubt keeping them out of trouble."

Anthony's face hardened. He could be as brutally

frank as Camelbourne when opposed. "The goal is to keep them alive, in body and spirit. I wish I could make you understand that."

"Come, Anthony. We passed an act only three years ago to limit work hours, and there have been improvements in the Poor Law, not to mention the movement under way to stop children and women from working in the mines altogether."

"It's a start," Anthony said, not giving an inch.

Camelbourne pulled on his gloves, then over them a costly assortment of rings. "Social changes take time."

"Even one day of a child consigned to hell is too long," Anthony said.

Camelbourne gave him a condescending smile. "Perhaps, Anthony, but it surely isn't worth you and I arguing over. I respect your passion, even if I do not share it. Farewell, and congratulations to you both. Lady Pentargon, I trust you will send me a copy of your father's work when it is published."

Then he was gone. Morwenna sat down on the sofa, holding Ethan's book to her like a lifeline. She looked lost and hurt, more confused than angry. "Children, Anthony? Do you have children you are trying to protect? Is this some sort of blackmail scheme?"

"They are not my children, Morwenna," Anthony said. "Most of them, in fact, belong to no one. But a long time ago, when I was a young man healed of a condition that rendered me a practical cripple, I made a vow that I would do something to help other children who had not the means to help themselves. In return for Abandon, Camelbourne has ensured the passage of two acts that will fulfill this promise. He is the most powerful friend I have in the political world."

"Is there no other way?" she asked, not moving. "Is there nothing you and I could do together?"

He sat down beside her. "Our efforts would be a drop of water in the ocean. He can influence more people than I have ever met."

When he finished explaining to her the extent of the child abuses he'd witnessed, he felt as if a burden had been lifted off his shoulders. There were tears in her eyes, and he knew she had been as deeply affected as he was by the cruelties inflicted on the most helpless members of society.

"Do you think that anything could change his mind?" she said quietly.

He smiled. "If your charms did not sway him, then nothing will. Do you still hate me?"

He was so intense, so magnetic, so unlike any other man she had met. "How could I now? Even before, I did not hate you. If anything, oh, Anthony, this only makes me proud of you."

He wanted to take her in his arms and make love to her. She had only belonged to him for a day, and he could barely keep his hands off her. But just as he drew her into his arms, Vincent appeared at the door to remind them that the vicar expected them in an hour for the dinner in their honor.

As they rose, Anthony confided in Morwenna that he could not imagine a worse torture, lusting after his own wife while pretending interest in religion over dinner.

She kissed him in the doorway, explaining she needed time to change into her evening dress and mantle. He thought she wanted to be by herself, and he understood that. She had taken Ethan's book upstairs with her. Anthony had meant to ask her if she had noticed anything peculiar about the illustrations, but the time had not been right.

The dinner at the vicarage proved to be worse than Anthony had anticipated. The vicar's daughter played the pianoforte while his wife sang, inappropriately enough, a solid hour of battle hymns. The food tasted awful, standard British fare—boiled beef, lamb, green peas, and a lardy raspberry trifle.

Anthony didn't eat; he was too engrossed with his wife, concerned by how white and withdrawn she was. She kept looking at the window, almost longingly, he thought, and suddenly he was afraid that something might happen to her, that she would disappear mysteriously as her mother had. He wondered now if Sir Roland had died of a broken heart.

"I suppose the marquess will have his own plans for the vicarage," the pleasant-faced reverend said as they sat together in the parlor for coffee.

Anthony nodded, not really listening. It took him a moment to realize the vicar was concerned about his own future on the island.

"I have recommended to him how crucial it is that the island's daily life remain unchanged," Anthony said. Which didn't mean Camelbourne would listen or retain the cleric, but the vicar look relieved that Anthony had gone to the trouble.

There was a sudden burst of rude knocking at the front door, and the sound of young people laughing and talking at once. The vicar's daughter jumped up, unable to hide her excitement.

"Everyone is here, Dad. I'm off for the revels. You will excuse me, Lord Pentargon, and you, Morwenna, I mean, my lady—you aren't going to come with us tonight, are you?"

Anthony was about to answer for her. He had plans himself for Morwenna, but she looked so wistful, almost beseeching, as their eyes met.

"Do as you wish, Morwenna," he said quietly. "As long as it's safe—it is safe on the moor at night?"

"You really wouldn't mind?" she said gratefully.

Yes, he would. He didn't want her out of his sight, for reasons that went beyond how much he enjoyed her company, but he also felt he owed her this last indulgence. "I don't mind."

"It's innocent enough, my lord," the vicar said, "if a trifle too pagan for my tastes. Still, once or twice a year, I turn a blind eye to their revels. To serve these people is to respect their beliefs. Of course, this may be my last summer as their spiritual adviser, depending on the marquess."

For an instant, Anthony tried to picture Abandon as a hunting retreat, without the Oxford-educated vicar visiting cottages with his dogs at his heels, without the revels on the moor. It was a bleak image. He caught Morwenna's hand as she reached for her mantle.

"Wait."

They had followed the vicar and his wife down the narrow hallway to the door, crowded now with restless dogs and the vicar's daughter.

"I don't want you to go."

"Why?" Morwenna whispered. "You said you didn't mind."

"I'll worry about you."

"Oh, how sweet, Anthony."

"It isn't sweet. It's irrational, but I'm afraid something is going to take you away from me."

She laughed. "I'll come back."

"Promise?"

"Promise."

"On King Arthur's grave—wherever it might be?"

"Oh, Anthony—yes, on his grave."

He pretended to scowl. "Should I meet these friends of yours first, to see if I approve?"

"Don't you dare!"

"Then wait." He reached into his vest for a small velvet box. "I have a birthday gift for you."

"You remembered," she said, deeply touched.

"Of course. Here."

It was a gold chain embellished with pearls and a center pendant rose-cut diamond. "I have never loved anything more," she said, her gaze meeting his.

"Then let me put it on you, so at least you will remember me while we are apart."

Her heart beat faster as he fastened the chain around her throat and drew the mantle over her shoulders. He touched her now whenever he could, not caring if anyone saw them. He had the right, and he loved her. But even Anthony could not understand her attachment to Abandon, and she needed to be alone. Just to think clearly, to regain her sense of self.

"I only want to be with my friends for a few hours."

He stared at the group of young people talking in the doorway. He wanted to remind her that this was their honeymoon. He didn't say the words because he knew what she must be feeling, that she had the rest of her life with him. But there would probably never be another magical Midsummer Eve for her again, at least not on Abandon.

"Well, all right, then," he said. "But stay with them. Don't go off alone in the dark."

"Of course, Anthony." She smiled as if his overprotectiveness amused her. "But don't you expect me back for a time, and by the way, the vicar cheats at cards."

Her friends pulled her outside, into the evening mist and festive atmosphere, into the unknown. "When?" he said, following her like a worried parent. "How long will you be?"

"The young people will be fine, my lord," the vicar said behind him. "The island boys are a sturdy lot. They'll protect the girls, although on a night like this, it is not the mortal things one must fear."

Anthony turned. He didn't like the idea of sturdy island boys protecting his wife. "What do you mean, not the mortal things?"

His wife, plump and friendly, bustled between them. "He's referring to the legend of the Wild Hunt, my lord. When King Arthur and his knights awaken for a phantasmal chase across the moor. It's an annual affair."

"What do they chase?" Anthony stood in the doorway, hearing his wife laugh in the mist. He could barely see her. All one could pick out were the torches, held aloft by a band of strapping young men. He felt a stab of possessive jealousy.

"I don't know," the vicar said. "The only person on the island who claims to have seen them is Annie Jenkins."

"The woman is more than a century old," his wife said, gently closing the door. "The mist is cool, is it not, my lord? Come sit by the fire."

The vicar led the way back into the parlor. "It was on a night like this that Sir Roland's wife disappeared, or so I've heard. I wasn't here at the time. The old vicar is dead five years now. He presided over the funeral."

His wife frowned at him from her chair. "Her ladyship is not going to disappear, so let us discontinue this conversation. And that was only a rumor, anyway, Miles. What a gossip you are. No one really knows what happened to Lady Pentargon's mother."

The vicar grunted, pushing three dogs from his path. "Well, I'll tell you what is not a rumor. John Hawkey was dismissed tonight."

"Dismissed?" Anthony said. "Already?"

"The marquess's man came to the digging site and berated him in full view of everyone." The vicar unbuttoned his vest. "I say good riddance to the troublemaker. Hawkey threw his pickaxe in a rage and vowed revenge, but I'm glad he's gone."

His wife shivered. "Indeed. We'll see an end to the petty thievings now. I hear Carew is back in charge."

"What petty thievings?" Anthony asked.

"A hen stolen here and there. The new supplies in the barn, blankets and lamps."

The vicar patted his protruding stomach. "I say it was Pasco playing tricks again. He's got it in his stupid skull to flaunt his powers, and he has a pair of obnoxious cousins working for him."

"And I say it was not Pasco." She pulled out a chair for Anthony at the card table. "We'll see now, won't we? Either the trouble will end, or it will not."

15

By midnight, he could not stand it. He wanted to find her, ignoring the vicar's invitation to pass the night, his wife's warning that the mist was uncommon thick, the knowledge that John Hawkey had been dismissed. He set out on his horse with only the bonfires on the hill to guide him. Mist twisted around the granite crags in weird shapes. The moor looked beautiful if a little eerie and disorienting.

He never thought he'd be chasing down his bride on their honeymoon, and when he finally found her on the hill, he was horrified and amused. Slightly drunk, and barefoot, she was dancing in a circle of young people. Someone had strung a garland of lilies around her neck, and her long golden-brown hair curled around her hips. She looked like a virgin sacrifice, except she was not a virgin, as of last night. She was his, Lady Pentargon.

He pushed forward to remind her of that fact.

*　　*　　*

Nearly all of the married couples had gone home, and only the most reckless of the revelers remained, savoring the last hours of Midsummer madness. A fiddler perched on the rocks played away. The dance, the Snail's Creep, grew wild, unrestrained. Young girls passed from boy to boy, a kiss stolen here, a hand straying where it should not.

Morwenna grimaced as Jonathan Illugan, Pasco's young apprentice in black magic, grabbed her by the waist and planted a slobbery kiss on her mouth. He was the one who helped Pasco cast his awful spells.

"Toad!" She rubbed her mouth in distaste. "I'm probably going to break out in warts."

He grunted, swaying from side to side, then suddenly fell backward as a fist flew over the top of Morwenna's head and crashed into his startled face.

She turned, whispering, "Anthony," in dread and delicious terror.

"You were expecting the Spanish ambassador?" he asked wryly.

Her friends had parted to allow him through, not willing to take on the dark and dangerous-looking earl who owned the earth beneath their feet. And now he claimed their magical child, the girl born of a Midsummer storm who brought rainbows and lilies to the island.

Then someone, too drunk on elderberry wine to note the forbidding set of Pentargon's face, gave Morwenna a friendly push into his arms. "Dance with your husband."

He caught her before she could stumble over Jonathan Illugan, rising groggily on his elbows to ask what in God's name had hit him. Anthony's strong arm lashed around her waist like a rope. Yet when he spoke, his voice was tender, not angry as she'd expected. No. His rueful self-control was far more powerful than force. She had more to fear from this man's gentleness than his wrath. "Am I so displeasing that you would rather dance with brainless clods than endure my company?" he said.

She drew back in self-defense, but their eyes locked in a battle she had already lost. "You know that is not so, my lord."

"Then why did you run out the vicar's door like an escaped convict?"

"I always dance at the Midsummer revels."

"You might have danced with me instead." His eyes gleamed darkly. "I missed you, bride."

If he had commanded her to come, she could resent him. But he was too clever, wooing her with words. She knew exactly what he wanted, and her heart began to pound in anticipation. She no longer had the right to deny him anything.

"I wish to stay, my lord, for the fortune-telling."

He pulled her even closer. "There's nothing you need to know about your future. I am your destiny, Morwenna, from the moment we first met."

She caught her breath. Every year in Annie Jenkins's cottage, the girls would gather to beg the old wise woman to read their fates in a turf fire. Nearly every girl asked the same question: Who will I marry? Who will my true love be? And hadn't the flames last year predicted that Morwenna would marry the next man who took possession of the castle?

"I want to know whether I will find Arthur's cave," she said suddenly.

His smile taunted her. "But I could take you there."

"If?"

"If you promise never to leave me alone with the vicar and his wife again."

Without warning, he pulled her around a massive dolmen, kissing her face and shoulders and the swells of her breasts until her head swam in a sweet haze of desire. "Don't leave me again," he said, punctuating his words with stinging bites on her neck. "Ever. Ever." He bit gently at her breast. *"Ever."*

She felt so deliciously weak, not even resisting when he ran his hands all over her body. "Anthony."

"I want you." He groaned into her hair. "Here."

"Oh." She giggled, floating on a cloud of bliss. "Not here."

Her friends had begun their final dance, forgetting the enemy in their midst. Faraway thunder rumbled across the sea, and the mist shimmered against the cliffs, silvery green. On such a mystical eve, people had been known to witness supernatural events that haunted them for the rest of their lives.

"The circle, Morwenna!" a masculine voice shouted, a fisherman just realizing she had vanished from sight. "Dance with us for luck."

She did not respond, could not, captive in Anthony's arms, his mouth at her breasts, hot, hungry. Time passed in a blur. He pulled her down the hillside, down, down, away from the fire and the people, onto the moorland grass. He'd unfastened her frock, and she felt like a wanton, praying no one would see them.

"Morwenna," a group of revelers called from a distance. "Where have you gone to?"

"Anthony," she whispered, trying to raise her head. "Someone might come."

He pulled off his coat and spread it out on the ground. "I certainly hope so."

"Surely you don't mean to—to—not in the open."

His white teeth flashed in a grin. "Surely I do."

"But someone might see us."

"Everyone else has shown the good sense to go home, except me, who cannot resist his own wife."

It was true. She glanced around at the moor, foggy and abandoned, with a boulder rising here and there like a giant frozen in time. The flames of the bonfire had burned almost to ashes.

"Your presence chased the lesser beings away," she said quietly.

"Good." He unbuttoned his trousers. "Because I wouldn't want them to hear you scream."

He raised her skirts up around her waist, ignoring her indignant laughter until he kissed her into surrender. The moorland grass felt damp and prickly against her skin as he nudged her legs apart, pinning her beneath him. She twined her arms around his neck. She saw a shooting star fall from the sky and closed her eyes, wishing he would love her forever, all hope of resisting him lost. Her heart belonged to him. The next thing she knew, the tip of his shaft pressed inside her. She arched her back, her body opening to sheath him. She felt swollen from the night before, and she gasped at the sensation of fullness, the power of his male body.

"Please," she whispered, biting her lip.

He smiled as he stared down at her, her breasts gleaming where he'd just kissed her. "Please what?"

"Anthony." She gripped his arms. "Stop torturing me."

"Sweetheart, you're still so very tight. I don't want to hurt you again."

"Do it."

"Are you sure?"

"Yes."

Dazed, she moaned deep in her throat as he stretched her wide, penetrating her in one practiced thrust. The mist spread a curtain of privacy around them as he lost control and practically pummeled her into the ground. One flesh, a man and woman caught in Midsummer madness. They found release within moments of each other, Anthony using his body to shelter her as she began to shiver. The dampness of the earth seeped through the coat he'd laid beneath her. They lay together in silence under the canopy of stars, his arms wrapped around her.

He gave a contented sigh and lifted her to her feet. "That was very gratifying."

"It was wicked of us, behaving like a pair of adolescents." She pulled down her skirts, starting to laugh again. "I don't know what it is about you that makes me lose my senses."

"I'll take that as a compliment." He pulled her back into his arms for another kiss. "In fact, I'll take anything you'll give me."

"Oh, Anthony, not again. Can we make it over the causeway first?"

"I'm not sure. When we get home?"

She peered over her shoulder. "*If* we get home. The mist is coming in like cream."

He took her by the hand, leading her down the hill to his horse. The air smelled of burned herbs mingled with sea mist, and something intangible. A presence. "They roasted an effigy of the marquess in the Midsummer bonfire," she murmured.

He slid his hands down her body, possessive, openly sexual. "At least it wasn't me."

She flashed him a grin. "Actually, it was. I made them change it."

"How thoughtful of you."

"There's a strangeness in the mist tonight," she whispered. "Take me home."

"Of course."

"I meant to the farmhouse. *My* home. It's closer."

"The castle is your home now, Morwenna."

"Not for long. We'll all be evicted before the summer ends."

He hoisted her into the saddle with no effort at all, his hand lingering on her bare leg. "No stockings, child. You do need taming." He swung up in front of her. "Hold on to me."

"There's no need."

"Then don't." The stallion lurched forward, on purpose, she suspected. She was forced to grab hold of Anthony, clinging to his muscular back to keep from falling.

"You made the horse do that."

"Morwenna, sweetheart, you give me too much power."

"You have too much power."

His deep laughter floated out across the unearthly landscape, the granite cromlechs glistening, looming like frozen monsters in the fog. "After last night, I believe the power between us is shared. I am your servant, Lady Pentargon."

She laid her cheek on his shoulder, confused by her reaction to his confession. "It's Midsummer Eve, my lord, and we're alone. Do you know where we are?"

"Almost to the cliffside road. Where are the cats tonight?" he asked conversationally.

"Locked up in the castle where Pasco cannot steal them."

His face darkened. "His apprentice stole a kiss from you."

"And paid for it with a broken jaw to judge by the blow you gave him."

"Lucky it wasn't his life," he said unsympathetically.

Vapors swirled around them as the wind rose. Every so often, the mist would lift, revealing a ridge or hill ahead. For the most part, they were wandering in a world of shifting images, trusting instinct to guide them.

"My father told me that long ago, the giant Thunderbore walked this land, throwing down his hammer where he would."

"Pity he didn't throw down a few road signs on the way," Anthony muttered.

"But there *are* road signs here," she said quietly. "Unless your men removed them."

He grunted.

"Those oddly stacked slabs of granite ahead, Anthony—yes, the ones that you are about to ride straight into—are also said to be the work of a giant's hand."

"Then you do know where we are," he said.

"Goodness, no. The giants left such earthworks everywhere."

"Busy old buggers, weren't they?"

She sighed again. "One asks oneself, did Arthur ever find the perfect world he searched for? Did it exist, or was the quest in itself both goal and end?"

"One asks oneself, where the hell did the road go to? Never mind the perfect world."

She cuddled up against him. "If one passes naked through a holed stone three times at high noon, one can be cured of ersipelyas."

"Of shyness too, I'd think."

"I can just see Morgan rowing Arthur to safety on a night like this."

"I can't see a damn thing."

"People used to pray for shipwrecks on misty nights."

"Now, that's a charming piece of history." He paused. "Morwenna, if you keep rubbing against me like that, you'll find yourself on the ground again, mist or not."

"This isn't right," she whispered.

"Of course it's right. That's why I married you."

She leaned around him. "No, not that. I meant—I think we're almost to Cape Skulla."

"That's impossible. It's five miles from the vicarage."

"Yes, but it's the only part of the island I'm not intimate with. Nothing looks familiar here."

The mist lifted for a few moments.

"Look up that hill, Morwenna. There's a man."

"I believe it's only a dwarf oak," she said. "The wind twists them into strange shapes. Some of them appear to be elves dancing in a circle."

"It's a man crouching on the ground."

"Perhaps you need spectacles," she said gently.

He raised his brow. "I'm telling you, it's a shepherd. I thought I heard a sheep bleating a minute ago. Stay here. I'll ask where we are."

"Be careful, Anthony. It could be Pasco making a sacrifice to his satanic majesty."

"It could be a shepherd too, Morwenna. Did you think of that?"

As Anthony disappeared from sight, Morwenna felt acutely alone in the cocoon of mist. It was suddenly so quiet, so lonely without his presence. She could detect the pounding of the waves in the distance, muffled by the coastal fog. Closer, she could hear the dripping of moisture from the granite slabs of a dolmen, the whicker of Anthony's horse beside her.

The fine hairs rose on the nape of her neck.

She wasn't alone.

She turned slowly, her breath trapped in her throat.

Something had moved behind the upright stones of the dolmen, something watching her, stalking her in the shadows.

"Anthony?" she said, the word almost a prayer.

The stallion swung its head around, forcing her back, back, toward the hill where her husband had disappeared. She stumbled over a pile of loose stones. The horse moved with her like a shield. She thought she saw a gleam of silver, then heard the clank of metal against rock.

16

By the time Anthony had reached the rise of the hill, the shepherd he'd seen had vanished. Disgruntled, he turned to shout down to Morwenna, only to realize he could not discern either her or his stallion in the mist.

"Where are you, Morwenna?"

"I am a few steps away from where you left me, my lord."

"And where might that be?"

"Here. Several feet from where I was. I thought I saw something," she added sheepishly. "The mist plays tricks on the imagination."

"Can you give me a hint as to your location?"

"Do you want my precise location in degrees longitude?"

"How about waving your little hand over your head?"

"Oh, fine. How's that?"

"How is what?"

"I'm waving my hand."

"Are you?"

"How about this?"

"What?"

"I am waving both hands like a windmill."

"I do not see you, Morwenna. Now I am waving my neckcloth in the air. Do you see it?"

Her voice grew fainter. "I think I do. No, it was the mist. Could you climb the hill again? It might help."

"I could climb the hill if I could find it," he muttered, feeling as if he were talking to himself. He walked beneath an overhanging crag. "Morwenna, keep talking to me. Do not leave the horse."

No answer. He swore.

The mist parted again, revealing bleak moorland that looked the same as before yet somehow different. There was no sign of Morwenna, but in the shadows below he thought he heard a horse whickering, and a soft glow fell over everything, an incandescence like candlelight.

He turned his head in disbelief as a hunting horn from the hilltop broke the spell of stillness. Before he could recover from his surprise, he heard the creak of a rusted gate being opened and the pulsing hoofbeats of riders across an invisible bridge or causeway.

"What in God's name—Morwenna, where are you? Get out of the way—*hide yourself!*"

They thundered down the hillside, a party of knights in mail armor, chasing what or whom he could not guess. They did not glance his way, but strangely he began to feel their bloodlust and excitement; he could sense the determination of the broad-shouldered rider on an iron-gray charger who split from the group to corner the quarry they chased. The knightly figures were almost translucent. Their energy seemed all too real, pulsing in the air.

He watched the solitary horseman dismount, a spear in hand, and walk cautiously in a widening arc across the moor. There were trees now, which Anthony knew had not been there a few minutes earlier. None of it made sense, but suddenly he was too caught up in the fervor of the hunt himself to question the logic of this illusion.

Even when a boar appeared from the fringe of mist, charging the knightly huntsman from behind, he could not restrain a shout of warning.

"Behind you—look out! Look out!"

Whether the hunter heard him or not, Anthony couldn't tell. The man turned, his spear raised, seconds too late. The animal's tusks impaled his left hip to the boulder, and he fell with a groan of agony that could have been torn from Anthony's own throat.

He could even feel the searing pain in his own side, the struggle for his life's breath. He could smell the fetid animal's scent, and as his sight dimmed, he saw men in mail armor crowding around him, their voices low with concern and admiration.

He *was* the wounded knight, watching himself as if in a play.

A gentle but strong hand, the king's gauntleted hand, removed his helmet, and Anthony saw his own face revealed as if in a looking glass; he saw *his* features contorted in pain and the stoic acceptance of death.

"Brave knight," the king murmured. "You shall have your reward yet in another world."

The scene faded into the mist, blurring into nothingness.

Anthony stepped back, away from the dissolving

mirror of time, stumbling, then falling, rolling, over heather and scratching gorse and hard rock until he came to a stop. Turning onto his back, he felt an incredible pain in his hip and saw his wife standing over him with a look of uncertain amusement.

"Oh, Anthony." She threw herself down upon him with such force that he released a roar of agony.

"Hell," he said. "What happened?"

She laughed; obviously, she had no idea how much pain he was suffering. "You fell down the hill. It was the silliest sight."

"I never climbed the hill. I never found it."

"But you must have—oh, my God, there is blood on your trousers, Anthony, and I have been laughing at you. Let me see."

"It's nothing. I'm fine." He stood, suppressing a groan. "Where did they go?"

"Who, my lord?"

"The hunting party—you didn't see them?"

She stared around the mist-shrouded landscape, her voice puzzled. "Did you?"

"Morwenna, this is no time to make jokes. There was a hunting horn and a rider on an iron-gray charger who was attacked by—"

She backed away from him, her face white. He meant it. She could see that he was serious. "The Wild Hunt. You actually saw it. This is so unfair."

"There was a boar. The huntsman did not see it charge in time, and—" He put his hand to his hip, staring at the clump of congealed blood on his fingers. He didn't remember hunting himself, and he had no memory of falling. In fact, the images were already fading, so faint he questioned whether it *had* been a hallucination.

You shall have your reward yet. The deep voice echoed in his brain. Where had it come from? he wondered. And what kind of reward was an aching wound in the arse?

"We need to go home now, Anthony. I do not want to leave you here while I fetch help." She bit her lower lip, glancing back at the dolmen. "I believe we may have wandered into an enchanted hollow."

"A what?"

"An enchanted hollow. A place on the moor where one may pass into another time or encounter restless spirits."

He nodded, in too much discomfort to argue with such nonsense. Even worse than his pain was the limp that accompanied the first few steps he took to the stallion.

He prayed it did not mean a return of his childhood disability, and that his wife had not noticed it.

The Marquess of Camelbourne cursed as his coach drew to a halt at the edge of the road. It was an isolated spot, fringed with trees, not an area he recognized or cared to explore.

He rapped his cane on the roof. "What has come over you, coachman? We are ripe pickings for footpads, waiting here in the evening mist. And why have you taken a detour? This is not the way to Penzance."

When there was no reply, he let himself out of the coach. The driver had disappeared, presumably to ask directions. Camelbourne took out his fob watch and cursed. The carriage that bore his secretary was nowhere in sight, and—

He looked up slowly at the rather intriguing figure

of a woman in a white cloak at the side of the road. He might have been disturbed by her appearance, his armed driver missing, but he carried a pistol for protection in his own coat and the two footmen waiting on the coach.

He glanced back. The footmen had also disappeared.

"Do not be alarmed, my lord." The woman approached him, her voice more alluring than anything he had ever heard. Did they know each other? Stunned, he thought that it wasn't, no, it could not possibly be Pentargon's bride, and yet he was reminded of her.

She stopped before him.

No, not Morwenna, but similar enough that he could be forgiven the mistake. Beneath the hood of her cloak he saw a face of classical beauty, wisdom where Morwenna's features had shone with innocence.

"What do you want?" He was fascinated by her, not frightened at all, and curiosity had replaced his impatience even if in the back of his mind he realized this was an unusual situation. Midsummer madness, he thought.

She took his arm and led him through a thin stand of trees into a bare field. There was a sign in the distance. *Barnstaple Coal Pits*, it said, which he knew could not be possible. The area looked like a scene from hell, wheelbarrows clattering, the thudding of picks, lanterns strung on poles, and children, half-naked, their eyes vacant and hopeless, huddled together outside a tent. Deplorable, primitive conditions. How could this be?

He walked away from the woman and approached

the children in front of the tent. One boy, perhaps seven, looked so much like his own son that Camelbourne almost called to him by name. The boy ignored him, dipping his fingers into a bowl of gruel and eating as if it were his only meal of the day.

Then, from the depths of the tent, Camelbourne heard a young girl's cries, saw the silhouette of a man upon her, their bodies moving in a violent mating. Outraged, he shouted at the man to stop and made a move around the boy. The woman caught his arm. "They cannot see or hear you," she said gently.

"But how—" He stopped, suddenly realizing he would receive no logical answer to his question and that it didn't even matter *how.* "This is not right," he said, shaking his head in sickened disbelief. "There are laws to prevent this sort of thing. Why are they not enforced? How can it be allowed?"

"Indeed," she said with infinite sadness in her eyes. "How can it be allowed, my powerful lord?"

She motioned him back toward his coach, and through the trees he could see the driver and footmen positioned in their proper places. Around him the mist rose as the clamor of the coal pits faded into silence. He walked ahead, aware that she had not followed.

As he reached the road, he turned once to look at her. "Who *are* you?"

"A friend, my lord. Only a friend."

17

By the time they reached the castle, clumping over the causeway in the silence of the wee hours, Anthony had convinced himself he'd imagined the hunting scene. Morwenna kept questioning him in detail about what he had witnessed until he refused to answer; it disturbed him to realize that he, pillar of privacy, logic, and self-restraint, could succumb to the same superstitious drivel that had lured Ethan to his death.

"Did you see Sir Bedivere, my lord?" she asked excitedly. "Sir Galahad is said to have ridden a gray charger. Did you see the king?"

"I do not wish to discuss it again tonight." The pain in his hip had eased slightly, but he feared his limp had become more pronounced. Was he to become a cripple again? He wondered when Morwenna would notice and how she would feel about being married to a physically imperfect man.

He made a point of following her up the staircase.

In their bedchamber, he watched her undress, then drew her down onto the bed beside him. "Anthony, I haven't even put on my night rail."

"Why bother?" He ran his hands down the graceful curves of her back. Lovemaking seemed a perfect antidote to the supernatural, an earthly tumble to counteract the unsettling soul-memory he had met in the mists of time.

"I thought you were injured," she said.

"I am." He kissed the hollow of her throat, breathing deeply of her scent. "Make me better," he whispered.

She reached down between his legs and touched his organ. He narrowed his eyes, his voice deepening in approval. "Lord have mercy, Lady Pentargon. I might live after all."

Shyly, she closed her fingers around the bulbous head of his shaft, stroking gently. "How do you feel now?"

"Definitely closer to a complete recovery. In fact—" He put his hands around her hips and raised her to straddle him. She caught her breath as he lowered her onto his rod. His hands encircled her waist, lifting her up and down until she began to follow the rhythm on her own. Groaning with pleasure, he folded his arms under his head and watched her. Her small breasts bounced with her efforts. After several minutes, he gripped her bottom and flexed upward with all his might, bringing them both release.

She craved sleep afterward, lily petals still caught in her heavy mass of hair, her body curled around his. He drew the coverlet over her.

"My pagan bride," he said tenderly. "I am bewitched by you."

"I think I am the one bewitched." She closed her eyes, releasing a sigh. "My friends were right. You are possessed of supernatural powers, and Abandon did not come to you by accident. Tomorrow, before you forget," she murmured sleepily, "we will begin to explore the caves."

"We are not married two days, Morwenna. I would like to spend our first week of wedded bliss bedding you, not rowing you about like Wynken, Blynken, and Nod, searching for Ali Baba's cave."

She giggled. "You have confused a nursery rhyme with Arabian Nights. My father would be appalled." She opened her eyes, struck by a sudden realization. "I do believe my earlier theory is the answer."

"Was there a question?"

"I suspect what might have happened to you tonight occurred because of something known as a time shift. You must have passed through a hidden portal of a hollow hill."

"Of course," he said. "It happens to me all the time. I was a Roman gladiator last week. Who knows? When you wake up tomorrow, I could be Joan of Arc. May I borrow your sword and Bible?"

"Oh, Anthony. It's so ungrateful of you to mock your gifts."

"My gifts, Morwenna, are a pain in the posterior. Literally, I might add."

"I should gladly die for a chance to see what you have seen," she said in a burst of youthful enthusiasm.

A chill went through him. "Don't say that."

"Why not?"

"Because the thought of anything happening to you is more than I can bear."

"Hold me, Anthony," she whispered, touched by his confession.

He did, and after a few minutes they managed to fall asleep, their breath mingling until she gave a startled cry. Pale filaments of dawn broke through the window. He stirred and looked at her.

"What is it?" he asked in concern.

"I had a dream, about Elliott. He was calling me, Anthony. He needs me."

"It was just a dream, sweetheart. Go back to sleep."

"You think he's dead, don't you?"

"It would seem so," he said gently.

He didn't tell her then about finding Elliott's helmet in Pasco's cottage. She would only want to confront Pasco again, and he would not allow it. Still, after an hour or so of sleep, he and Vincent would go out once more to comb the caves around Pasco's home on Cape Skulla.

Morwenna relaxed against him, her breathing even as he settled back against the pillows.

No sooner had he closed his eyes than another chill went through him, the sense of a presence in the room.

He turned his head.

On the nightstand sat a tarnished silver goblet, embellished with a medieval hunting scene. He sat up, careful not to disturb his wife, and lifted the goblet to his nose. The contents smelled enticingly good, like mulled wine, honey, and herbs.

The sort of beverage an ancient warrior might drink when he returned from battle. Or from a hunt.

There was a piece of parchment beneath it, with the words:

**The wine is healing to your wound.
Sweet dreams, young lord.**

"Young lord," he said aloud, and in his mind he was suddenly returned to the past, to a forest clearing, a clumsy, half-crippled boy who lacked courage and confidence. A green-eyed woman stood above him with a branch, bestowing bravery upon his timid soul.

"You," he said, rising naked from the bed to stare around the room. But it was empty, except for his sleeping wife and three cats in a basket beside their bed. "How is it possible? It *isn't* possible."

A sudden impulse compelled him to taste the potion; he did not know if it were poison, if Morwenna would find him dead on the floor when she awakened. But only a deep sense of tranquility came over him as it took effect, and he slept.

He dreamed until he awakened several hours later. Strange dreams that made no sense, the vicar's wife talking, Morwenna on the moor, calling to him for help, but he could not reach her. He was crippled, deformed, and she would laugh at him as his father and friends had.

He was lame, limping across the moor, wandering lost around a series of burial chambers, a bird cawing above his head, leading him, urging him to hurry—

He opened his eyes to morning light. There was no goblet on the nightstand, no note. Morwenna was also gone, and he heard the flapping of wings at the window. By the time he got out of bed, there was nothing there, a shadow in the blue sky that could have been anything.

He looked down past the causeway. In the bay sat a small steamer, and men bustled back and forth unloading furniture onto the beach, brocade settees, a marble bust, a china cabinet. Searching for Elliott, at least for his body, would apparently be delayed a few more hours.

He dressed and hurried downstairs. His limp had returned to its barely noticeable existence, and there was no evidence of injury to his hip. For a moment, he felt a profound relief.

He met Mrs. Treffry in the hallway. "Where is my wife?"

"Gone with Mr. Vincent, my lord."

"Gone?" He visualized Morwenna and Vincent catching butterflies on a cliff edge. "Gone where?"

"A baby was taken sick, my lord, in the Lanreath cottage. She went to help."

"Are you certain that Vincent accompanied her?"

"Absolutely, my lord. He insisted he ride with her every step of the way."

"Well, I suppose it's all right, then. I think I shall join them, though."

"Without breakfast, my lord?"

"Nothing, thank you."

Vincent was a formidable bodyguard and no one's fool. Furthermore, he genuinely cared for Morwenna. Still, Anthony didn't like the idea of her gallivanting about without him, even though she had done so all her life. Rainbows were pretty occurrences, but they did not offer much protection from the dangers of the world below.

Magic had not saved Abandon.

A loud knock at the door announced the arrival of Camelbourne's furnishings. Within a quarter-hour, the castle's understated elegance gave way to the ornate appointments of the era: papier-mâché chairs, a stuffed baroque sofa, a rococo sideboard the size of a cliff.

He was almost glad, as he walked into a Loo table, that Morwenna was not here to witness this crime against good taste. And if—

The missing book sat on the marquess's table.

Without thinking, Anthony started to reach for it, stopping as he reminded himself that he could examine it in detail after he found his wayward wife.

Open me.

Read me.

He took a step away from the table, wondering if he *had* lost his mind. Drinking strange potions, imagining phantasmal hunts in the mist. And yet the strongest feeling had seized him, the irrational sense that the book had called to him as if trying to impart a message he refused to accept.

He turned resolutely and saw the white cat sitting at the door, waiting.

"You again," he said in annoyance. "Oh, what the hell—"

He picked up the book.

The vellum pages flew through his fingers as if by magic. A prickle of fear crawled up his nape as he stared down at the most recent illustration.

The artist had depicted the maiden in chains, Morwenna, water rising to her waist in a sea cave.

The image so sickened him that he did not even hear the footsteps behind him. "My lord, thank God I have found you. I saw the yacht and wondered—"

Anthony turned, struggling to shake off the disturbing effect of the illustration. He saw Dunstan squeezing through the doorway between a pair of Grecian urns that had been deposited there.

He forced a smile he did not feel. "You do not look as though your meeting with Mrs. Winleigh went at all well. However, we shall have to discuss her situation this evening, unless we are both to be buried in ostentation."

"Lord Pentargon—"

"Walk me to the stables, Dunstan. I am about to look for your niece and do not wish to waste a moment."

Sir Dunstan did not return his smile. "I rushed back here as soon as I could. Tell me she has not left the castle alone."

Pasco huddled within the triangle of black candles, his face terrified beneath the medieval helmet. He wanted to believe that Morwenna deserved what had happened to her. He'd wanted to see her suffer for rebuffing him all these years. But now he shook with horror at what he had done.

He hadn't meant for her punishment to go this far. Even the infernal spirits refused to speak to him, and he had found his one-eyed crow dead in its cage this morning, a portent of what was to come. During the night, the toads in his garden had multiplied and crowded on his doorstep so that he could barely escape the cottage, or his conscience.

He was terrified suddenly that the darkness he had served all his life would turn on him, if Lord Pentargon did not tear out his throat first. For surely the earl would hunt him down and kill him unless Pasco could find the hidden cave that would soon become Morwenna's grave.

18

The illustration in the book had shaken Anthony to the core; although he did not believe in such things, where his wife was concerned, he refused to take a chance. Furthermore, Dunstan's distress underscored Anthony's own anxiety. Without apologizing, he ordered two horses saddled and insisted that the man explain himself on their way to the cottage.

"I take it all did not go well with Elliott's wife," he said as they crossed the causeway.

"His wife is dead." Dunstan's voice was hoarse with fatigue and fear. "According to Elliott's mistress, the young Mrs. Winleigh had a rowing accident—she went out in a boat one day, she was carrying his child, and she drowned."

"A rowing accident? *Another* rowing accident?" Something terrifying tried to work its way through Anthony's mind. A possibility that had been there all along, but now it was coming together, and he did not like the conclusion. "And he kept a mistress, before his wife died?"

"He *keeps* a mistress." They slowed their horses at the end of the causeway, the sea crashing against the cliffs below. Dunstan looked unwell; he wasn't a young man, after all, and he was frightened for his niece. "He is not dead, my lord, that is what I hurried back to tell you."

"Then you saw him in St. Ives?"

"No, but the young woman I found in his lodging house was drunk and angry enough at his bizarre behavior to betray him for the few pounds I gave her. She said he cared only about his art, that it was a sick obsession with him, and she was fed up with it."

"A sick obsession." Anthony read a world of horror in those three words.

"The more I thought about it," Dunstan continued, "the more I realized that my brother had tried to warn me about Elliott on his deathbed. Roland had suffered a stroke, and his speech was practically incoherent. I thought he meant I was to protect Morwenna *and* Elliott, because Elliott was so sensitive about his art."

"Oh, God," Anthony said.

"Now I understand that Roland was trying to warn me to protect Morwenna *from* Elliott. His mistress said that Roland and Elliott had fought over the illustrations for the last book. Elliott threatened to sue him, but Morwenna and I knew none of this."

"Why would Elliott stage his own death?"

"I don't know. His mistress thinks it was part of a plan for revenge. You see, Elliott recently learned that Roland had privately advised the Crown Council against commissioning Elliott to paint the Queen's Robing Room. The work would have guaranteed him artistic immortality. But Roland suspected, rightly so, that Elliott was unstable, that his art reflected a private madness."

Anthony shook his head. "I thought his sketches were quite incredible."

"So did I. Until his mistress showed me what he considered to be his masterpiece. It was a drawing of a young woman chained to the Wheel of Fortune, near death. It was Morwenna, my lord, and I am terrified for her."

Anthony fought down a wave of panic. "But you said Elliott was in St. Ives."

"Last week. His mistress thinks he has returned to Abandon, that he is hiding in a cave."

"I'll find Morwenna. Go back to the castle in the event she returns. Keep her there." Anthony spoke with calm deliberation, needing to believe it was not too late. "I'll make sure she's safe, and then we'll hunt Winleigh down. The gangers can organize another search party, but everything else can wait until she's safe in the castle. She'll be all right, Dunstan. I will not let anything happen to her."

"Yes. Yes, of course, my lord. I've no doubt you will keep your word."

Anthony sighed in relief when he spotted the barouche parked on the sandy road above the granite cottage. There were children playing outside, chasing ducks around a pond; Gunther was on the beach, dozing, and the sun shone down on the pleasant scene. A few crab pots had been left on the rocks to dry, and flower crates were stacked high by the door, to be filled and shipped the following day.

It was a peaceful setting, reassuring, but Anthony would not breathe easily until he saw his wife. He knocked at the door. He could hear Vincent's chuckles of laughter from within, and he exhaled as a young woman opened the door, a baby in her arms.

"Yes—oh, it's you, my lord." She dropped a curtsy, flustered, glancing back over her shoulder at Vincent, who rose in embarrassment from a carved oak bench. The baby began to cry.

Anthony glanced around the cottage, barely hearing the woman whisper, "Hush now, Ethan. Don't be afraid. Lord Pentargon is a good man, like your dad. He's a good man."

"Where is my wife?" Anthony said. He felt hollow inside, afraid again, all the fear surging back. Was she in another room? That was it—she was in the garden, with the other children—

Vincent glanced at him in confusion. "But her ladyship is with you, my lord."

"With me?" No, no, *no*.

"You sent the note—" Vincent reached for the folded paper on the windowsill. "I know your script, my lord. The most illegible in the kingdom."

Anthony unfolded the note and stared at the most perfect forgery of his own handwriting he had ever seen.

> *Morwenna,*
> *I want to show you Arthur's cave, as a wedding present. I am waiting on the cliff path. The magic is for you alone.*
> *A*

Only an artist could have duplicated the swirls and loops unique to Anthony's impatient scrawling, and suddenly he remembered Elliott bending to pick up the letters that Morwenna had knocked from his desk. "But you weren't supposed to let her go, Vincent. How could you have been so unbelievably stupid?"

Vincent and Jane exchanged alarmed looks. "I saw

you on the cliff, my lord," Vincent said in disbelief.
"You waved to us. I recognized your cloak—"

Anthony went to the door, his eyes black with
anxiety. "The cloak I lost on the beach, Vincent. It
was not me you saw. It was Elliott Winleigh."

He did not need to elaborate. Vincent was
instantly at his side, understanding enough from
Anthony's uncharacteristic behavior that Morwenna
was in grave danger. "What do you want me to do?"

"Meet Dunstan on the moor with Carew, and
break up into three separate parties to cover the cliffs.
He won't take her near the cottages, but someone
needs to watch the water for outgoing boats."

"My brothers will help," Jane said. "Do you want
to take these with you?"

She had laid the baby in a cradle and opened a
drawer to remove a pair of handsome Italian pistols.
Anthony stared at them in surprise for a moment,
wondering why they looked so familiar until he realized he had brought them back from Florence for
Ethan two years ago.

"Ethan wanted me to keep them for protection,"
she explained quietly. "I told him I'd never need
them. We were waiting for the right time to tell my
family about the baby, and to get married."

And Ethan had died instead. Anthony glanced once
at the baby in the cradle, his nephew, but this wasn't
the time for introductions or strengthening family ties.

"The pistols aren't loaded," he said. "But I do need
a rowboat. Can you help me?"

"Of course. Just follow the path from the door
down the cliff. My brothers will help you. They'll do
anything you ask to save Morwenna."

19

Morwenna stood chained to the wall of the sea cave, her hands in manacles as water rose around her. How naive she had been to believe Elliott's excuse for forging Anthony's handwriting. Why had she ignored her instincts when Elliott explained, in the face of her shock and hesitation, that he wanted to share the mystery of Arthur's cave with her before the rest of the world destroyed it? Why had she not run from him on the cliff when she had the chance? Vincent had been watching her.

She'd been so relieved to see Elliott alive that she had refused to question the inconsistencies of his story. "His cave, Elliott—how do you know?" she had asked as he gripped her hand, tugging her with him. "Where have you been? We thought you were dead. Why didn't you at least let us know you were alive? How did you find Anthony's cloak? Where are your spectacles?"

He told her he had been hiding to finish his greatest work ever, that finding the cave had sent him into a frenzy of inspiration and he did not want to lose it. Hadn't she gotten the note he'd written the day of his disappearance, explaining that he was going into seclusion? He had paid one of Pasco's boys to deliver it to her in person, but the little beggar had probably pocketed the money instead.

And now she knew it was all a tangle of lies, a knot of ever-tightening evil from which there was no escape.

"This isn't Arthur's cave." She spoke to herself, if only to retain a hold on her sanity. The ancient king had not betrayed her. She stared in scorn at the ugly granite walls that closed around her. The legendary cave was said to be composed of porphyry, tourmaline, chalcedony, and hornblende, illuminated by a holy light.

No rare rose or white crystal brightened the dark interior, only a circle of stolen lanterns that cast a dull glow on her captor's face.

"There is no cave, you fool." His voice was detached, almost bored. "There was no Arthur, or Merlin, or Camelot. Lyonesse is a legend. Your father wasted his entire life weaving fairy tales into scholarly works, and in the process, he destroyed my career."

"That isn't true—"

"It is. He told the royal commission I was mad, that I would offend the queen. He didn't want me to illustrate his last book, but he was afraid to tell me to my face. He thought I might hurt you. He didn't realize I knew he had betrayed me."

Help me. Help me. Someone help me.

She closed her eyes, trying to block out his face,

his voice, the icy numbness that crept up her legs into her spine. When she looked into Elliott's eyes, there was no soul, no humanity, no hope. The sea water had reached her waist, and he sat above her on a ledge, sketching her in frowning concentration. A hermit crab scuttled across his papers, and she could feel red seaweed washing against her ankles. Her voice sounded faint.

"Elliott, the tide is going to be at my shoulders soon."

"Good. There isn't much oil left in the lamps, and this cavern is as dark as"—he glanced up and smiled at her—"a tomb."

"Oh, my God, Elliott. You aren't going to do this. Please tell me you only wanted to frighten me."

"Stop moving your head," he said in annoyance. "And if you want to be rescued, then use your magic. What, it doesn't work? What a shame. Then I suppose your half-lame knight will have to come. But how will he ever locate you, in a forgotten cave slowly filling with water? No one will find you, Morwenna, until you are quite dead."

She stared outside at the endless wash of ocean water, the castle etched against gray-blue sky, a sight that had always lifted her spirits and inspired her dreams. Now there was only a living nightmare, and she would die, knowing all the magic she had believed in was an illusion. Her arms ached from the strain of being forced above her head, and the manacles had cut into her wrists. Her loosened hair was saturated at the ends, the water slowly rising.

Nothing bad ever happens on Abandon.

She should have listened to her husband. She should have done what he wanted from the start, instead of obeying her headstrong nature. Her heart twisted at the thought of how he would grieve for both a brother and a wife. He was a good man, and she had been wrong to question his judgment, believing in some elusive magic.

Magic. Oh, Papa, it isn't real.

She closed her eyes again, then opened them in wonder as the muted clamor of church bells penetrated the cavern walls. Drawing a breath, she stole a glance at Elliott's face to gauge if he could hear, but he appeared unaffected, his thin face composed, almost serene, his spectacles reflecting the lantern light.

Anthony had heard the bells before when she had not. Would they summon him now? Had he even guessed what had happened to her? For all she knew, Vincent was still at Jane's cottage, unaware of Elliott's deception, and Anthony assumed his wife would come home in due time.

She listened to the bells and told herself again that their faraway music was a magical lifeline, a sign that everything would be all right. If she gave in to her terror, if for a moment she let herself believe she would die . . .

Fighting panic, she pictured Anthony's face when he had told her about the children who worked in the mines and the abuses they faced on a daily basis. She had never known a man who cared so deeply about others. If he appeared hard, it was only because life had forced him to behave so in self-defense. What a wonderful father he would make, and when she thought that she might even be carrying his child, she had to bite her lip so she wouldn't break down.

The bells gave her courage, and she concentrated on them, knowing then that Lyonesse was real, that her father had not been a fool. That thought uplifted and saddened her at the same time, and something strange must have shown on her face because Elliott put down his pencil and stared at her for a long time.

"I had never seen that expression on your face before," he said after several moments. "It is intriguing, but nothing like the look on a woman's face as she draws her last breath. If we had more time, I would show you my sketches of my wife before I killed her. They really are quite fascinating."

20

Anthony shoved the boat out into the water with all his might. The surf was rough, breaking against the craft, but he welcomed the chance to channel his energy into a physical confrontation. An eel darted between his legs as he climbed over the gunnel; he could hear thunder in the distance, a storm approaching, and the clatter of a dog cart on the cliffs above. Many of the islanders had already begun to look for his wife.

He might never find his way around the island as well as Morwenna, but he knew that half the cliffside crevices, the hiding places, could be reached only by boat at high tide.

"Lord Pentargon! Lord Pentargon!"

He'd just leaned into the oars when he saw Pasco running helter-skelter across the sand. His first impulse was to ignore him; he wouldn't waste a moment on the little bastard. But Pasco chased after him, wading, then swimming up to the side of the boat when he saw that Anthony wasn't going to stop.

"I don't have time for this," he said between his teeth.

"You have to take me with you." Pasco pulled himself into the boat, shivering, but with a look on his face that made Anthony reconsider.

"Do you know where she is?"

"Somewhere on Cape Skulla." Pasco wiped his eyes on his dirty lace sleeve and picked up the other oar. It was a fisherman's boat, and a net sat on the bottom beside a knife encrusted with fish scales.

"I didn't mean any harm in helping him, my lord." Pasco looked terrified, possibly more for himself than Morwenna, and with good reason. Anthony felt a wild fury unleashed inside him as he listened to his pathetic confession. "I didn't know he was mad."

"You helped him? Do you know where he took her?" He was rowing against the wind as he fired off questions, and if he'd had time to spare, he would have put his hands around Pasco's neck and squeezed the answers out of him. "Are you telling me you knew he was alive?"

Pasco refused to look at him. "Yes. I caught him out on the moor early one morning trapping game, and he persuaded me to play a prank on you and Morwenna. I have no future on the island once the marquess comes. I stole your cloak from the beach. I brought him the things he asked for."

"Such as?"

"Food, a blanket, charcoal." His voice shook. "Manacles."

All the fear Anthony had held inside threatened to break through his self-control. "Manacles. You piece of filth. If he's hurt her, if—"

Pasco started to cry.

Anthony swallowed, turning his face to the cliffs. "Where do you think he has her?"

"I'm not sure." He wiped his eyes again. "He told me he had found the cave and that there were treasures inside it. He said he would reward me for helping him."

"He didn't find the cave." Anthony couldn't explain why he was so sure, it sounded like something Morwenna would say, but he believed that nothing ugly or malignant could occur in the sacred cavern he had found. "How many other caves could there be?"

"Maybe seven. Most of them will be filled now. You wouldn't want to stay inside."

Anthony looked at him with disgust in his eyes. "Unless you were chained and unable to escape. How much farther?"

"I think—"

They both looked up at the same moment to see a large black raven circling the cliffs. Despite what the islanders insisted, dozens of other birds like it had to exist on Abandon, solitary scavengers that bred on the seacoast. Still, he couldn't help feeling it was the same raven that had warned him and Morwenna from the path that day.

Anyway, he had little else to go on. He was desperate for any sign to show him where she was, desperate enough to believe in a superstition that proclaimed a common bird to be the incarnation of an ancient warrior king.

"Is the raven flying above Cape Skulla?" he asked Pasco.

"Yes, but the waters below are dangerous for a boat, full of undercurrents and rocks like razors. I

don't know how close we can get. The caves are
flooded by now."

"Could we swim?"

Pasco stared at him. "Possibly you could. I haven't
the physical strength."

"Start finding it, Pasco. I need your help."

She was drifting away, so cold, so numb, her eyes
closing just as she noticed a shadow move at the
mouth of the cave. Moments later, she heard a splash
that broke the rhythmic slapping of the waves against
the cave walls.

Anthony.

She caught the briefest glimpse of him as he sur-
faced from the submerged rocks for air, a much
slighter figure beside him. Then, as suddenly as the
pair had appeared, they vanished, swallowed up by
the dark green shadows. Had she imagined them?
Was she having a hallucination? Her arms and shoulders ached. There was no feeling in her lower body,
but suddenly hope moved through her system like an
electric shock, lending her the energy to turn her
head.

"Morwenna," Elliott said, frowning at her. "Don't
move."

She saw him again, her husband, recognizing his
profile and upper torso as he crawled across the
rocks. The look on his face was so deadly that she
shivered, in relief and anxiety. His presence seemed
to fill the cave—didn't Elliott sense it? Anthony had
almost reached the ledge now. He pressed his forefin-
ger to his mouth, signaling her not to give him away.
She swallowed; her throat was so constricted she
couldn't have spoken, anyway. All she could do was

breathe out a sigh, not daring to glance at Elliott again.

"Bored, Morwenna?" he murmured. "Would—"

Anthony sprang out of the water like an ancient sea god, a knife between his teeth. He hit the ledge with so much force that two of the lanterns fell from their perch into the water; barely enough daylight penetrated the cave for her to see what was happening. Anthony seemed larger than life, his hair dripping on his shoulders, his linen shirt and black trousers molded to his muscular frame as he straightened to take on Elliott.

Elliott had been caught off guard, but he reacted quickly. He flung a bottle of turpentine in Anthony's face before he reached for the medieval sword at his side. Anthony had dropped his knife; she saw it glittering on the ledge, and she felt so helpless, so frustrated; the only thing she could think to do was force her legs through the water to kick spray into Elliott's face as a distraction. The effort cost all the energy she could summon.

"Be careful, Anthony!" she cried. "He's stronger than he looks."

Another shadow obscured what little light illuminated the cave. At first, she had no idea what had happened. Then she recognized Pasco, and she swallowed a sob of panic. Elliott had bragged how he had persuaded Pasco into helping trick her. Had Pasco followed Anthony here to kill him?

Pasco hauled himself out of the water onto the ledge, and she cried out again as he reached down behind Anthony for the knife. Only one of the lanterns burned above them now, throwing eerie flickers of light around the cave.

"Pasco is behind you with the knife, Anthony!"

He had thrown himself at Elliott, fighting for the sword, and he seemed so intent, she doubted he had even heard her.

The sword flew from Elliott's hand, shattering limestone as it hit the cave wall. She saw Pasco charge, pushing against Anthony, and a man's groan of surprise and pain. For a moment, she felt sick, violently ill. Her mind did not register that Pasco had stabbed Elliott. Frozen in horror, she watched Anthony draw back a step, waiting for him to fall before she realized he had not been hurt. She stared in disbelief as Elliott staggered between the two other men, his hand to his throat; then he plunged into the water.

"Oh, Jesus, Pasco, what did you do?" It was Anthony's voice, low with panic, but she really didn't care what he was saying. All that mattered was that he was alive, and here.

He dropped to his knees, struggling to drag Elliott's body from the water before the current claimed him. "He had the key to her manacles," he said in a desperate voice. "How are we supposed to get her free now if he's hidden it somewhere?"

"I have the other key," Pasco answered.

"With you?"

"Yes. It's here in my cuff. I'll get her free. You'd better stand in the water below her to be there when she falls."

Anthony looked up at her then. "My God," she heard him mutter. "Whatever you do, don't drop the key," and there was so much love and concern in his voice that it broke her self-control. She felt tears on her face, and she knew that she could fall apart now.

Suddenly she was shivering, in gratitude and pent-up anxiety, then her wrists were free, the blood stinging as it rushed back into her veins, and she was slipping, down, down, into darkness, into the strongest pair of arms in the world.

The relief in her eyes as Anthony caught her filled him with fresh rage. Now that he could breathe again, knowing she was safe, he burned with bitter regret that Pasco had killed Elliott, depriving Anthony of the privilege. His face taut with worry, he lifted Morwenna onto the ledge and climbed up beside her, pulling Elliott's blanket over her shoulders.

"Better, love?"

"Yes. But don't let me go."

"No. Never. It's all right now—are you hurt anywhere?"

"My arms. My back." She was too tired to talk. "Sore, but nothing bad."

Bad enough, he thought grimly, staring in hatred at Elliott's body, bobbing against the walls of the cave. Let him rot there forever. Let the eels devour him and the sun bleach his bones. He had shackled her to the wall like a human sacrifice, calmly sketching as the water claimed her, inch by inch. The tide had almost reached her throat when Anthony found them, and in another few minutes, it would have been too late. He put his free hand over his eyes as if he could erase the image, but he knew it would haunt him forever. How could the man's mind have been so twisted? How could *he* forget what he had felt in that hellish interval when he couldn't find her?

"Did you hear the bells?" she murmured, fighting

to keep her eyes open. "I thought that they would bring you to me."

She laid her head on his chest, and he could feel his heart beating with the same desperate fear as when he had seen her, pale and helpless, not knowing if he was in time. "What bells?"

A hint of a smile moved across her face. "You didn't hear them. Well, finally, I'm the one. It's only fair."

"It was the raven who brought us here," Pasco said, his voice thick with emotion. He was sitting farther down the ledge, hesitant to intrude.

"The raven?" she said in surprise.

"I am sorry, Morwenna," he said quietly.

"I'm the one who should be sorry," she said. "I thought at first you'd come here to help Elliott."

Anthony looked away. He wasn't going to upset her by explaining that Pasco *had* been helping Elliott before his conscience won out. She'd been through enough already, and forgiveness would prove a better balm than anger.

"Elliott ransacked the farmhouse to hurt Papa," she said, her voice muffled against her husband's chest. "He hated him even after he was dead."

Anthony tightened his hold on her, knowing they ought to move before long; by the dry appearance of the cavern walls, he judged that the water level rarely reached the ledge, but he didn't want to stay the entire night there. She needed warmth, food, and the comfort of the castle.

"Perhaps I could find another way to help the children," he said without thinking. "Perhaps I could persuade Camelbourne he would be happier on some secluded Scottish isle."

"Anthony."

"What?" He looked down at her anxiously. "Is something wrong? Are you still cold? Are you sure he didn't hurt you?"

"Don't doubt your decision," she whispered. "We are committed to the children, Anthony. We can't fail them."

We. He buried his face in her hair, overwhelmed by his feelings, unable to express them. Tears stung his eyes. "I'd do anything for you, Morwenna."

"Anything?"

"Anything."

"Take me to Arthur's cave."

"Dear God," he said, clearly startled by her request when he was himself emotionally reduced to rags. "Dear, dear God."

Then he started to laugh, and so did Pasco, because they were all alive and magic was still a possibility. But there wasn't time for any more discussion about the cave. A fleet of fishermen had sighted Anthony's boat outside, and within moments a rescue crew headed by Carew appeared around them, bearing ropes and lanterns.

21

Morwenna sat on the floor of the library, awash in a sea of papers, sketches, and research books. Anthony, fluent in several languages, had promised to help her translate some obscure Latin passages describing little-known details of Arthur's court.

She had almost completed her father's book—after deep thought, she had decided to include Elliott's illustration of Arthur's cave, but in the four days she and Anthony had searched, they had not found the cave itself.

Tomorrow they would try again, and then the marquess would take possession of the island. Her heart was broken, but she knew that whatever magic existed on Abandon could not be destroyed, only hidden, and perhaps that was for the best.

"You look far too pleased with yourself, Lady Pentargon," Anthony said as he came into the room.

She watched him remove his coat and gloves, thinking how handsome he was, how his presence enthralled her. She smiled now remembering she had thought him uncaring and arrogant when they'd first met, beautiful outside, empty within. But she had never been so wrong about anyone in her life. He was the strongest and most unselfish man she had ever met, the embodiment of all the knightly virtues in King Arthur's court. Some force for good had brought him into her life, and she was grateful.

He sat down opposite her, sifting through the piles of literature. A copy of the fourteenth-century *Book of Talesin*. A pamphlet entitled *Shape-Shifting: A Lost Art?* by Sir Roland Halliwell.

"Shape-shifting," he murmured. "Good God. What next?" And his next question was answered by the second pamphlet in the series, called *Raising a Storm: A Celtic Talent*. "Why are you smiling anyway, Morwenna? Is the book finished?"

"If only it were. Uncle Dunstan has held off Papa's publishing firm for three months now. They're promising advanced copies and an endorsement from Prince Albert, but the ending isn't right."

"What's wrong with it?"

"There isn't one," she said in exasperation. "Not without the cave, and a promise or prophecy that Arthur will—" She sat up, her forehead creasing in a frown. "You have sand on your boots, and you're getting it all over my books. Where have you been?"

"At the cottage becoming acquainted with my nephew, and his mother, and her family, all of whom I suppose are my family now. They're very worried about what the future holds." He looked past her into the fire. "And so am I. If Camelbourne decides to invite his friends to spend the summer here yachting, then even the profits from the last pilchard catch will be lost."

"Spoken like a true islander," she said gently. "How is your hip? I have not heard you complain once. Are you better or just being brave?"

He stood, pulling her from the pile of papers. "I'm well enough that I can carry you upstairs to bed."

"It really isn't bothering you?"

"No." He lifted her into his arms and carried her to the door, out into the hall, and up the stairs. "Does my lameness bother you?"

"I never even noticed it until you claimed to have been injured by a wild boar on Midsummer Eve."

He smiled down at her, seeing the mischief in her eyes. "*You* are doubting my story, Lady Pentargon— you who lured me into this magical world to begin with."

She rested her head against his strong neck. "Well, Anthony, it is rather a lot to believe, a boar going about in a frenzy on Abandon. Perhaps you do need spectacles, as I suggested, and by the way, did you know your book is lost again?"

He kicked open the door to their bedchamber, gratified to find a fire lit and the bed turned down for the night. "No, I didn't, and by the way, I don't need spectacles for what we are about to do."

She gazed up at him guilelessly as he deposited her on the bed. "Which is?"

He leaned over her and unhooked the back of her gown, peeling it off her shoulders. Half-naked, she sat up and said, "Anthony, there's someone at the door."

He pushed her back down, pulling off her petticoats and skirts. "The door is locked. Don't worry."

She tried to sit up, but he was kissing her all over, the man had no shame, and he was making her shiver in anticipation. "I think the cats are crying to come in," she whispered.

"I do not want an audience for what I have in mind, thank you very much," he said as he undressed.

He eased her back down onto the bed, bracing his forearms at her sides to hold her in place. She wasn't going to get away from him, not now or ever. He kissed her, slowly and deeply until she relaxed, and she allowed him to do whatever he wanted, and what he wanted was to worship her, to replace all the horror she had gone through with a sweeter experience.

With heartbreaking gentleness, he kissed the bruises on her throat and wrists. He kissed her entire body until she was begging for mercy in one breath, then demanding more in another. A perfect gentleman, he was only too happy to please his wife—his talented fingers soothed her even as they seduced. The gentleness of his touch set her nerves on fire and banished the memory of her ordeal. He possessed the power to heal as well as delight, and he did both.

"Anthony," she said, a moan escaping her. "I am dying of pleasure."

His kisses branded her breasts and belly. "Shall I stop?"

She bit her lip as he raised his head to give her a wicked grin. "Don't you dare."

Their eyes met, not in battle but in a bond of mutual love, desire, and commitment. Her body shivered beneath his, opened, recognizing his mastery.

"My wife," he said, his voice rough when his feelings for her were so tender, he trembled with them. "I love giving you pleasure." And he embedded himself in her body, moving inside her until she reached a climax that shattered his own control. Sheathed in the silk of her, he shuddered with a satisfaction so intense, he felt his heart stop. He gripped her to him afterward, unable to express how much she meant to him.

She looked exhausted when they recovered enough for conversation, and he was afraid he might have done something to hurt her. But she only smiled when he asked her if she was all right and gathered her against his body.

"Are *you* all right?" she asked. "You haven't hurt the other hip overexerting yourself, have you?"

"Madam, I am a good deal older than you but hardly too decrepit to fulfill my husbandly duties."

She laid her head on his chest, her legs entwined with his beneath the muddle of covers and sheets. "I cannot disagree with you on that point."

"If we continue like this, we will have as many children as we do cats, Morwenna."

"I wouldn't mind." She ran her hand over his flat stomach, marveling at how he was built. There was still a bruise on his hip but no scar, no wound. He had to be teasing about the Wild Hunt. "Would you?"

"I would love nothing more. There is a good chance you are pregnant right now."

"Do you think so?" she said in delight.

"If you aren't, you will be by tomorrow."

"Tomorrow," she said, her voice suddenly sad. "Camelbourne is supposed to be here, isn't he?"

"Tomorrow or the next day. His last message was rather odd." He frowned, staring across the room as she closed her eyes, already drifting off to sleep. A world of worries weighed on his mind. His nephew,

Ethan's son, needed a secure future, and he felt compelled to see the other island families settled, meeting their basic needs should Camelbourne fail to help them.

"You knew all along that Ethan and Jane had a child?" he asked, kissing the top of her head.

"Everyone guessed," she murmured. "They seemed to love each other. Annie Jenkins said Ethan intended to marry her, but then he had the accident. It's such a shame."

"Did she really love him?"

"Why would she not, my lord? Why is that difficult for you to accept?"

"My brother seemed to feel his disability put him at a disadvantage with women."

"Silly." She was almost asleep; she could not imagine any Hartstone male at a loss with a woman. Charm flowed from their fingertips. "Oh, Anthony, I did so want to find Arthur's cave—what did you do with the waxen figures of us you found in the tower?"

"They disappeared from my desk several days ago."

"Disappeared? Isn't that peculiar? I thought they were rather sweet."

When he looked down again, she was asleep, but his mind would not rest. The entire time he had been on Abandon, he'd neglected his business affairs at home, and now this burden of finding gainful employment for one hundred and sixty or so basically unskilled people?

Gently disengaging himself from his wife, he dressed in a lawn shirt and trousers and went to the desk in the corner. But he couldn't concentrate on anything. A pair of moths fluttered about the small lamp in the corner, and as he reached to swat at them, Morwenna sat up from a dead sleep, crying, "Oh, don't kill them. They're the secret folk."

"The secret folk?"

"Yes, Anthony. They possess souls just like us. It's cruel to kill them, and bad luck besides."

"I'll let them out the window, shall I?"

"I think they prefer the garden."

"Did the moths actually tell you that, Morwenna? Do you really believe bugs can talk?"

"Do you really believe a boar attacked you, Anthony?"

"Is there a particular place in the garden where I should release them?" he asked wryly. "Do the moths have a preference?"

"I don't suppose it matters—as long as there isn't a hedgehog nearby. Or frog."

"Oh, good. That makes my job so much easier."

"You don't mind, do you?"

"Why should I mind?"

"Some men might," she said sweetly.

He sighed and told himself he would have to get used to this, and so just a few minutes after midnight, he found himself creeping downstairs to release the small furry insects into the night.

He was almost to the garden when he saw another figure lurking behind the rhododendron. His first thought was irrational—that Elliott had returned, that he hadn't been dead, or that it was Pasco, on some mission of black magic. At any rate, Anthony was protective enough of Morwenna to tear the intruder apart with his bare hands.

22

"Come out, whoever you are. I have a pistol."
Which he didn't, actually. He only had the garden
trowel he had grabbed from the bench, because the
average nobleman did not make a habit of nocturnal
prowlings around his home with a gun in hand, nor
the moths he had gently released into the night.

"Oh, goodness, my lord," a horrified voice said.
"Do not shoot. It's only me."

"Vincent? What on earth are you doing here at
this hour?"

"Releasing the moths that gathered around the
kitchen window. Mrs. Treffry insists I wait until the
cats are settled before I let the creatures go." He crept
out from behind the bush, his face sheepish. "It is my
last duty of the night."

"I see." Anthony covertly set down the trowel.

"And you, my lord, you were unable to sleep?"

"Something like that."

Vincent nodded. "Ah. I thought perhaps you and

Lord Camelbourne were discussing private affairs in the library."

"In the library?"

"Yes, my lord—didn't you know? He arrived an hour ago, made himself quite at home, which is his right considering the castle is now his."

"Is he still there?"

"As far as I know. The yacht was in the bay when I last looked. Shall I see to his comfort?"

"No. I'll take care of him."

Anthony glanced at the tower where his wife slept before he made his way back through the darkened castle. This was a meeting he dreaded, but it seemed pointless to postpone it.

Camelbourne was sitting in the corner, staring out the window when Anthony came in. "I expected you tomorrow, Lloyd."

The marquess turned his head. There was something different about his face, a change in his eyes, but in the dark, Anthony could not tell what. He did notice that the castle's elusive white cat was curled up in the man's lap. "Do you mind?"

Anthony shrugged. "It is your island."

Camelbourne said nothing for a few moments, his beringed fingers stroking the cat. Something across the sea appeared to have caught his attention. "I did not want to disturb your wife. Has she recovered from her ordeal?"

"Physically, I believe so," Anthony said shortly. It irked him that the man was so impatient to take possession, he could not even give them their last night alone. "The horror of it lingers."

"Of course." Camelbourne took a sip of whiskey with his free hand. The room was furnished as before, but the bookshelves were denuded of the books Anthony had packed yet again. "Did she ever find the cave?"

"No." Anthony looked pointedly at the clock. "And I suppose now she never will."

"Why not?"

"Because—damnation, Lloyd, can we discuss this tomorrow?"

"Of course, Pentargon, it is your home. You are the host."

"Actually, I'm not."

"Actually, you are." Camelbourne sat forward, his craggy face solemn in moonlight. "I have no idea how you feel about this island. Your wife has made herself quite clear on the matter, so at least one of you will be pleased by this."

"Pleased by what?"

"I've changed my mind. The atmosphere on Abandon is not what I had originally envisioned. Do you know, I thought I heard bells ringing right before you walked in? I do not need another castle, anyway."

Anthony looked stunned. "But what about your promise to me? What about the passages you agreed to support?"

"Your precious children will be protected," Camelbourne said calmly. "In fact, I think I shall make it my personal cause for the next year. I have already written a speech to present to Parliament about how current laws are being evaded, about the need for stricter enforcement. It really is quite brilliant. I might even make a mark in history."

Anthony stared at him. "I'm sure you will."

"Go back to bed, Pentargon," he said with irony.

"If I had a lovely wife like yours, I would not be prowling about the place like a lost soul."

"No?"

"No. Now, tomorrow, if she is well enough, Morwenna may take me around the island before I set sail. I wouldn't mind being able to tell the queen I'd found Arthur's cave myself. The legend is quite the thing at court and in artistic circles." He tapped the heavy book on the table. "If it's anything at all like the illustrations here, it is a sight to behold."

That damn book again.

"What illustrations?" Anthony asked.

"Call it vanity, Pentargon, but I fancy I see myself in one of these book plates—the one of the rather handsome older knight slaying a dragon."

"We are all of us subject to vanity—" Anthony broke off as the white cat jumped off Camelbourne's lap and darted through the door. "There is something odd about that animal."

"She's a strange one, isn't she?" Camelbourne said with a smile.

Anthony went up the stairs, overwhelmed by his good news, but just before he reached the bedchamber, he stopped, listening to the haunting melody that floated down the hall.

The music lured him to the tower, and there he found the lady by the fire, playing a silver harp. Her slender white fingers stilled when she saw him, and the expression on her face was wicked and wise at once, so reminiscent of his wife that he caught his breath.

"The Wheel of Fortune has turned in your favor, my lord."

Her voice was the same as he remembered, deep, ironic, patient, from his childhood. "So it is you, Morgan, or Mildred. My governess, or guardian angel."

"Or murderess, as the stories go," she said in amusement.

"Why is Morwenna unable to see you?" he asked.

She turned from her harp, a flicker of sadness on her face. "Not yet. She is only coming into her powers and has not learned to control her emotions. She would want to be with me, and that is not possible."

"Then why me?" Anthony said. "It doesn't seem fair. If she is your daughter—"

"You have always placed others above yourself, my lord," she said with a gentle smile.

"I have only done what was right. Nothing more."

"But more than most. Merlin and I are impressed by your single-mindedness. Not every man can vanquish evil."

He stared at her.

"You have heard of Merlin, my lord?"

Anthony blinked. He was dreaming, that was it. In reality, he was fast asleep in bed with his wife, and this was not happening at all. "Merlin, the wizard— your enemy, as I recall."

"Another distortion. Merlin and I will have no rest ourselves until the world is returned to rights." Her eyes were mournful. "In every century, we leave a few descendants behind to stand guard and fight for the values our beloved king embodied. It is a sacrifice I cannot describe."

Leaving descendants across time? Anthony decided it was a sign of his superior intelligence that he had invented such an elaborate dream. And what a hell of a job for the descendants, he thought. Fighting for Arthur's values, indeed.

"Which is why powerful souls such as yours are chosen to help them," she said with a sly smile.

He straightened. Had he spoken the thought aloud?

"The potion I left for you has healed your wound?" she asked in concern.

"Yes. Yes. But—"

"—a hint of the limp remains. Shall I heal you again? It is only fitting that I grant you a boon for your noble deeds. Do you desire physical perfection?"

He laughed at that. "Once, yes, but now—no, if you have the power to grant wishes, all I ask is that my children not be born with the disability that afflicted me. I have more than any man needs for happiness. My wife seems to find me attractive enough."

"Then why are you not in bed asleep with that wife?" an amused voice asked behind him.

He turned in surprise to find Morwenna standing in the door, a half-afraid, half-teasing look on her face. Suddenly he realized there was no fire burning, no woman at a silver harp. Just Anthony alone, apparently talking to himself, not even sure if he imagined the elusive scent of lilies that lingered in the air.

"What is it, Anthony?" Morwenna asked. "Why aren't you in bed? Was your hip hurting you again?" She came into the room, shivering in her silk dressing robe. "It's damp in here, and you sounded so serious." She gave him a teasing grin. "Were you having a nice conversation with yourself?"

He looked up from the fireplace.

"Oh," she said, suddenly understanding. "You heard her music again, didn't you?"

He led her back to the door. "I was only securing our castle for the night, Morwenna."

"Our castle? For a few hours more, at most. I can almost feel the bite of the executioner's ax."

He put his arm around her shoulders, guiding her to the stairs. "I have something to tell you that will put your mind at rest."

23

Summer passed. The pilchard harvest was the most bountiful Abandon had ever known. The fish practically begged to be caught. The island flourished. Flowers continued to grow out of season, and three French businessmen had struck a deal with Jane's family to distill the lady's-fan lily into a perfume, which they described as "capturing the hope and innocence of a bridal wreath."

On the moor, the ancient stones had settled back into their original places.

Pasco Illugan soon resumed selling ill wishes from his cottage on Cape Skulla, although he was forbidden to trap any animals for his spells. Some people grumbled that Lord Pentargon should get rid of the pellar once and for all. But Anthony owed Pasco a debt for helping him save Morwenna, and Anthony was a man of honor above all else.

Morwenna came and went at will over the coves and beaches; Anthony made a habit of following her at a distance, priding himself that she was unaware of his covert missions as chaperone.

He watched over her as she visited her friends, Annie Jenkins in particular. The old woman's health was fast failing, and before she died, she yearned to share her secrets with Morwenna. Many of these included remedies for infertility. He guessed Morwenna grieved a little every month that passed without sign of a pregnancy. But she was less concerned since Ethan's mysterious book had reappeared for one more night, and he had showed her the final plate.

"Look, Morwenna." He pointed to the illustration of the knight and his lady with their five children. Three of them were clearly male, jousting and tilting in play. The last two were infants, all bundled up in white lace, of indeterminate sex.

As before, the book had only revealed one chapter of their lives at a time. The remaining pages had been sealed, and Anthony found it suspicious that on the same day the white cat disappeared from the castle, the book vanished too. He wondered whether either would be seen again.

For the moment, however, the prospect of five children was quite enough to contemplate.

By the end of October, Morwenna told Anthony she thought she was pregnant, but her happiness was overclouded when Annie Jenkins took a turn for the worse and died.

He and Morwenna were walking along the cliffs together, from the old woman's cottage, and Morwenna had been crying for an hour, but to Anthony her tear-stained face was the most beautiful sight in the world.

"Everything was so perfect," she said. "Why

couldn't she have lived another few years? I wanted her to see our children. Oh, Anthony, I'm going to miss her so much, I cannot stand it. Who will I turn to for advice?"

"I'll always be here for you, Morwenna."

"Not when I want to complain about female problems." She pulled off her straw bonnet, smiling at him. "She was troubled by a vision the night before she died."

"Not about us, I hope."

"No. Do you remember the legend about how King Arthur would reawaken only when Britain fought its greatest battle?"

"Is she predicting another war for us? In our time?"

"She said our grandchildren will join his army." She turned to the sea. "A battle will rage across the world led by a monster who will inflict evil of unspeakable proportions. It was a vision of this inhumanity that broke Annie's heart. She died of grief for what the world would know."

"But you said—*she* said—Arthur will return to fight this battle for Britain. And we will win."

She nodded. "She said a queen would knight him for his heroism."

"What is this warrior's name?" Anthony asked. "Where is he supposed to come from?"

"I don't know. She was too befuddled and weak to explain in a way I could understand. She kept saying something about a church on the hill."

"Church? Hill?"

"I don't know what it means either."

"Perhaps her vision was wrong," he said. "Perhaps it won't come true."

She raised her brow. "She predicted you and I would be together forever."

"Ah. Then the woman was a true mystic."

He didn't want to think about the future. He wanted to hold this moment forever, and if that was impossible, then he wanted to hold what they felt for each other. Life would change them. There would be more battles, but they would grow together like the honeysuckle that grew on the wind-twisted yews of the Cornish coast. He would protect her with all the strength he possessed.

He took her into his arms and held her. "Come back to the castle."

"Not yet. Let's walk for a while longer." She stared up at him in concern. "Unless your leg is bothering you."

He kissed her as the breeze rose around them. "It isn't. It's you I worry about. The path to the beach is steep."

"But this is Abandon, Anthony, and by the way, I know you follow me everywhere. It's really very sweet."

He laughed. "How do you know I'm following you? I'm as subtle as a damn French spy."

"Oh, Anthony. I just know."

There were some things he would simply have to accept as long as he was to stay happily married to Morwenna. Things like flowers growing out of season, in the strangest places—masses of lady's-fan lilies had sprung up in the castle's cannons and in the cavities of the stones returned to the moor. Things like hearing harp music in the middle of the night and learning to sleep with a half-dozen cats draped over one's various body parts.

He shook his head, smiling, and followed her down the cliff to the silver sand. It had rained earlier in the day, and now a rainbow stretched across the sky above them as he took her hand to begin the walk home.